Book Cover by GetCovers

1st edition 2026

# The Girl Who Came Before

EMMA NEISS

For my husband, who never once doubted me. Thank you for being my biggest believer, my safe place, my home.

# Contents

# CHAPTER ONE

# Serendipity

Shadows dance across the prints scattered around me, each photo a moment suspended in time. I brush a stack of them with my fingertips as I reach to massage my legs, pins and needles shooting through my flesh. I should buy a rug to keep me comfortable, and to muffle my movements in this too-quiet apartment.

Muscle memory guides me to where my coffee mug should be, but my fingers close around air. Hmmm. I spot my mug sitting on the far edge of the table, a brown ring staining the wood beneath it. When I narrow my eyes at it, lightning strikes behind my eyeball, fracturing my vision into prismatic shards. I'd swallowed two pills at 8am, then one more at noon, but the jackhammer in my skull keeps pounding, and now I can't even locate a mug that's a few feet away from me. Perfect.

"It's probably just a brain tumor the size of a golf ball." I force out a dry chuckle. One of these days I'll call around and find a doctor in my network. But first things first. I need to put these photos away before I leave, or Toast will turn them into his playground. Last time, I found my prints scattered from the kitchen to the bathroom, their surfaces marred with paw-shaped smudges.

As if summoned by my thoughts, a warm weight presses against my knee, and I look down to find wide amber eyes fixed on me. They swivel meaningfully toward the empty food bowl in the kitchen, and Toast lets out a meow that sounds more like a rusty door hinge than a cat.

I groan, glancing at the clock. It's fifteen minutes past his dinner time. Toast follows my every move as I wobble to the kitchen and peel back the foil lid of the can, releasing a fishy smell that seems weirdly appetizing. The spoon clinks against ceramic as I scrape every morsel into his bowl, remembering the note a neighbor slipped under my door last week: *"Some of us don't appreciate your beast's howling every night. Kindly feed it or re-home it."*

Toast's purr rumbles through the apartment, his pink tongue darting methodically as he devours his food. Sounds of chewing and swallowing fill the kitchen, and the wet food disappears in greedy bites.

I give Toast a quick pat and sink back to the floor amid my sea of photographs, then rub at the back of my neck, squeezing the muscles like I might wring the ache from them.

"Focus, Tessa."

I go back to sorting through the prints from last week's shoot. Prints of a model in bright lipstick holding a white balloon spread out before me, their sea of colors blurring before my eyes. As I'm flipping through the photos and trying to select the best ones, my eye catches on a man in a blue parka in the background. I must have missed him during the shoot. Ugh. My headache grows tenfold as I think of all the edits I'll have to make in Photoshop later.

"It's fine." I mumble, tossing the photos onto the growing maybe pile, and pop a vitamin from the pill organizer on the coffee table.

The label says Tuesday, though I'm pretty sure today's Thursday. The vitamins are the only thing that works for these headaches. I don't know what's in them; probably caffeine or some kind of miracle root. All I know is that the bottle is expensive and a pain to special order, but I've been popping the pills like candy.

I rummage through the rest of my portfolio, but my movements slow when I realize there's an out-of-focus figure haunting other images as well. The person is leaning against a brick wall at the Johnson wedding, then half-hidden behind a potted fern at a ribbon-cutting ceremony. I continue to flip through photos, and sure enough, there he is again, near the exit of a charity auction. In any single shot, he'd be just another blur at the edges. But seeing him across multiple events creates a pattern, like someone who keeps drifting into view before melting back into the shadows when he notices the camera pointed his way.

I examine the photographs one by one. Is that the same blue parka man from the model shoot? He's just beyond the camera's focus; a smudge of a person with shoulders curved inward and head cocked at an angle.

The similarities are there, but it's impossible to tell if I'm looking at the same person. Chances are, these photobombers are all different people. After all, I've photographed hundreds of men and women at dozens of events. Coincidences happen. A few random people must have just walked into my shots without me noticing.

I shake my head, promising myself to scan the edges of every frame more carefully next time. No more strangers wandering into my perfect shots. No more hours wasted in Photoshop erasing some random man's elbow or profile.

A blur of orange fur launches across the living room floor, and my heart nearly stops as Toast torpedoes through my carefully arranged work, sending photos flying in all directions.

"TOAST, NO!" My voice echoes off the walls as the cat darts away, tail held high in pride.

I squint after the furry menace, my temples throbbing. "Is this what I get for saving your butt from the shelter?" I grind my teeth. "Should have gotten a dog instead..."

With a defeated exhale, I go to collect the scattered photos. I am sweeping my work into a messy pile and grumbling under my breath when an unfamiliar picture slides free from the stack. This one's smaller, thicker, with a distinctive white border all instant photos have. Its edges look yellowed, like a memory that's been fading for some time.

Huh. I lift the print to the light, inspecting the two figures pressed together on what looks like a balcony, city lights blurred behind them. It looks like the photographer positioned the camera behind the couple, capturing a candid moment without their awareness. The woman's head is thrown back in laughter. I recognize the black dress with those distinctive ruffles; I still have it hanging in my closet, wrapped in dry cleaning plastic from the last time I wore it.

The man's face is half-hidden against my neck in the picture, one hand splayed possessively across the small of my back, bunching the fabric. I flip the picture over. There's no date. No caption.

I rack my brain, trying to place the scene. Was this taken at some reception or a corporate event? I bring the photo closer, my nose almost touching it. The balcony railing looks like the one at the Carlyle Hotel. But whom was I with? I study the man's dark hair, broad shoulders, and the way his hand curves around my waist with such familiarity. I should remember him, but I'm drawing a blank.

"It doesn't matter," I mutter, although my fingers linger on the photo's edge. Something about the curve of the man's neck against mine feels... almost familiar.

"If he was important, I'd remember him," I decide, letting the instant photo slip from my fingers. It lands facedown on the discard pile with a soft tap.

I'm quite the photographer, I think bitterly. Overlooking strangers lurking in the backgrounds of my photos, forgetting men who touched me in such familiar ways. I suppose that's what happens when you spend your nights with your cat and a bottle of wine. Or when your romantic life has become so nonexistent that even the men in your photographs remain completely out of touch.

My phone alarm blares with its shrill wail, magnifying the ache in my temple. I gather the remaining photos into a messy stack, corners jutting out at odd angles, and stuff them into a manila folder that's already bulging at the seams.

The gallery opening starts at seven, giving me just enough time to shower and make myself look presentable. It's an important gig that will allow me to blend into the background and focus on photograph-ing the art and the space, while avoiding the need for too much social interaction. Exactly the type of job I like.

I cringe when I catch a glimpse of myself in the hallway mirror. My hair's sticking up in tufts like something's been nesting in it, and my oversized t-shirt sports a coffee stain shaped like Texas. The gallery curator would have a stroke if I showed up like this.

After a quick shower that is hot enough to burn the skin off my bones, I dab concealer beneath my eyes, blending the edges with my ring finger until the shadows retreat. The waxy scent of the red lipstick fills my nostrils as I trace the outline of my lips, transforming them from bloodless to bold.

The gallery crowd will wear Chanel and discuss Beethoven. I won't fit in with my thrift store clothes, but at least now I won't look like I've been exhumed for the occasion.

My fingers curl around the camera bag's strap, the leather worn smooth in the middle where it's pressed against my collarbone day after day. Its familiar weight feels comforting as I loop it around my shoulder. The perfect finishing touch.

I hesitate at the threshold of my apartment, checking to make sure the lights are off and that the apartment is cat proof. My eyes travel across the room to where the manila folder bulges with photos on the coffee table, and then to the nearby trashcan where the instant shot peeks out among the crumpled rejects. Something about that photo makes my heartbeat flutter like a trapped bird beneath my ribs. I rub at my sternum and tear my gaze from the stack, feeling off balance.

Inhale. Exhale. I close my eyes and draw air into my lungs until my pulse slows.

Tonight's my big night. I'll be shooting Guzman's comeback after his decade-long disappearance, and the exhibition has art critics frothing at the mouth. The check they're cutting me will cover three months' rent on this shoebox apartment. I can't afford to let some photo and a migraine derail what could be my big break.

Keep your head in the game, I remind myself.

I don't glance back again at the pile of photos as I let the door close behind me with a decisive click that echoes throughout the hallway.

***

The gallery is a contemporary building with enormous windows, lavish chandeliers, velvet benches, and marble polished to perfection. It is brimming with the clang of wine glasses and the hush of expensive shoes tapping against the floor. I spot Marissa, the gallery's owner and my employer for the evening, gliding from guest to guest, her silver dress a streak in my periphery and her lips a shade bolder than my own. I keep my head down and kneel by the coat check to swap my sneakers for heels, then adjust the well-worn camera strap on my shoulder so it won't wrinkle my top.

Tonight is supposed to be easy and lucrative. Shoot the art, shoot the crowd, then cash a check and disappear. The migraine's a low thrum now, blood pulsing behind my eyes, which is manageable as long as I stay under the radar. I breathe through my nose and line up the first shot of two ladies frozen mid-laugh, next to a sculpture that looks like a pile of horse manure.

*Click. Click. Click.*

When I find my rhythm, the ache at the base of my skull and the crowd's chatter drain away. I slide along the wall's perimeter, shooting from low angles and quick flanks, invisible as a ghost. It's only when I step back for a wide shot that I slam into something warm and hard.

Correction: someone warm and hard. I rebound off a tailored torso and watch in slow motion as a splash of red arcs out, gravity pulling the liquid onto a man's dazzling white shirt. I freeze, horror and humiliation fighting in my chest.

"Oh my god. I am so, so sorry." I scrabble for a paper towel, but there aren't any. Of course there aren't, because this is an art gallery and people are supposed to hold their liquor.

The man towers over me, dark hair falling just so, framing features that belong on a billboard. Eyes the color of expensive whiskey and moss meet mine, revealing nothing at first. Then something shifts, and warmth swirls through their amber. A devastatingly handsome smile breaks across the man's face and leaves me momentarily speechless.

"That's one way to make an impression."

"Not the best one, to be fair." I chuckle awkwardly. "Here, let me—"

"It's all good. It was my fault anyway. I should've paid more attention to my surroundings."

The man's gaze pins me in place, warm and attentive, as if I've done something fascinating instead of ruining his clothes.

"I'm Tessa," I offer, because not saying anything feels even worse. "Tessa Grey, the event photographer."

"Adrian Mercer. Pleased to meet you." He shakes my hand, then glances back at the spreading stain on his shirt with mock gravity. "And I'm here to see the new exhibition. I'd hoped to avoid *becoming* part of the art tonight, but here we are."

I don't know if I should laugh or cry, so I settle on, "Maybe the red suits you."

There's a spark in Adrian's eye as his gaze lingers on my hands, which I notice are now flecked with wine... Jesus, I'm a mess. I wipe my hands on my pants, which earns me a raised brow. "Let me buy you a drink after you're done working, to replace the one I'm wearing."

I shift my weight. "My boyfriend won't appreciate that."

"You don't have a boyfriend." His voice is certain, matter-of-fact.

"No?" I raise an eyebrow. "How could you possibly know that?"

Adrian's gaze darkens, a muscle working in his jaw. "The way you're studying me isn't how someone with a boyfriend looks at a stranger."

My pulse hammers in my ears so loudly that I'm certain he must hear it too. I take three steps back, holding the camera up as a shield. "Either way, you don't have to buy me a drink. But you could let me take your picture as penance. You know, for the gallery photos."

"I'm afraid the drink is non-negotiable. But I'll let you take my picture if that'll make you feel better." Adrian leans into the lens, the ruined shirt on full display. "Tell me how to stand."

"Just... just act natural and look at me," I tell him, wondering why I thought this was a good idea. He follows my instructions, and the moment is more intimate than I expected, the focus sharp on his broad form as it fills the viewfinder. I click twice and lower the camera.

Adrian doesn't move. "You're good at that," he says, voice low. "Capturing people like you already know them."

"It takes some practice to find what makes you "you" behind the camera. There is something in every person that shines as long as you capture it at the right moment."

"I like that. So what do you do when you're not in high demand at gallery openings?"

The actual answer is sleep, swallow vitamins, try not to google symptom clusters, or obsessively read romantasy until I have finished every book in the series. "This, mostly. Freelance gigs. Small stuff. I take a lot of pictures of my cat."

Adrian tilts his head, studying me a beat longer than seems comfortable. "Can I see one?"

"Of my cat?"

"Of anything. I'll trade you." He pulls his phone from his pocket, scrolls with long fingers I can't look away from, then holds out the device. "Here," he says, angling the display toward me. "Caught this while hunting for new ideas." The screen shows a photo of the city skyline at dusk, impossibly crisp and blue.

"Wow," I whisper, impressed. "If I didn't know any better, I'd say you're a professional."

"I am professional at a lot of things." He gives me a grin that makes my cheeks go hot. "But no, not a professional photographer. I am an architect, actually, which is similar in some ways. We both frame the world in a way that moves people."

"I don't think I've ever met an architect before."

"Well, seems like tonight's your lucky night." The look he gives me suggests I might get lucky in more ways than one, and my blush deepens. "Alright, come on. I showed you mine, now you show me yours."

I huff out a laugh, then grudgingly scroll through my photos. I skip the ones I've just taken, along with some bad mirror shots, before landing on a picture from a wedding last month. "Here," I say, and pass the camera over.

Adrian's thumb ghosts the edge of the screen. "Interesting choice," he observes. "Being responsible for capturing the perfect moments must be quite stressful."

"Not necessarily," I say, watching his face as he studies my work. "A groom in love looks at his bride like she's the only person who's ever existed, which is pretty easy to capture. Everything else blurs away for them except that perfect bubble of happiness they're sharing, and I'm fortunate to be there to capture that."

Adrian's eyes flick up to meet mine, a half-smile playing at the corner of his mouth. Our hands almost brush as he returns my camera. He's standing closer, enough that I can smell his cologne; something woodsy and rich, like cedar and citrus.

Marissa sweeps by, clutching three VIPs in her wake, their laughter loud and bubbly. She sees me and flashes a double thumbs-up before vanishing into the noise. Reality crashes back, and I realize I've barely worked, too caught in Adrian's presence.

"I should, uh—"

"Get back to it," Adrian finishes, but doesn't move away. "I'll be here, waiting for you when you finish."

The way he says those words so smoothly is almost enough to restart the ache at the base of my skull. My face flushes deeper, and I give him a quick nod before shuffling down the room.

I photograph a red-plated installation, then a sculpture that looks like a blowfish. I can feel Adrian's presence behind me, a little too close. His attention makes my skin flush, as if I was standing next to a space heater on full blast.

I hide in the alcove near the restroom for a minute to let my adrenaline settle. My fingers are trembling, so I form them into fists to steady them. The jitters are from too much caffeine, I tell myself, and definitely not from the way Adrian's eyes seem to strip me down to the negatives.

I peer out and watch him drift through the crowd, already deep in conversation with a woman in a sequined jumpsuit. She's laughing, with one hand stroking his arm, and for some reason I feel a twinge of something sharp and petty in my chest.

I tear my gaze away from Adrian and the woman, and snap another dozen shots, staying on the move so I won't get ambushed by Marissa. I keep thinking I'll catch Adrian watching me again, but when I turn, he's absorbed in the surrounding people, schmoozing with a wineglass in hand. It's only when I review my camera roll that I realize he's in some photos, angled so his face doesn't quite look at the art, but at me.

The show blurs past in a melody of shooting and sidestepping. When the crowd thins and the lights dim, Adrian reappears, materializing at my elbow with a half empty drink in his hand and a shirt that's still dotted with wine. "Gallery's winding down," he says. "Let me buy you that drink you promised me earlier."

I want to remind him I made no promises. I want to tell him I need to upload photos, or that my cat will perish without treats. But

I nod instead, grab my shoes from the coat check, and follow him out into the cold. The gallery's glass door swings behind us, and Adrian falls into step beside me. It takes only a block for us to find a narrow, candlelit bar with pressed-tin ceilings and music that's more mood than melody.

Adrian leads me to a booth in the back. The seat is deep, nearly swallowing me whole. He slides in next to me, his body heat seeping into my side instantly. "What are you having? Wine? Champagne?" he asks, signaling to the bartender.

"Just water for now." I squeeze my hands together under the table.

"You don't like to drink?"

"I do. But I get migraines sometimes. It's easier not to tempt fate tonight."

Adrian leans forward, elbows on the table. "I get them, too. Cluster headaches are the worst. Sometimes they hit me so hard I can barely see straight. Have you tried those heated eye masks with the vibration?" When I tell him no, he looks genuinely distressed on my behalf. "You're missing out. They are an absolute game changer."

I nod, reaching for my water glass. "Maybe I'll buy one. Or I'll find a better way to manage my stress. But honestly, my whole life is stress, so that's probably not gonna happen." I smile ruefully. "If I weren't always running around like a chicken with its head cut off, I don't know what I'd even do with myself."

Adrian huffs in amusement. "For what it's worth, pain sharpens you. That's what my father used to say." A little darkness moves behind his eyes, almost a flicker, before he gives a slow, weighted laugh. "He's a terrible person though, so probably not the best source for words of wisdom."

I find myself leaning forward, curiosity knotting in my gut. "He sounds... colorful."

"More like insufferable. I haven't spoken to him in years." Adrian's gaze refocuses on me. "But enough about him. We're here to talk about us, to get acquainted on a deeper level."

I look at him askance, unsure of what to say.

Adrian grins. "Okay, I'll start. I've always liked people who put things in their own terms. I think that's what drew me to you."

"You barely know me."

"I know enough, and I like what I see." His words are so direct and unapologetic I almost choke on an ice cube. "You seem like a problem solver, someone who observes and documents everything. I noticed how you mapped the gallery in phases." He taps the table, illustrating with quick, neat beats. "You're systematic. But only until you see something you want, then you break pattern for it."

I bristle, maybe just a little, because who enjoys being read so quickly?

"I guess that's true," I admit at last. "If you miss the shot, it's gone forever. People change the second they know someone's looking at them. I like catching them off guard."

He nods, considering. "Most people hate being surprised. Myself included, if I'm being honest. Unless, of course, the surprise is running into a beautiful woman like yourself." He raises his glass, and I clink my water against it.

Adrian asks about my favorite artist, and I try to think of an answer that isn't *the lady who painted the custom sneakers I bought on Etsy a while back.* I tell him about Lewis Shantel, about the importance of angles and lighting, about the things that inspire me.

I let myself talk. Adrian doesn't interrupt, and he doesn't look bored. He chases my thoughts, asks smart questions, hazel eyes so intent and focused that I can't look away for long. I'm so drawn in by him that the rest of the bar could collapse and I wouldn't notice.

Somewhere between the first and third drinks, I switch to wine despite my better judgement, and the air between us shifts. It's still charged, but there's a sense of shared intimacy now, a feeling of warmth in my belly. Adrian tells stories about designing buildings, and about the time he built a model of a high school gym out of sugar cubes for a class project. When I laugh, it's less awkward than before.

A basket of fried pickles lands on our table. Adrian lifts one between two fingers, dipping it into ranch, then pops it into his mouth. "You ever notice," he says between bites, "how the best food is always the most terrible for you?"

"That's the entire point of bar food," I say, crunching into my own pickle. It's so hot I nearly burn the roof of my mouth. "Wow. These are hot but delicious."

"There's a fine line between pleasure and pain," Adrian says, voice low. "Fries, cheese, fried anything. All designed to soothe us, even as we know it's slowly killing us."

"We're all slowly dying anyway."

He wipes his fingers and leans in, elbows on the table. "That's a morbid thing to say... But I suppose you're right, so we might as well enjoy the ride."

"Amen to that."

We clink our fried pickles together in a greasy toast.

"So you said you're an architect. What's your favorite building?"

"Hmmm. That's like asking a parent to pick a favorite child. But if I had to choose one, I'd say it's a building I once saw in California." He pulls out his phone, flicks through a few photos, and shows me an image of a glass-walled home floating over a glowing city. "I love the illusion of openness, but the structure is fundamentally about protection."

I study the photo, and then him. "I get it," I say. "You design open spaces because you want to see everything, but at the same time, you want strength and control. Something beautiful on the outside and unbreakable on the inside."

"See? Very observant," Adrian says. "You notice details. Are you sure you're not secretly psychoanalyzing me?"

"Um... I'm way out of my depth with normal people, let alone people with... depth."

Adrian laughs, bright and genuine, and I can't help but smile back.

"I'm glad you think I have depth. That might be one of the most interesting compliments I've ever gotten." Adrian leans back in his seat. "So tell me. Are you from around here?"

I take a sip of wine. "No. I grew up in a small town, two hours north of here. My mom taught third grade for thirty years, and my Dad worked the railroad. I'm an only child. Guess they figured one kid was enough trouble."

Adrian nods, swirling his drink. "That sounds like an idyllic upbringing."

"It was. What about you?" I ask, leaning forward. "You strike me as a city boy."

"Guilty," he says, his lip tugging up at the corner. "I'm a city kid through and through."

Adrian tells me he grew up in an upper-class family and his mother was the glue that kept everything together... until she wasn't. I try to say something sympathetic, but he just shrugs, and somehow the subject changes before I have time to get sad about it.

The crowd in the bar thins out. My headache dissolves into something electric that runs just beneath my skin, leaving me caught between the urge to fidget and the desire to lean closer. Adrian's smile is lazier now, less practiced, as if he's relaxing into the evening. He's let his jacket slide off onto the seat, and there's a tiny wine stain on his cuff I hadn't noticed before.

He checks the time and sighs. "I wish tonight didn't have to end, but I've got an early client meeting tomorrow. I'll have to be on my A game because this client is notorious for putting people on the spot. Last time they asked me to name the Pantone values for the conference room carpet. Can you believe that?"

"That sounds serious." I chuckle, but my chest tugs. I don't want the evening to end either. "It's been a long day and I better get some rest too," I say, knowing it's for the best.

Adrian stands, and I step out of the booth to follow.

The city feels vivid and close outside. Adrian turns to face me. "Can I walk you home?"

I almost say no out of habit. We just met. Adrian knowing where I live probably isn't the smartest idea. But there's something earnest in the way he's watching me, the wind tousling his hair, making him look almost boyish. "Sure," I hear myself say.

The night air bites at my skin as we walk in companionable silence, and I cross my arms tight against my chest. Adrian glances over, shrugs out of his jacket, and holds it open for me. When I start to refuse, he just raises a brow, as if daring me to question his motives.

The fabric of the jacket is still warm from his body as he drapes it over me. I breathe in the scent of cedar and citrus clinging to the collar.

"Thank you," I mumble, hyperaware of every inch between us.

"My pleasure. It's a rare night I get to save a damsel from hypothermia and red wine simultaneously."

I snort. "Chivalry isn't dead, then?"

"Not tonight, at least." Adrian's eyes catch the streetlamp's glow as he looks down at me. "I know I'm just a stranger to you, but—" He stops, shakes his head, then smiles. "I'm glad you're here."

I can't think of a clever response, so I just nod with a smile and keep walking. When we reach my building, I shift from foot to foot under the awning, twisting the keys in my hand. The cold is seeping through my pants, and I remember Adrian's jacket is still hanging off my shoulders.

"Thanks for the drink," I say, slipping out of the warm fabric and handing it back to him. "And for the jacket. Next time I'll try to remember to bring my own."

Adrian watches me for a second, then takes the jacket and folds his hands into his pockets. "You're welcome. And for what it's worth, you have an open invitation to borrow my clothes anytime."

I feel my cheeks flame despite the cold. "That's... awfully forward of you."

"Just stating facts." Adrian steps closer. "Can I see you again?"

"Yeah. I'd like that."

His grin is dazzling. "Tomorrow?"

My breath hitches, not because it's an eager ask, but because I want to say yes so badly that it scares me. I'm not used to being wanted quite so blatantly. It's an intoxicating feeling that I shouldn't like so much. "I'll see if I can pencil you into my schedule."

Adrian holds my gaze, waiting for me to backpedal, but I don't. I feel my mouth pull into a smile that's probably lopsided and a little idiotic.

"I'll hold you to that."

I watch as the city lights catch along Adrian's cheeks, sharpening his features and making him look more handsome than he has any business being. With his hands jammed into his pockets and a loose, confident tilt to his frame, he looks relaxed. Not quite leaning in, but very much not leaving.

There's a long beat where neither of us moves. The world feels a little too quiet, like it's holding its breath too.

"You have a good night, Tessa," Adrian murmurs at last, still holding my gaze.

"Yeah. You too, Adrian." My mouth can't decide if it wants to say something else, and I settle for a weird little half-nod, like I'm bowing in an Elizabethan play.

Adrian's grin tugs at the corners. "I'll text you later," he says, and then he's gone, hands still in pockets, footsteps receding into the thrum of the city.

I watch his form disappear into the darkness, and a small, irrational wish that he'd turn back one more time tugs inside me.

The elevator is slow tonight, and I'm tired enough to just stand inside it with my eyes closed, the hum of the ballast lights droning overhead. My phone buzzes as I open my apartment door.

> *Liz: Did u survive? Is the art any good or did the gallery host a glorified wine mixer?*

And then, five seconds later, another text:

> *Liz: Tell me you wore the dress. Did you talk to any hot guys??*

I smirk, toes scrunching against the cold floor as I balance my phone and try to not step on any stray toys Toast scattered around the living room while I was gone.

*Me: Wearing pants. Spilled wine on a hot guy in the first five minutes*

*Liz: Ugh I told you to wear something sexy*

*Liz: Did he at least spank you?? Or ask for your number?*

*Me: He asked me out*

*Liz: OMG!! Pics??? Or at least a link to his Insta, come on, give me SOMETHING*

I scroll through my camera, looking for the two shots I snapped of Adrian during the *penance portrait* part of our interaction. Adrian's grinning in the first photo. In the second, he's smirking at the lens, his eyes dilated against the hazel, one eyebrow slightly raised. My thumb hovers over the image for a moment too long, and I have to swallow twice before I can breathe normally again. I hesitate, then send the second photo, daring Liz to psychoanalyze him. She responds in ten seconds flat.

*Liz: HELLO DARK AND HANDSOME*

*Liz: His jaw could cut glass. When are you seeing him again?*

I laugh out loud, startled by the force of my voice echoing off the walls. I lean against the couch, phone pressed to my chest, and try to steady my hands.

> *Me: I'm glad you approve. I will see him again tomorrow*

> *Liz: Ooooh! I want every detail!!*

> *Me: I promise to report back to you*

The migraine trickles back to life as I undress, a slow auger behind my left ear. I pop two more vitamins, realizing as I do that this is the fourth or fifth time today that I've taken them. That can't be good. I wash them down with cold water and squint at the manila envelop laying on the table. I'm trying to calculate how many hours I have until I need to be functional again tomorrow, when another beep from my phone draws my attention.

> *Unknown: It was great running into you tonight. Looking forward to tomorrow*

I don't remember giving Adrian my number. Did I? I must have. I tap out a reply, fingers sticky with anticipation.

> *Me: Likewise*

I should say something else, shouldn't I? But before I can type, delete, then re-type another message, my phone beeps again.

> *Unknown: Do you usually eat breakfast?*

> *Me: Sure. Why do you ask?*

> *Unknown: Because I'd like to meet you at the Plum Pot at 9am tomorrow for breakfast*

I read, then re-read his message. The Plum Pot Cafe is on the next block. It's a tiny joint with odd hours that sells Turkish coffee so strong it makes your brain vibrate. It's been my little heaven, a secret hideout away from the world that only the locals frequent. But suddenly I want to be there with Adrian. I want to see if he orders for me or if he lets me do it myself. I want to watch his face in the flat morning light.

> *Me: 9am sharp. Don't be late, I'm not patient when it comes to caffeine*

> *Unknown: Noted. See you then*

I grin, feeling the stretch across my cheeks, and save Adrian's number in my phone under *Wine Guy*. I stare at the contact name, imagining it lighting up my screen tomorrow, and feel a flutter low in my stomach.

The manila envelope continues to judge me from the table, swollen with work, but I leave it there. I should import the gallery photos, I should tag and cull and retouch, but the thought of sitting hunched over the harsh light of my laptop screen feels unbearable right now. For once my thoughts are soft and pliant, and I can't stand the idea of work intruding on my good mood.

I brush my teeth for a full two minutes, floss, and even massage moisturizer into my face, which is a luxury I usually skip when I'm tired. I climb into bed in just a t-shirt, the sheets cool against my shins. I stare at the ceiling, trying to remember the last time I was this excited for the next morning.

A flutter of something restless and eager makes me reach for my phone, then stop. I could text Liz again, or even call my mom... but what would I even say? That I'm excited, but considering canceling my coffee date because I'm nervous? No, that won't do. There's something about Adrian that feels different. He's not like the men whose messages grew further apart until they stopped altogether, or the blurry faces I can barely recall after nights of too much Cabernet. No, I get the sense Adrian isn't like the rest.

There was something in the way his eyes found mine across the crowded space at the gallery. Every time he was around, my attention narrowed, and the background noise faded to a distant hum.

I should be cautious; I should take things slow. But when I think about canceling our plans for tomorrow, my fingers refuse to type the words. I'm setting an alarm instead, already wondering what I'll wear in the morning. My gaze lingers on Wine Guy's name in my contacts, and I know I'm already in too deep to pretend I will not show up.

My body feels light, almost effervescent, as I slide under the covers and dock my phone on the charger. I haven't felt this electricity sinc e... well, maybe ever. Ridiculous, really, over a man I barely know. But I surrender to the warm current of anticipation anyway, drifting into a restless sleep with my lips curved in a half-smile.

# CHAPTER TWO

# Freefall

I wake up well-rested, which is a sensation so foreign that I have to check my phone to see if I've blacked out and slept through the weekend. Friday glows at the top of the screen, the digits too bright, but my head is clear for the first time in months. For a moment I just float, listening to my heater wheeze and to the distant thump of someone's morning playlist.

I flip onto my back and let my eyes adjust to the light filtering in through the blinds, then reach for my phone. The first notification is a text from Adrian, time-stamped eight minutes ago.

> *Wine Guy: See you soon. Counting down the minutes*

I smile at the message, then blink at the string of blue bubbles above it. I must've messaged Adrian again last night, because there's a "*Can't wait to see you*" and a row of cat emojis, none of which I remember sending. There's also a midnight "*LOL ur cute*" message, and most damningly, another bubble time-stamped 2:04am: "*Promise you'll show up tomorrow?*"

I cringe and clutch the pillow to my face, mortified. I am that girl. The eager, emoji-slinging maniac. If Adrian has any sense, he'll draft a gentle let-down about how he's busy with work for the next decade.

I set the phone aside and will myself to breathe. It's cool and gray outside, which is the perfect weather for staring at nothing for a luxurious hour or two, but nerves won't let me sit still. So I shower, and even shave my legs for the first time in weeks.

After trying on three outfits, I settle on the navy dress Liz likes, with built in spandex that makes my waist look smaller, and pair it with thick beige tights. I line my lips with the faintest bit of color before completing my look with a cardigan and a pair of boots.

In the hallway mirror, my reflection surprises me with her shoulders back and chin lifted. The woman staring back looks ready for something good to happen. With my purse clutched tight against my hip, I force myself out the door before doubt can creep in. My phone buzzes against my palm just as I reach the stairwell.

> *Wine Guy: Are you a donut person or a scone person?*

> *Me: Surprise me*

I'm not sure if I mean it as a challenge or a test, or just a way to stop myself from saying something insane. I coast down the stairs, avoiding the elevator and the stale perfume of my neighbor, and hit the street.

It's only a couple of blocks to the Plum Pot Cafe, and my nerves ratchet up with every step.

The little cafe is busy, with a line of grad students and retirees tucked inside under a painted sign. I spot Adrian through the frosted glass. He's at a table, reading something on his phone. He looks polished in his cable-knit sweater and jeans. My gaze lingers on his freshly shaved jaw, then travels to the small frown tugging at his lips as he reads. I wonder if he's reading the news, or if perhaps he just got some bad news at work. His shoulders fill out the soft wool, and I can't help but admire the muscles shifting in his arms as he lifts his cup.

I want to run my fingers through his perfectly styled hair, to mess it up until it matches how I feel: with my nerves frayed and heart beating out of sync.

But what if he doesn't like who I am in the light of day?

My feet carry me forward while my thoughts spiral. Last night the wine flowed and the candlelight was forgiving. It was easy to feel desirable. It was easy to forget that my shirt came off a clearance rack, or to pretend I was someone worth crossing a crowded room for. But morning is different. Morning is harsh and honest, and I'm not sure I hold up under that kind of scrutiny.

*Calm down, Tessa. Everything's gonna be fine.*

I take a breath. Then another. Adrian spots me before I can finish composing myself, stands, and waves me over. His smile is welcoming as I walk up to him, not at all like someone who's been bombarded with desperate 2am texts.

"Hey, beautiful!" He rounds the table to pull out a chair for me.

"Good morning." I try to sound casual as I slide into the seat. "You're punctual."

Adrian sits across from me, eyes bright. "I might have planned my morning around our date," he admits. His gaze trails over me appreciatively, and I feel my shoulders loosen a bit. "And I brought options." He gestures to the table, where there's already two mugs of coffee, a glazed donut, and what looks like a poppyseed scone, cut in half.

I hope my grin looks flirtatious rather than unhinged. "So you're a man who believes in contingency plans. Nice."

Adrian nods while drumming his fingers against his mug. "You can never be too prepared." He leans forward, elbows on the small, wobbly table. "I suspected you'd pick the donut, but then I figured, maybe you're a wild card. Maybe you'll pick the one I least expect."

I break off a piece of scone and pop it into my mouth, the flavor lemony and tangy. "Seems you've figured me out already. Most donuts are way too sweet. I'll take a scone over a donut any day."

"Good to know. I'll remember that next time."

Next time. I like the sound of that.

We spend the next hour chatting. Adrian tells me about a client who wanted an office building covered in mirrors, even in the restrooms. I tell him about an eccentric accountant, who hired me to photograph his pet rat in a Santa hat for the staff holiday card.

Adrian nearly spits out his coffee at that. "Please tell me you kept a picture of the Santa rat."

I do, and I show him. Adrian grins, thumb grazing the screen right next to mine. "That definitely gives the team mascot a whole new meaning."

When he looks up, he's closer. I see the green flecks in his hazel eyes, and something about how he holds the coffee cup, fingers curled just-so, makes my own hands itch with the urge to photograph him.

"So, be honest. Did you regret sending me those texts last night?"

I groan at the change of subject, which only makes him smirk. "I didn't even remember sending half of them until this morning. Talk about feeling mortified when I woke up."

"You shouldn't have cared. I actually liked your texts. They were…" Adrian pauses, searching for the word. "Unfiltered. I like that you say exactly what you mean. That's rare these days."

I trace the rim of my mug. "More like rarely unfiltered…" I chuckle. "That sounds like it belongs on a T-shirt, actually."

"It does, doesn't it? It would make the perfect punny shirt." Adrian rubs his jaw in contemplation. "I'll market it. We can split the profits fifty-fifty."

I almost snort coffee out of my nose at that. That's the thing I'm quickly learning about Adrian. Just when I start to overthink the way I'm slurping my coffee, or the way my fingers won't stay still, he says something that breaks the tension, and suddenly I forget to be nervous.

The windows cloud with mid-morning chill as we talk. I study the way Adrian's lips twitch when he's trying not to smile, my gaze drawn to the dimple that appears in his right cheek.

He catches me looking. "Do I have something on my face?"

"Just your face," I say, and his smile widens. Two women at the next table glance over, their stares lingering on Adrian's profile. I can't blame them. Heck, I can't seem to tear my gaze away from the man either. Adrian holds my gaze, seemingly oblivious to the female attention around him. I consider asking if he's always this present and intense with everyone he meets, but catch myself.

"So," I say, fidgeting with my napkin, "what does the rest of your day look like?"

Adrian glances at the clock on his phone, then shrugs. "Work meeting in an hour. Another after that. The rest is just busywork if I'm lucky. Then a networking dinner in the evening."

"You call busywork lucky?"

"Only because it keeps my mind off you for longer than two seconds. But if I had the choice, I'd stay here and have coffee with you all day instead." His gaze flickers over my face, open and searching.

I avert my eyes, a hot flush creeping up my neck as his words hang in the air between us. Men before him would glance at their phones mid-conversation, their attention drifting away if I paused too long between thoughts. I'd memorized the furrowing of eyebrows that meant I'd said something odd, the subtle shift in posture when they began planning their exit. I'd learned to fill silences, to laugh at the right moments. But with Adrian, the rules have changed, and I'm not sure how to navigate these uncharted waters.

Our knees bump under the table. Adrian's phone vibrates, but he ignores it, eyes on me as I finish the last bite of scone. "What about you? You have a busy day?"

I take a long sip of coffee. "Some editing. I need to finish organizing my portfolio and send Marissa the gallery photos. But honestly, I'll probably try to nap at some point."

"Ah. There's nothing better than a mid-day nap. Do you get tired a lot?"

"All the time. But it's mostly my fault. I stay up too late, obsess over photos, and read books instead of sleeping. I'm actually terrible at being a grown-up."

Adrian hums in agreement. "Growing up is overrated."

I like how he says it, like he gets tired of pretending to be an adult some days too. I want to ask him why he finds me so fascinating. Why does he look at me like I'm a puzzle he wants to solve? Why did he say last night that pain sharpens you, and what did he mean by that? But the words get tangled up in my mouth, turning into something safer. "So, um, are you naturally a morning person, or is your early morning enthusiasm reserved just for me?"

Adrian's lip tugs at the corner, and he studies me a beat too long before answering.

"Maybe I couldn't wait to see you again..." The dimple makes its appearance. "Maybe I've been thinking about that smile of yours since the moment we met. The way it starts slow, like you're deciding whether I've earned it." Adrian's gaze drops to my mouth as I wipe at it with a napkin, then back up. "And when you blush like that, I lose my train of thought completely." His thumb grazes my wrist across the table. "I hope that doesn't scare you away."

"It doesn't," I mumble, feeling my flush deepen. I don't know why admitting that feels like jumping into the deep end of a pool.

Adrian's eyes crinkle at the corners. "I was hoping you'd say that." He drains the last of his coffee, then spins the mug in slow circles, fingers drumming once, twice. "You want to walk for a bit before we both have to go play grown-up?"

I can't think of a reason to say no. "Sure."

The air is brisk outside. We fall into step easily, and I note the way our strides match, the accidental synchrony of Adrian's arm brushing mine when we cross the street. We talk about random things for a while, like bad architecture and the worst foods to eat on a first date. Adrian goes with soup dumplings, and I tell him it's buffalo wings, hands down.

I'm lighter than I have been in ages, like the sum of my gravity changed direction the moment I met Adrian.

A few blocks down, we slow at the corner. "I don't want to make you late for work," I tell him. I know we should head back, but a tiny, traitorous voice in my head wants to see what would happen if we just kept walking all day.

Adrian shrugs. "The world won't end if I miss a meeting or two."

"If you're sure," I say, and that settles it.

We stroll towards a park a few short blocks away, then down a path lined with the last shreds of autumn. Fallen leaves curl and spiral around my boots. The park is mostly empty except for a man with a dog and a couple jogging in tandem.

"I wish I was more like those people," I say, gesturing at the couple pounding the path. "But I can't run unless something is actively chasing me."

"I hate running too," Adrian confesses. "I tried to force myself to like it. Then I realized life's too short to do cardio you despise."

I give him a look. "So what do you do to stay... you know." I wave my hand, gesturing toward the breadth of his shoulders, the way his jeans fit in a way that makes my brain lose all function. "Fit?"

He shrugs. "I try to hit the office gym a couple of times a week." His gaze slides toward me. "You could join me sometime."

I snort. "Not sure if that's an insult to my physique or just your way of asking me out again."

Adrian leans closer, his voice dropping. "Would you be offended if I told you, I'd just like to see you in a pair of workout shorts?"

"Dream on. You'll never catch me in one of those skimpy workout sets."

"Good," he murmurs. "I'd hate to spend my workout punching every man who can't keep their eyes to themselves." He gives me a heated look, and I fumble the next step, nearly tripping on a warped section of sidewalk.

Adrian steadies me with a hand at my elbow. "Whoa," he says, "careful."

I laugh to cover my embarrassment. "See? This is exactly why I don't run."

"It's a good thing I'm here to catch you," he says, and his hand lingers just a moment longer before letting go.

At the center of the park, we wander to the water's edge and watch the ripples dance across the surface. When Adrian turns to me, his face looks softer, but also older, like the sunlight has carved new lines into his expression. He shifts his weight from one foot to the other.

"There's something about you," he murmurs, voice lower than before. "I swear there's this pull between us. Like we were meant to find each other." His fingers brush against mine. "Tell me I'm not imagining this. Tell me you feel it too."

I want to deflect with humor, but something in his gaze keeps me anchored in this moment. "I don't let people in easily. But with you," I shake my head, "being with you feels easy. So yeah, I feel it too."

The words would normally mortify me to death, but today, with him, they hang in the air and feel oddly right. "I must be honest with you, though. I don't do relationships. I'm terrible at them."

"Me neither. But I think we have something worth exploring here." Adrian steps closer, his hand finding the curve of my waist. "I can tell by the way your heartbeat picks up when my skin grazes yours," my heart stutters when Adrian's fingertips brush mine, "and by the way your cheeks flush when you're thinking about me." Heat blooms in my cheeks despite the chill in the air, proving his point. "Or when you imagine what it'll feel like to have my lips on yours."

Time seems to slow as Adrian pulls me closer, and I suck in a breath at the shock of his cold lips. Then warmth blooms between us as his lips soften and his tongue finds mine. He kisses me deeply, and I lean into him, losing myself in the sensation. His groan of approval vibrates through me, the sound sinking into my belly and pooling liquid heat in my core. I curl my fingers into the front of his coat, holding on, because I'm certain my legs will give out any second. The city blurs around us, the sounds muffled, until there's nothing but Adrian's mouth, his hands, and the heat of him bleeding through my clothes.

I'm dizzy, my skin feeling electric, aching for Adrian's hands everywhere at once. And when he finally pulls back, just far enough to look at me, his breath uneven against my lips, I wish we could stay here all day and explore where this pull between us could go.

A bell rings somewhere. It's faint, maybe coming from a church a few blocks away, but the sound rings through me. "You'll be late," I whisper against Adrian's lips.

"I'm exactly where I want to be." He presses another kiss to my mouth, then another. "Can I see you again tomorrow night?"

I nod, probably too fast. "Yes."

"Good girl." Adrian's grin breaks wide, and his body relaxes against mine as he kisses me one more time. "Let me walk you home."

"You really don't have to," I tell him. "I've kept you long enough. And besides, I want to stay out here a little while."

Adrian gives me a long look. He looks so thoroughly kissed, with his pupils blown wide and his lips swollen, that I'm half a second from pushing him down onto the nearest park bench. Jesus. Yes, I definitely need some more cool air.

"Fine. I'll text you later," he promises, then releases me slowly. "Enjoy your nap, Tessa. I hope you dream about me."

"You've given me plenty to dream about." I laugh too loudly and too openly, nothing like myself. And for once, I'm not embarrassed about it.

I linger after Adrian's gone, letting the cold press into my skin. I look at the pond and think of the glow of the bar last night. I think of Adrian's charming smile and the red wine stain on his shirt. Then

I think of the kiss we just shared, of the way he consumed me, and the promises I tasted on his lips. A tremor of anticipation stirs inside me, making my skin feel new, like I've shed some old version of myself.

Back home, I trade the navy dress for an old sweatshirt and pull my hair up in an untidy knot. The manila folder of photos continues to glare at me from the table, a sullen reminder that adulthood is still my full-time occupation. But I don't want to think about work yet. Not when I can still feel the heat of Adrian's hands on my skin and the taste of his lips against mine.

I flop onto the sofa and check the notifications peppering the home screen of my phone. I silence a reminder to buy cat food, clear out a handful of missed spam calls, then tap open a message from Liz.

> *Liz: So I did some online stalking. This guy is a HOTTIE. And he owns more than one suit jacket? SOLD!*

> *Liz: Please tell me you went to second base with him*

> *Me: None of your business*

> *Liz: That's all the answer I needed*

> *Me: Haha very funny. If you must know, he kissed me today and it was amazing*

The three dots pulse on my screen, and within seconds, Liz's next text slides into view.

> *Liz: Of course I must know!!!*

> *Liz: I'm proud of you, Mother Theresa.*

> *Liz: Hey, let's do dinner tonight? You bring the deets and I'll get a bottle of cheap Merlot to celebrate your romantic glow up*

I debate for a minute. Liz is a force of nature and will wring the details out of me, but I kind of want to talk. I kind of want to bask in this newfound sense of excitement for a day, maybe two.

> *Me: Sure. Ramen at 7? I'll bring the tea*

> *Liz: Perfect. I expect a full tea party with a PowerPoint!!*

***

By 11pm, Liz and I have demolished two bowls of ramen, a plate of gyoza, and the better part of a bottle of cheap Pinot Grigio she served in Yeti tumblers labeled *Boss Babe*. We're sprawled on her couch, with our stomachs distended, and limbs draped like we've survived a culinary battle.

"So, let me get this straight," Liz brandishes her chopstick like a baton. "First date? You publicly humiliate yourself and spill wine on him. And he still asks you out. Second date? He buys you breakfast and stares at you like you're the last woman on earth. Then he kisses you like a starving man." She leans in, blue eyes glittering. "And you're still single because...?"

I throw a napkin at her. It bounces off her forehead and lands in the empty takeout box. "Because it's only been two dates. Also, he's too perfect. No one is that perfect..."

Liz almost inhales the last bite of her gyoza as she snorts. "Tessa. Babe. You just met this guy and you've already got a running list of red flags? Just once, let yourself enjoy something without sabotaging it."

"I am enjoying myself," I protest, but Liz cocks her head like a therapist who's caught you in a lie. "No, I am! I enjoy talking to him. He listens, and he texts me back. And he's not allergic to commitment, or at least I don't think he is."

Liz sips her wine and nods. "Sounds pretty good to me. So what's the problem? Worried you'll find something damning about him? Wait... tell me you've looked him up online to make sure he isn't a serial killer before you went on a date with him."

"Of course I looked him up. I'm not a savage." Adrian's social media is as blandly successful as you'd expect. It shows the names of an architecture firm, grad school, and one of those charity marathons I always say I'll donate to and never do. "There's not much about him online, but I did find a high school yearbook photo where he's got braces but still looks like a fairytale prince. He's just so... wholesome."

Liz rolls her eyes. "You say that like it's a bad thing. Seriously, your relationship with this guy could be the start of a cheesy romantic movie if you weren't so neurotic."

"Or the crime documentary that follows," I retort, which makes Liz shake her head so hard she spills wine on her leggings.

We watch some reality show with everyone wearing capes and plotting murder, but I can't keep my focus. My phone keeps buzzing with

Adrian's name, and I have to fight the urge to check it. Liz notices, of course.

"Go ahead," she says, grinning. "Text your boyfriend. You know you want to."

"He's not my boyfriend—" but she waves me off, already absorbed in whatever twist is unfolding on the screen. I check my phone under the throw blanket.

> *Wine Guy: I hope you're having fun. Tell your friend I said hi*

> *Me: She says you owe her a bottle of wine for endorsing you*

> *Wine Guy: Deal. But only if you bring her to dinner one day soon. She seems like a smart wing woman and I could use all the support I can get*

I grin, thumb hovering over the screen. "Adrian says hello."

Liz salutes the air with her nearly empty glass. "Tell him he needs to step up his game if he wants to get into your pants."

She sets her drink down on the coffee table, watching me for a moment. "Actually... never mind. It makes me happy seeing you glow like this, Tess. If this guy's got you all heart-eyed in twenty-four hours, he must be doing something right."

I look away, a little embarrassed by how right she is. "Weird, right? It's like I'm already in too deep and I barely know him."

Liz tips sideways into me, her arm looping around my shoulders. "Nah. You deserve to feel wanted. And when the right person comes along?" She squeezes me tighter. "You just *know*."

When I get home, later than I meant to, I find myself reluctant to turn on the lights. The city outside is silent, and my living room is clean for once, except for spilled kitty litter and the photo equipment I forgot to put away earlier. I find Toast curled up in my half-open camera bag, his orange fur coating my expensive lenses. He squints at me as I step over him on my way to the couch, shedding my boots and jacket as I go.

I curl up under an old quilt, my phone warm in my palm, and scroll through the day's texts, re-reading them with a dorky grin I can't seem to suppress.

> *Wine Guy: Still free tomorrow night?*

> *Me: Are you worried I scheduled a date with someone else since we last talked*

> *Wine Guy: Just making sure you aren't getting cold feet*

Before I can respond, another message pops up:

> *Do you like pasta?*

> *Me: It depends. What kind?*

> *Wine Guy: Freshly made tagliatelle. Will that do, or is that too basic?*

> *Me: I suppose that will do. Are you trying to seduce me with carbs?*

> *Wine Guy: Maybe… Is it working?*

> *Me: It is*

By the time we finalize our date night plans and I text Adrian goodnight, my cheeks hurt from smiling. The sensible part of me whispers I should pump the brakes because this thing between Adrian and me is moving too fast. Yet here I am, calculating hours until tomorrow evening, and taking mental inventory of my good underwear.

My phone glows in the dark as I tap through my nightly routine. I set the alarm, clear out junk emails, then start doom-scrolling social media until I go blind. I'm about to switch to social media when Marissa's name jumps out from my inbox.

*Tessa,*

*Just started paging through the proofs and I'm obsessed. You made that ghastly sculpture look expensive (maybe there's hope for my taste after all). Come by Tuesday at noon for a quick meeting? I want to talk about future projects, if you're available.*

*Xoxo,*
*M*

It's the first time a client used the word *future* with my name attached to it, and for a second I just sit there, blinking at the screen. The idea of having more well-paying gigs lined up, and something better than work waiting for me on the other side of the day, is a rush that makes me feel downright bubbly.

I soak in the feeling, lost in thought, and watch as the lights of the city flicker against my window. The bed is calling my name, but there's a blissful feeling about tonight that makes me want to just sit here and breathe it in. I want to hang onto it, to memorize it. Just in case.

When my eyes begin to drift closed, I migrate to the bedroom and start to draft Adrian a clever and flirty goodnight message. But my thumb hovers, paralyzed by the million ways I could make myself sound nuttier than I am. I delete, re-type, delete again. In the end, I opt for a GIF of a cartoon lasagna doing the come hither finger wave, which seems about right for the level of dignity I've managed so far.

Adrian responds with pasta emojis and a winking face.

I set the phone down and bury my grin in the folds of my duvet. I don't reach for my vitamins, and I don't lose myself in a book boring enough to lull me to sleep. For once, my mind isn't racing with anxiety about tomorrow or replaying old embarrassments. Tonight I just close my eyes and let thoughts of the way Adrian's lips felt against mine, and the rasp in his voice when he laughed wash over me. My last thought before sleep claims is, I can't wait to see what tomorrow brings.

# CHAPTER THREE

# Deja Vu

**M**y head is full of static in the morning, but there's no pain, and that feels like a win. I get up and make coffee, letting the earthy, bitter scent drag me back to the world.

I find a follow up email from Marissa waiting for me, along with another from a client who wants a set of staff headshots, nothing fancy. There's also and a long-winded newsletter I don't remember subscribing to. I delete the newsletter, respond to the clients, and bask in the rare pleasure of not being behind on life for once.

I spend the rest of the afternoon editing, the photos from the gallery flickering across my screen. Every third shot looks crooked or overexposed, but in the best ones, you can feel the whir of the crowd and the crackle of the room. Adrian's in a few. He's always on the edge of the frame, like he's caught between one space and the next. My eyes hover over one photo, snapped at the exact moment he was grinning at Marissa's joke, the red stain on his white shirt impossible to miss.

I crop the photo and adjust the contrast. I file it away, then open a text to Liz.

> *Me: Send me your best hangover cure. Hypothetically, if I drank too much wine last night*

> *Liz: Liquid IV, greasy food, and a long walk. Preferably with company… wink wink*

> *Me: Speaking of which, if I invite you to meet Adrian at some point, promise not to interrogate him?*

> *Liz: Hell nah! I'm not promising that*

> *Me: Not even a little bit?*

> *Liz: Absolutely not. It is my duty as your only family nearby to make sure your man is up to snuff*

Liz's words stir a deep ache inside my chest, and I glance at the fridge where my parents beam from their Tampa postcard. They are wearing matching visors, their paper umbrella drinks raised in a toast to their well-earned retirement. Mom and Dad are living the life they planned, and I'm thrilled for them, even as I feel the miles stretching between us.

Thank goodness for Liz, who barged into the empty spaces of my life with her chaos and unflinching loyalty. She's become like family, if family came with zero obligation and twice the volume. Three months of friendship and already she knows exactly which buttons to push and which wine to bring. Sometimes the people who weren't there for the beginning of your story understand the middle chapters better than anyone.

I still have the ridiculous purple yoga mat Liz convinced me to buy when we first met at the yoga studio. It's gathering dust under my bed, a $49.99 reminder of the single class I attended before realizing downward dog was not for me. But I will never regret the friendship I found that day.

Last month, when I couldn't stop vomiting for three days straight, Liz had me prop my phone against my bathroom sink and stayed on FaceTime while I dozed on the bathmat. "If you die in there, I am dressing your corpse in the frilliest dress I can find," she told me. Her threat was enough motivation for me to haul myself off the bathroom floor and into bed.

My phone pings with another message from Liz, bringing me back to the present.

Liz: Also, tell him I eat men with weak handshakes for breakfast, so he better have a respectable grip

Liz: I'm just looking out for you. You want a man with strong and nimble fingers

Me: You're deranged, but I love you

Liz: As you should. Men come and go, but BFFs are forever

> *Liz: Just wait till we're wrinkled ladies sharing a beachfront cabana and scaring the pool boys*

> *Liz: Speaking of which, I could use a vacation*

I snort into my half-empty cup, then remember I haven't showered yet. Those beachfront cabana plans will be in jeopardy if a client FaceTimes me in the next ten minutes and sees what a fright I look. I hustle through a rinse, drag on the least-wrinkled thing I own, and pull together a semi-professional-looking outfit.

My afternoon would bore anyone else to tears, but it makes me feel competent. I meet Marissa to talk about her next gallery project, ship off an invoice, answer emails, and even clean my apartment. On a whim, I text Adrian a photo of my peanut butter sandwich and caption it, *The food of sophisticated artists everywhere.* Adrian replies with a selfie a minute later. He's in a hard hat and construction vest, eyebrows raised, holding an enormous sub like it's a newborn child. The filtered sunlight gives him a wholesome halo, and I have to bite my lip to keep from grinning.

I start prepping for our dinner around 6pm. I haven't had a proper date-night (not counting the evening I met Adrian) in actual years, so I spend a full ten minutes deliberating between dress or pants, winged eyeliner or none, lipstick or no lipstick, hair up or down. I go with a dress and leave my hair down, then second-guess my decision, pinning my hair back into a messy bun.

I'm so on edge about being late that I arrive at Adrian's apartment building fifteen minutes early. I'm about to take a seat in the lobby so I can collect my composure, but the front desk attendant already has my name and lets me up. Despite my attempt to project confidence, I can see every fidget, every nervous tug at my sleeve in the elevator mirrors.

When I reach the top floor, the doors open to a hallway brighter and sleeker than any place I've ever lived.

Adrian waits at the end of the hall, leaning against a door with a hand in his pocket and another holding a beautiful bouquet. He looks tired, like he's been running all day, but that fatigue melts into a bright, open smile when he sees me.

"Hey beautiful," he says, "these are for you."

"Hey yourself," I smile shyly, stepping up to him. "These flowers are so pretty. Thank you."

I take the bouquet, careful not to crush the tissue paper around the stems. I recognize the fat, ruffled peonies in every shade from blush to near-white, with a spritz of eucalyptus and sprigs of baby's breath. "How did you know I love peonies?"

Adrian's cheeks dust pink. "Lucky guess," he shrugs, but I know it's not that. He probably noticed the handful of peony photos I'd posted on my social media, or remembered some offhand comment I'd made in passing.

I set the bouquet on the shelf by the door, and Adrian is beside me, his fingers brushing mine as he helps smooth the wrinkled edges of the wrapping.

"I wanted to make a good impression," he murmurs, his breath warm against my ear. "I know it's just dinner, but—"

"I like that you made the effort." I turn to face him. "But you're setting a dangerous precedent. Sure you can keep this up? I'll be expecting breakfast in bed by next week."

Adrian's hands settle on my waist, pulling me into him. "Good." The word is a low promise. "I'll bring you breakfast in bed every day you'll let me."

And then he kisses me. His lips move confidently, like he's fantasized about this moment as many times as I have. I taste wine and desire as his fingers thread through my hair, tugging just enough to send shivers down my spine. He explores the soft inner curve of my lip, each lick slow and sensual. I lean into his firm chest to steady myself against the sudden weakness in my knees, aware of a warmth spreading through me that has nothing to do with the temperature of the room.

When we break apart, Adrian's eyes are dark and hungry. He runs his tongue across his bottom lip, and the sight of it sends a hot current straight through me. "You have no idea what seeing you here does to me," he whispers, voice rough at the edges.

I press closer, feeling the unmistakable evidence of his desire against my hip. "I think I have some idea," I breathe, and his smile curves slow and deliberate, like he's already undressing me with his mind. It's official; I'm going to need a cold shower to get through this dinner.

Adrian's fingers thread through mine, and he tugs me inside. "Come on. Let me give you the tour before I decide to skip the pasta and have you for dinner instead."

His home is neater than I expected. I take in the modern lines and the exposed brick. The view of the city through Adrian's floor to ceiling windows makes my place look like a broom closet.

I'm relieved to see a few signs of real life, too. My eyes land on stacks of books and a potted fern with a clearly beloved cat toy half-buried in the dirt.

"You have a cat?" I ask, raising an eyebrow. I don't know why the idea of Adrian owning a pet is so surprising, like finding a teddy bear in a CEO's briefcase. Perhaps it's because he's all masculine and sophisticated. It's hard to picture him picking out cat treats at the store or letting something furry sleep on his pillow.

"Fostered one for a while. Couldn't bring myself to toss the toys yet."

"Huh. That's actually really sweet."

""Don't look so surprised. Even I have a soft spot or two." His eyes hold mine for a beat before he ushers me along. "And besides, you'll learn soon enough how sweet I can be when properly motivated."

I swallow hard, willing the heat in my cheeks to subside as I let my gaze wander over the rest of the apartment. I take in the leather couch with seasonal throw pillows, then my gaze wanders to the shelves lined with strange architecture models and paperbacks. The living room is open concept and connected to a kitchen that makes my apartment look like a 24-hour truck stop.

Adrian gives me space to discover his home at my pace. He tells me about the building's original beams and how he likes to find unique decorations at street markets around the world. I take it all in with wonder, stopping by a ceramic vase that is so lopsided I'm not sure how it stays upright.

Adrian follows my gaze. "That's actually not a real piece of art. I made that in a pottery class. I was terrible at it and dropped out after three weeks."

"Isn't that the whole idea behind art though? Something unique that you created? Although no offense, but it looks like the vase is melting into the shelf."

"It's sort of a metaphor for my life," Adrian laughs, and my heart does a stupid little flip.

Adrian moves toward the kitchen, uncorks a bottle of champagne with practiced elegance, and pours us each a glass. I take a slow sip, surprised at how good the drink is. It goes down easily and has a toasty aftertaste.

"You like?" he asks, watching me closely.

"I do. It's dangerously drinkable." I let myself relax as I continue to sip my drink, settling onto a barstool at the kitchen island.

Adrian goes to prep our meal, humming under his breath as he reaches for pots and pans. It's so domestic, I half expect him to slap on an apron. He hands me a salad to toss and busies himself at the stove with a confidence I find unfairly attractive.

Before long, the garlic and onion are sauteing into a heavenly smell. "Where'd you learn to cook?" I ask, hoping he doesn't hear the atrocious growls my stomach is making. I should have eaten a snack earlier.

Adrian glances back, smiling. "My mom taught me. She used to say that if you can make a meal and tell a joke, you'll never eat alone. She wasn't wrong."

He lifts a pan lid, checks the contents, then lowers his voice. "I started cooking more after she died. Her absence seemed easier to manage when I did things that reminded me of her, you know?"

I nod, and there's a moment of silence. "I'm sorry for your loss. She must have meant the world to you."

"I appreciate that." Adrian stirs the sauce slowly, the wooden spoon circling the pot in rhythm. "My mother was a complicated woman. She was the one who got me into art, and took me to all the museums around town. She loved beautiful things, but didn't really believe she belonged among them. My father, on the other hand, is not like that." He laughs, a quick, flat sound. "My father grew up in luxury and believed he deserved anything he wanted, and he aways got whatever that was."

Adrian focuses on the food, and I watch the way his shoulders move under his shirt, the confident line of his back tapering down. My mouth goes dry, and it has nothing to do with the champagne. If there's a circle of hell in the afterlife reserved for people who fantasize during the most inappropriate moments, I've just booked my spot.

"They split up when I was a kid," Adrian continues, oblivious to my ogling. "Father married his mistress before the ink dried on the divorce papers. Then immediately moved into a new house with his new family. The whole thing felt premeditated, like he'd just replaced us." His grip on the spoon tightens. "My mother lasted about a year after that. She couldn't find her footing... I tried to help, but it was like trying to stop someone who's already decided to jump."

"That's... I can't imagine going through that," I murmur, and I mean it. It's clear how much Adrian's mother meant to him. I picture Adrian as a child, first watching his family splinter apart, then watching his mother fade away, and my chest constricts painfully

"You'd think I'd hate my father for it. Maybe I do; I'm not sure." Adrian rakes a hand through his hair, leaving it disheveled in a way that makes my stomach tighten with an inappropriate emotion. "Anyway, he got his wish. Got a new son, Marc, who was perfect in all the ways I wasn't."

Marc. I can't place why, but the name sounds familiar, as if I've heard Adrian mention him in passing before. "So you got a stepbrother?"

"Yeah. Half-brother."

"How did that make you feel? That must have been difficult to process."

Adrian nods, turning down the flame under the sauce. "After Mom died, I moved in with them. Marc wasn't a bad kid, really. Dad finally had the son he'd wanted. And I had someone else for him to focus on." His jaw tightens as he stirs. "But in that house? I was always the outsider. They had their little circle; Dad, his new wife, Marc. And then there was me, this reminder of a life they'd all rather forget."

My heart hurts for Adrian, and I want to tell him as much, but my mouth runs ahead of my brain, and instead I blurt, "You talk about Marc like he's not around anymore."

"Marc died," Adrian says so simply that it takes a second for his words to register. "A couple of years ago, in a car accident."

"Oh." I want to say something comforting, but my tongue feels like sand. "God, I'm... so sorry." I reach across the counter and touch his arm. "I can't imagine the pain of losing both your mother and brother."

Adrian's hand finds mine, his thumb brushing my knuckles. "It's easier now. Time lessens the pain." He looks up, and there's a tightness around the edges of his eyes. "Sorry. That got heavy, huh?"

I shake my head, earnest. "No, I... thank you for telling me. I would rather you share the truth than a watered-down version of your life. You can talk about your family any time if that lessens the pain... Or not... Whatever you need."

"I'd rather talk about you, if that's okay."

I nod, relieved to be back in a territory I know how to navigate. "There's not much to say. My life is a series of photography jobs and a cat who likes to cause havoc everywhere he goes."

Adrian raises a brow. "Tell me about the cat."

So I do. I tell him about the time Toast honest to God smacked my keys into the toilet, and the time he ate an entire pizza roll and threw up on my favorite pillow. Adrian is rapt, asking questions as if my cat's misadventures are the most fascinating thing he's ever heard. The tension slowly drains out of the room, leaving behind something light and easy.

After a while, my stomach growls again, and Adrian slides a plate of what looks like rolled up lettuce stuffed with meat in front of me.

"Try these?" he asks, then, before I can answer, adds, "Don't worry, it's tofu that contains zero pork. I checked the ingredients twice."

I blink. "Have I mentioned my pork allergy to you?"

Adrian hesitates for a split second, mouth quirking. "It's just a force of habit. My coworker has a gnarly allergy, and his face swelled up like a balloon the one time he ate bacon, so now I ask everyone about potential allergies. I should've checked with you sooner." He laughs a little self-effacingly. "Any other allergies I should know about? Gluten? Lactose? Wait, don't tell me you have some weird moral objections to arugula."

I snort. "Just cilantro... and kale. I will not eat kale. It's like chewing on punishment." I fork a piece of the lettuce wrap and pop it in my mouth, surprised by the subtle spice and the hint of lemon zest. "This is amazing. Did you make it?"

Adrian grins. "I did. It's actually a neAnd thank you for validating my anti-kale stance. We're off to a great start."

A laugh escapes me, and it hits me how easily I could get used to this banter. To the feeling of being not just accepted, but welcomed.

When the appetizer is gone and we are both feeling warm and relaxed from the champagne, Adrian exclaims that dinner is ready and scoops pasta onto my plate. The long ribbons are glossy and perfect, and I nearly moan at the first bite. "That's ridiculously good," I say around a mouthful, and Adrian grins, pleased.

We eat at the counter, elbows touching, talking about everything and nothing. I learn Adrian's irrationally afraid of clowns, and that his guilty pleasure is crime documentaries in the bath. I admit to my own smut addiction, and he makes me promise to send him book recommendations, which I do, sitting there in his kitchen, glass in one hand and phone in the other.

I notice his bookshelf has dog-eared copies of the same novels I've read to tatters. When I point at them, Adrian grins and says, "Great minds," and I feel a strange flutter, like maybe the universe isn't as random as I thought.

When the pasta's gone, we drift toward the couch. The windows are dark, reflecting the blurry constellations in the sky. Adrian puts on a jazzy and familiar playlist, and we sit shoulder to shoulder, melting into the music.

Adrian's thumb traces slow circles on my palm. The sensation is new, and so, so easy. I wonder what will happen next, if he'll kiss me again, if I want him to, if maybe I want it too much. I sneak a glance at Adrian, and he squeezes my hand, then shifts closer.

He lifts my chin with a gentle finger, and when our mouths meet, I swear I feel my whole body turn to liquid. Adrian angles his head, his tongue finding mine as if we've done this a hundred times before. The kiss tastes like wine, like everything good.

When we break apart, I'm breathless and a little dizzy. I bite my lip to keep from grinning like an idiot.

Adrian rests his forehead against mine. "You don't make it easy to go slow."

"Is that a complaint?" I mean that as a challenge, but my voice wobbles a little.

Adrian laughs, low in his chest. "Not even slightly."

We kiss some more and talk about random things, like our favorite movies and the best restaurants in town. Adrian's voice wraps around me like a warm blanket, and I barely notice the time. When I glance at the window, the city noise has quieted down, and the night has settled into a liminal quiet.

The clock on the wall reads 1:25am. I burrow deeper into the warm curve of Adrian's side, fighting the heaviness of my eyelids. "I should go," I tell him, but my chest tightens at the thought of saying goodbye.

"Or you could stay. There's plenty of room."

I want that. I want his sheets warm against my skin at dawn. I want to watch him move around the kitchen making breakfast, and I want his lips on mine when the world is still quiet. But Toast is probably knocking everything off my shelves right now, and something in my chest tightens at the thought of staying. If I let myself have this night, will I need all the nights? Will Adrian's hands on my skin become something I can't sleep without? And when this pull between us ends, because things always end, will I remember how to breathe on my own?

Adrian pulls me closer, his chest warm against mine. "I can see your thoughts racing a mile a minute. Don't overthink it. Just be here with me, Tessa." Then his lips graze my forehead in a gentle kiss.

The second his lips touch my skin, the world skips a beat, like a scratched CD, or a movie that jumps frames. It feels like déjà vu. A repeat moment that doesn't just tingle but clings to you, heavy and electric. The warmth of Adrian's arm around me and his lips on my skin are all so familiar. Maybe I lived this moment in a dream, or maybe just in some late-night fantasy.

I blink once, twice, and the room rights itself, swaying back into focus. Adrian is looking at me, his gaze soft and curious, and I realize he's waiting for me to say something.

I shake off the weird feeling of déjà vu. Maybe the universe is trying to tell me how right this is, how much I've needed something that feels this easy. Or maybe my brain is short-circuiting from the champagne and the way Adrian looks at me like I'm a secret worth uncovering. Either way, there are worse places to lose my grip on reality.

"What are you thinking?" Adrian asks, voice low.

If I dare to blink, I'm scared this will all be gone. But I don't say that. "I'm thinking that this is really nice."

Adrian hums, chin resting atop my head. He squeezes my hip in reassurance, and the sensation grounds me, replacing the vertigo with something sturdy and real.

We talk a little longer as if neither of us is ready for the evening to end. Adrian's fingers trace idle patterns on my skin as he describes a night market in Thailand where he ate something so spicy it made him hallucinate a little.

"Next week," he says, eyes crinkling at the corners, "I'll take you to this hole-in-the-wall Thai place. The chef knows me. And trust me, he'll make you cry in the best way possible."

"Next week? Why wait that long?"

"Have a big client presentation on Tuesday. I'll be living on coffee and anxiety until then."

"Oh." I nod, swallowing my disappointment.

"I'll miss you," Adrian adds, tilting my face up to his. His lips brush mine, soft and lingering. "Tuesday can't come fast enough. But I promise, it will be worth the wait."

The corner of my mouth lifts. "In that case, I suppose I can be patient."

Adrian insists on calling me a cab, his lips finding mine between each step down the lobby. Outside, the car idles at the curb, its head-lights carving golden tunnels through the mist. Before I can slide into the backseat, Adrian presses the bouquet of peonies into my hands, their stems still damp.

"Text me when you're home?" His breath clouds between us as he boxes me in against the open door, fingertips lingering on my neck where my pulse jumps. Then he leans in, his movement firm and deliberate, and catches my mouth in a kiss that is meant to claim, to devour. His lips are warm against mine, demanding, his teeth grazing my bottom lip as his fingers tangle in my hair. I taste wine and possibility on his tongue, and feel the curve of his smile against my mouth. I almost come undone at the satisfied hum that vibrates from his chest to mine, the city noise and the yellow car lights fusing into static.

After a minute, Adrian pulls back just an inch, breath warm and ragged. "Go, Tessa, or I will drag you back upstairs and throw away the keys."

I shiver at the promise in his voice.

I don't remember getting into the car or closing the door, only that the bouquet is in my hands and my lips are tingling, and the driver keeps glancing at me in the rearview mirror. The ride home is a blur of color and light, and the phantom taste of Adrian's mouth on mine.

Upstairs, I place the peonies in a chipped mason jar, which I fill with cold water, then set it on the windowsill. Then I text Liz to let her know I made it back safely.



I collapse on the bed and stare at the ceiling, thinking about the way Adrian said my name at the end. Thinking about next week and Thai food, and maybe, maybe waking up in his bed and letting our bodies tangle for hours. I want it so badly that my skin hurts. As if conjured by my thoughts, my phone pings with a message from Adrian.

*Wine Guy: Wish I could have kept you here all night. Sweet dreams, Tessa*

*Me: Next time, maybe don't let me go*

His reply is just a single, perfect promise.

*Wine Guy: I won't*

# Chapter Four

## Roots

The world's worst hangover arrives without warning, when you didn't even have the decency to get drunk first. That's how Monday morning finds me, with my skull feeling as if it's being pried apart with rusty garden shears. The room tilts when I try to sit up, and I fall back on the bed with a groan. Then, a jolt of adrenaline shoots through me as I remember that my website goes live today.

I roll out of bed and shuffle over to the laptop perched on the second-hand breakfast table I convinced myself I'd use for meals. The screen is open to the home page, and my eyes land on the whimsical text popping against a field of onyx. My logo, which cost more than my entire dinner budget last month, sits proudly at the top of the page. The pride that comes from publishing my very own website is worth every penny.

I don't bother pulling on anything but a hoodie before launching into my morning routine. I line up my vitamins, then make coffee with the aggressively bitter espresso machine my parents gave me when I graduated. I slide a pod into place and listen to the machine cough to life while eyeing the computer screen.

Toast prowls by my feet, swatting the counter with a paw until I fish out his breakfast. Heaven help us if His Majesty's breakfast is late by even two minutes.

I check the first trickle of hits on my website analytics. There's nothing for five minutes. Then I see twelve hits in a row, all from the same IP address. If I had to guess, I'd say it's Liz at work, obsessively clicking on my site. I smile and text her.

> Me: Heavy traffic on the new site. Should I invest in more bandwidth?

> Liz: Ha! I sent your link to my entire yoga group and all the girls at work. If that doesn't make you famous, I dk what will

I make a mental note to buy Liz lunch this week. Then I do the thing you're not supposed to do as a freelancer, ever. I check my bank balance. It's not pretty, but there's a four-figure deposit from the gallery, and that puts me on the right side of existential dread for at least a few weeks.

I'm halfway through dry-swallowing my second vitamin of the day when there's a knock on the front door. I freeze, startled. No one ever visits before noon, and even solicitors know better than to try my floor this early. I tiptoe over, hoodie zipped up to my chin.

When I open the door a crack, I find myself face to face with a bright eyed and bushy tailed Adrian. His hair looks wind-tousled, and he's holding two paper cups from the Plum Pot, along with a brown bakery bag. He is wearing a warm-looking sweater; the sleeves rolled just enough to show muscular forearms, and a charming smile like he's trying out for boyfriend of the month and winning in every category.

"Morning," he smiles, as if showing up unannounced at my apartment, a day sooner than planned, is the most natural thing.

I slam the door before my brain can catch up. The thud reverberates through the room as I press my back against the wood, fingers flying to my unwashed hair. My reflection in the hallway mirror confirms my worst fear. Pillow creases mark my cheeks, and yesterday's mascara is smudged beneath my eyes. Then I spot a brown splatter on my hoodie where I must have dribbled coffee on it. Awesome. I wipe my eyes and flatten my hair, knowing my attempts are futile.

Three knocks vibrate against my spine.

"I thought you were busy until tomorrow?" My words hang awkwardly in the air between us.

"The meeting got moved," comes Adrian's muffled and very much amused reply.

I inhale deeply, turn the knob, and peek through a crack just wide enough to see Adrian's grin, totally unfazed. "Also, I figured you'd forget to eat."

Steam rises from the coffee cups in his left hand, and the paper bag in his right's emitting the unmistakable scent of butter and sugar. "Let me in before I get frostbite?"

I reluctantly stand aside and swing the door open, mortified by the state of my living room. There are printouts and dirty laundry piled on the couch. "Sorry, it's a mess." I apologize, praying Toast is not about to streak across the room and puke his breakfast on Adrian's pants. "I wasn't expecting any company."

Adrian passes me a cup. "Don't sweat it. I like seeing the real you, in your natural habitat."

I cringe and take a sip of the oat milk latte, which has just enough cinnamon in it. Adrian must have noticed me shaking cinnamon over my coffee at the Plum Pot the last time we were there.

"You make it sound like you're describing a wild animal."

"More like a cute little pussy cat. Although, you do remind me of a wild cat when you glare at me like that."

"Are you always this hilarious in the mornings?"

"What can I say? You bring out my best qualities."

I roll my eyes and hide my smile behind the coffee cup. The caffeine hits my bloodstream for the second time this morning, and my fingers twitch around the cup, but the cinnamon-laced warmth spreading across my tongue makes the jitters worth it.

Adrian sets down the bakery bag and surveys my apartment. "It's cozy in here."

I almost choke on my coffee, dark liquid sloshing over the rim. "Sure, if you consider sparse furnishings and cat hairballs cozy."

Adrian's eyes crinkle at the corners as he steps over the empty Amazon box that has become a permanent fixture in my living room, thanks to Toast's obsession with it. He brushes his fingertips against a framed print leaning against the wall. "Are you planning on hanging this?"

"Sure, eventually," I mutter, kicking an inside-out sock under the couch. "Though I doubt my place will ever look as put together as yours."

"You know I don't care about what your apartment looks like, don't you? You could be living under a bridge and I'd still bring you coffee and breakfast just so I can see that look on your face when you take the first sip."

I scoff, averting my gaze. "Sure, if you say so."

Adrian closes the distance between us in two strides. His arms slide around my shoulders, and the soft material of his sweater slides against my chin. The scent of his woodsy cologne is so familiar and delicious that it makes my knees wobble.

"What?" I whisper, my gaze fixed on Adrian's collar.

His voice drops an octave. "You wanna know what I care about?"

I glance up just as his gaze drifts to my mouth. "You," he murmurs. "You're the only thing that matters to me." My heart trips over itself. "And if that means being permanently covered in cat hair, or always doing the laundry so you have more time for me?" His thumb traces my jaw. "I'll happily pay that price. Every day."

Adrian leans in, and despite the sweet moment, I'm acutely aware that I have not showered, nor have I brushed my teeth yet.

I duck under his arm and motion toward the breakfast table. "I love where this is going, but let's eat first? Then I could... you know." I mime brushing teeth, and Adrian's laugh fills the apartment. "Maybe we could do something together later?"

Adrian checks his watch. "I've got some emails to answer, but they can wait. I would much rather spend the day with you than at the office." His fingers brush mine as he reaches for the bakery bag, lingering a second longer than necessary.

"That's good, but I meant in the afternoon. I don't want to be the reason you're getting fired."

Adrian snorts. "Trust me, I don't have to worry about being fired. Besides, I've earned a day off after those all-nighters last week."

He hands me a scone that's still warm, the paper slick with butter, before biting into his own.

"You know, I'm starting to wonder if you brought breakfast just for me, or if you are secretly a scone person too, and this is just your excuse to indulge in them."

Adrian chews and hums under his breath. He watches me tear off a chunk of the pastry and pop it into my mouth. "You're adorable when you're suspicious."

An unladylike sound bubbles up in my throat, caught halfway between a giggle and a snort because my mouth is full of food, and for one mortifying instant I worry I'll choke and die in front of this very attractive man.

I swallow hard and say, "No one's ever accused me of being adorable before. My mother calls me spirited, and an ex boyfriend once said I was headstrong. But adorable?" I stick out my chin and cock my head. "You're the only one."

Adrian meets my stare, then takes a long, deliberate sip of his coffee. "I like the idea of being your only one," he says, voice dropping to a register that makes my stomach flip. His gaze drifts from my eyes to my hair, down to the coffee stain on my hoodie, then back up. The corner of his mouth twitches upward. "You're a lot softer than you let on. Especially when you look so rumpled and cute in the morning."

I scoff. "Rumpled isn't exactly the look I like to go for, but I suppose it could be worse..."

*THUMP.*

I turn to find Toast inching his way toward the pastry bag. "Don't even think about it!"

I reach out to shoo the cat off the counter, but Adrian beats me to it, scooping Toast into his arms. I expect the cat to squirm and meow in protest, but a moment later, the furry beast begins purring so loudly I can hear it from across the counter.

"Traitor," I mutter. "He likes you more than me already."

Adrian gives Toast a scratch behind the ears. "He reminds me of the cat I fostered. I miss that guy more than I care to admit." He sets Toast on the ground before turning back to me. "So, what do you want to do today?"

I take a sip of coffee while I consider his question. The drink's creamy with just the right edge of bitterness, exactly how I like it. Even the ache behind my temples is beginning to soften. Maybe today will be a good day after all.

"How about a hike?"

The words hang between us as my gaze drifts to the window, where raindrops are tracing jagged paths down the glass. I'm about to tell Adrian never mind when he clinks his cup against mine. "Let's do it. I'll swing by my place to grab gear and will be back in half an hour."

***

Within an hour, Adrian and I are loaded into his car with two raincoats and a bag of leftover scones. I am freshly showered, and my migraine has faded to a manageable hum, accompanied by a jittery warmth in my chest. Adrian tells me he is taking me on a surprise hike forty minutes outside the city.

Before long, the highway gives way to winding roads and tree canopies that drip with the last of the season's leaves. Adrian keeps one hand loose on the wheel, the other drumming the rhythm of the playlist he's put on. It includes my favorite songs, their order suspiciously reminiscent of the playlist I mentioned on a late-night call.

The rain stops about ten miles out. The sky stays heavy and gray, its colors saturated to their deepest pigments and the air alive with the scent of ozone.

I roll down the window a crack. "This is perfect. Just you and me, alone, and the mud will make this outing even more fun." I turn to Adrian, lips quirking. "So, is this your signature move? The secret hiking spot you save for when you want to impress someone?"

"Not exactly. This place is special to me. I've kept it to myself all these years, and now I'm sharing it with you. Only you, Tessa."

Something warm unfurls in my chest. "Good answer. I better not be following in some other girl's muddy footprints." Adrian shakes his head and grins as he navigates a sharp curve in the road.

We park in the secluded lot and lace our boots. I am ready to take off into the woods when Adrian swings a backpack out of the trunk with a practiced heft. It's double-strapped army surplus and about half his size. He slings it over his shoulder as if the backpack weighs nothing, then offers me a raincoat.

I eye the bag. "What do you have in there? Your entire apartment?"

Adrian gestures for me to turn, then zips me into the raincoat, as if I was a little kid. I can't help but laugh at the absurdity of it.

"It's another surprise," he tells me, tapping the top of the backpack. When he sees me squinting at him over my shoulder, he leans in, dropping his voice. "Can't reveal my secrets. If I told you what's in here, I'd have to kill you."

I snort. "Pretend I've never asked, then. I'm not ready to die at the hands of a man in a neon rain jacket."

The trail is muddy as expected, with leaves squelching underfoot. The first fifty yards are a steep grade, and I power-walk it, trying to hide just how hard I'm breathing. Adrian keeps pace without breaking a sweat, which I find both annoying and impressive.

We hit the ridgeline at the half-mile point. The trees thin, and the valley opens up to a river, and the overbuilt city skyline in the distance. I stop and catch my breath, resting my hand on a mossy trunk.

Adrian sidles up next to me. "Worth the hike?"

"The only thing better than this view is knowing how many people are missing it because they hate the mud."

Adrian snorts, stepping into my space. "All the better to have you here all to myself without anyone disturbing us."

I cock a brow and give him what I hope is a smoldering look. It works, because the next thing I know, he is leaning in and kissing me. It's a perfect collision, sensual and dizzying, making my whole body feel alive. Adrian tastes like rain and mint, and I'm left feeling winded when he breaks away, like I've just sprinted the ridgeline twice.

"Wow," I say, my voice ragged. "The air must be super thin up here."

"It must be, judging by that beautiful flush spreading up your cheeks." Adrian brushes a wet lock of hair off my forehead. There's a pause, where I think he might say something else, but he just holds my gaze, as if he's memorizing the way I look against the backdrop of the evergreens.

He glances around, then gestures up the path with a tilt of his head. "Come on. There's a spot I want you to see."

We follow the trail as it narrows, the trees crowding closer overhead. After a few hundred yards, Adrian veers off onto a barely there footpath until we reach a clearing under an enormous oak that looks like it's been standing since dinosaurs roamed the Earth. Moss covers the surprisingly dry ground underneath.

Adrian shrugs off his backpack, unzips it, and pulls out a blanket. He spreads it with a practiced motion, then surprises me by producing a fully packed picnic with all my favorite foods. He lays out cheese, chocolate, two little bottles of wine, butter, and a loaf of freshly baked bread wrapped in butcher paper.

"Wow, this is incredible." I'm unable to hide the delight in my voice.

"I'm glad you like it. Couldn't let my woman starve in the wilderness, now could I?"

His woman. Butterflies flutter in my belly at the casual way he claims me, and I press my lips together to contain the smile threatening to take over my face.

Adrian sits cross-legged and gestures for me to join him. The blanket is scratchier than it looks, but the comfort of sitting next to him, surrounded by the hush of the woods, more than makes up for it. Adrian uncorks the wine with a travel-size opener and pours it into matching mugs. I take a sip. The drink's heavy and a little too sweet, but I like the way it warms me from the inside.

I'm relieved to find that the alcohol doesn't trigger even a hint of the migraine that plagued me earlier. I wonder if it's the fresh air, or if Adrian keeps the pain at bay just by existing nearby, like some human analgesic.

He slices the cheese and the bread, and we eat in companionable silence, his body so close to mine that I can feel the heat radiating off him. The air is crisp and clean; the only sounds coming from the birds and the distant burble of water from somewhere below.

"This place is perfect."

"I'm glad you like it. It's one of my favorite spots to relax and reset my mind."

Adrian shifts so he's angled toward me, his forearms braced on his knees, and his face close enough that his breath ghosts over my cheek. "I've imagined you here with me so many times," he whispers, voice dropping. "Sitting right where you are now."

I open my mouth to say something coy, but he kisses me before I can. I taste the wine on his lips, and the world narrows to a pinprick of awareness. I want to get lost in the sensation of Adrain's hand at the nape of my neck and the roughness of his palm against my skin.

There is something about the way he devours me, like he's conquering every inch of my mouth. He tugs at my bottom lip with just enough pressure to make my fingers curl into the fabric of his jacket, pulling him closer.

Adrian moves down my jaw and peppers kisses along my skin, each press of his lips leaving a trail of goosebumps. I tilt my head back, my breath catching as his teeth graze the spot beneath my ear. But then Adrian bites into my skin harder, and my eyes snap open.

The forest canopy above us is blurring into a dizzying kaleidoscope as my eyes struggle to focus. The cold bite of air at my throat and the weight of a body pressed close suddenly feel like echos of a memory. The familiar sensations stir a restlessness under my ribs, and I push against Adrian's chest.

"Wait..." My voice is barely audible over the sudden rush of blood in my ears.

I break away, just enough to catch my breath, and scan the clearing for something that could explain my disquiet. My gaze lands on the gnarled trunk of the oak, just above Adrian's shoulder. A patch of scarred bark draws my eyes, and I squint at something carved into the wood, the letters half-obscured by lichen.

The world spins again, and for a moment I'm someone else, watching a man trace his girlfriend's name on the bark with a red razor. The memory is sharp and strange... But no, it can't be a memory... I'm certain I've never been here before.

"You okay?" Adrian follows my gaze. "You'd think this place would be too remote for teenagers to vandalize. But I guess if there's a will, there's a way."

I nod, my eyes on the carving. It looks like a heart, deep and jagged, not like the hurried graffiti you see on city park benches. Someone took their time here. Someone wanted the carving to last.

The wind hisses through the branches overhead, and I wonder if Adrian is thinking what I am. This place is too remote. If you didn't know where the trail was, you'd never find it. Would teenage couples really come all the way out here for fun?

I shake off the chill and force my attention back to Adrian's face. He's watching me, head tilted, as if he's waiting for something. His words are light and playful, but the intensity of his gaze makes my pulse surge.

"Sorry," I say, trying to laugh off these strange feelings, "for getting distracted by the tree. It's a little Blair Witch for my taste, you know?"

"I suppose it is. But I promise I'm not about to sacrifice you to the forest spirits."

"Good, because I left my pentagram at home," I chuckle, but the sound is brittle even to my own ears.

Adrian's hand finds mine again. He squeezes, then pulls me onto his lap in a motion that feels too smooth. His lips find mine with such confidence that I can't help but imagine all the women who've sat where I am now, receiving these same touches. My stomach clenches around the wine and cheese.

Deep down, I know I'm being unfair to Adrian with my thoughts, and I try to force them away, burying them under the weight of his embrace. He stretches the blanket around my shoulders and curls his arms around my waist before tucking his face into my neck.

"Tell me something about your past. Something you've never told anyone before," I whisper, hoping for a distraction. It would be so easy to get lost in Adrian's warmth, in the shelter of his body, if only I could forget about the sense of wrongness that still lingers in the air.

Adrian thinks for a second "When I was in first grade, my mother knitted me this orange monstrosity of a hat and scarf set. Complete with reflector patches that lit up like a construction zone whenever headlights hit them." Adrian huffs. "I conveniently lost them at school two days into wearing them."

"I bet you looked cute in them. You must have been the most visible six-year-old in the neighborhood."

"The most visible target for bullies, you mean." His voice softens. "Sometimes I think about those ugly things sitting in some donation box. I should have appreciated them, but I was too young to see all the work and love she put into them."

"You were just a kid, Adrian. You didn't know any better."

He hums, pulling me closer. "Your turn. Tell me something terrible you did as a child so I don't feel like the only jerk here."

"I was an angel." I snicker when Adrian tickles me. "Fine, fine. Except for the one time I ran away to the playground after fighting with my mom. I was eight, maybe nine. She found me on the swings an hour later, mascara streaking down her face. I'd never seen her cry like that before."

The memory of her asking if I knew what could have happened to me, if I understood how scared she'd been, still makes me feel guilty.

"This proves that all kids are little terrors," Adrian says, his breath warm against my neck.

"Yep. And some of us never grow out of it."

Adrian's lips brush my ear. "Do you ever think about having your own?"

"Kids?" I consider his question. "I'd love kids someday, when I'm settled. When I can afford to support a growing family." He is looking at me with such intensity that I have to avert my gaze. "What about you? Does this mean you want kids?"

Adrian's hips shift against me, and there's no mistaking his arousal. "I never thought I'd want them, but yeah, maybe... when we're ready."

When *we're* ready. His words make me flush from my chest to my cheeks.

Adrian traces slow, deliberate circles across my stomach, dipping dangerously close to my waistband. His lips brush the sensitive skin below my ear, making me shiver, and my skin prickle with warmth. I barely know this man, yet something primal stirs at the thought of starting a family with him. What is wrong with me? His suggestion should send me running, not melting.

"Good to know." I clear my throat, searching for steadier ground. "I've always wondered about your path to architecture," I say, the words coming out breathier than intended. "When did you realize you wanted to be an architect? Was that your childhood dream?"

Adrian laughs softly against my ear. "That's quite the shift in topic." He shifts his weight, readjusts, then wraps his arms around me again. "Yes, architecture was always my dream. I'd spend hours as a kid drawing buildings instead of people or animals. By high school, there wasn't really any other path for me."

Adrian's voice vibrates against my side as he talks about sleepless nights in school and about the scholarship he almost lost during his sophomore year of college. Then he tells me about his first year as an intern at a big shot architecture firm, where his boss made him redraw the same blueprint five times.

"Something in me just couldn't accept being average. I had something to prove to myself. Maybe to my father, too."

"And did you? Prove yourself?"

"Yeah. I've got my name on buildings across twelve states and enough money to retire if I wanted to."

"That's more than I've ever accomplished."

Adrian shifts me so we're face to face. "You know, my mom never worked a day in her life outside the house. She'd have laughed at the idea that she wasn't accomplishing anything."

"I know, I just—"

"You could do that, if you wanted."

I look at him. "Do what?"

"Stop working on your photo projects and stay home. I want to take care of you in every way, Tessa. Physically, emotionally, financially. You'd never have to work another day if you didn't want to." He finds my hand under the blanket. "I know it's soon. I just want you to know the option is there."

Adrian's words hang between us. I gape at him, trying to wrap my head around his offer. I'm flattered by his devotion, but beneath the butterflies, an uncomfortable pressure lurks at the thought of moving *this* fast. We just met, and Adrian's already talking about financially supporting me? I'm not sure I like the idea of giving up my work and relying on a man I barely know.

"I appreciate your offer to take care of me, but I need my job. Not just for money; for purpose. Even if we get serious, that won't change."

"You mean when we get serious," Adrian says, like it's already decided. His fingers trace slow patterns on my thigh, warmth bleeding through my jeans. "The offer stays on the table. I'll be here when you change your mind."

His declaration teeters between presumptuous and sweet, and I can't quite decide how I feel about it. So I nod in acknowledgement, then sink back against Adrian's chest.

The clouds drift by in silent procession, hurried along by a high wind neither of us can feel. After a few minutes, some of the tension starts to leave my body, and I find myself studying the way the veins rope under Adrian's golden skin, his fingers long and slightly callused at the tips. I want to memorize the feeling of his skin, so I can summon the sensation from memory later.

Adrian's phone chirps from the pocket of his pants, an abrasive sound that doesn't match the setting. He groans into my hair before untangling himself to check the notification, then lets the phone drop onto the moss a second later.

"I wish we could freeze time. Leave the rest of the world behind and spend the day here together."

It's an easy line, but it sounds like he means it. I wish I could tell him the same, but my eyes drift back to the carving in the tree, and the feeling of unease nipping at my consciousness returns.

After the wine and food are gone, we pack up and start back down the trail. I stumble twice, but Adrian is there to steady me. He makes a game of finding the slipperiest parts of the path just so he can catch me, and at the bottom he pulls me in for a kiss.

By the time we reach the parking lot, my hair is wild and my jeans are streaked with dirt. Adrian opens the passenger door with a flourish. "Allow me, my lady." I smile at how earnest he is as he ushers me in.

On the drive back, Adrian rests his hand on the gearshift, occasionally brushing my knee when he changes lanes. I catch his eye at a stoplight and he smiles. It's not the practiced smile from our first date, but something softer, more genuine.

I lean my head against the cool window and watch the trees blur past, not scrambling to fill the silence with clever observations or small talk. I love that I don't have to be a polished version of myself with Adrian. My thoughts can wander, my hair can tangle, and his eyes still find mine with that same warmth, as if I am the most beautiful woman in the world. It's an intoxicating feeling to be accepted and appreciated for who I am.

When Adrian drops me back at my apartment, he kills the engine but doesn't move to get out. He slides his hand across the console and curls his fingers around mine.

"I hope you enjoyed our hike."

"I did. Thank you for sharing your special place with me."

He looks at me like he wants to say something more. Instead, he pulls me into a hug. My face is pressed to his jacket, the spicy warmth of him filling every gap. I squeeze back, not caring that I'm probably smudging dirt all over him.

Adrian pulls back and brushes his lips against mine. "What are you doing tomorrow?"

"You're not sick of me yet?" I tease, but I cling to his jacket.

He tucks a strand of hair behind my ear, eyes never leaving mine. "How could I ever get sick of you? I could spend every day with you and it still wouldn't be enough."

Warmth unfurls in my chest, and I nod, unable to find words that won't reveal too much. We make plans for dinner the next evening as we reluctantly separate.

After Adrian's taillights disappear around the corner, I shuffle inside, kick off my muddy boots, and collapse onto the couch with my phone loose in my hand.

Toast saunters over, tail held high, and chirps a greeting. He inspects my clothes with delicate sniffs. I watch, amused, as his whiskers twitch in disgust at the forest debris still clinging to me. When I reach to scratch behind his ears, he gives me a wide-eyed look, like he can't believe I spent the day outdoors and want to soil his perfection with my filth.

I scroll through my messages and see a new one from Liz.

> *Liz: You disappeared on the Find My app. Tell me you didn't elope with Adrian already*

> *Me: Not yet. Went hiking. He packed a picnic with wine and cheese. Who is this man??*

> *Liz: Serial killer behavior TBH. But also romantic*

I want to laugh at that, but the sound dies in my throat. The tree with the heart carving flashes behind my eyes, and suddenly my skull throbs with a vise-grip, tightening from temple to temple. I wince, pressing my fingertips against the pain. So much for enjoying some wine earlier.

The orange vitamin bottle sits on my coffee table, its white cap reflecting the dim light. Two pills tumble into my palm. The doctor's offices are closed now, so I make a mental note to find a new primary care physician first thing tomorrow. No more putting it off.

# No Return

Adrian and I text all day, every day. It doesn't matter that I'm at my laptop with a mountain of edits or that he's in some endless design meeting. Every lull in our schedules means another message, a meme, a photo, or a pun that only we seem to find funny.

Adrian starts inventing reasons to see me. He comes up with an excuse to drop off a cactus he saw at a street fair because it looked vaguely like Toast. He invites me to a last-minute play he scored tickets to on Facebook Marketplace. Then, he delivers emergency soup for my alleged cold even though I told him three times it was just allergies. Eventually, I stop pretending I don't love his attention.

Adrian is a force of optimism, even when I try to sabotage our budding relationship with sarcasm or awkwardness. He tells me stories about his coworkers, like the junior architect who microwaves leftover fish in the break room every day. He meets Liz, too. I worry they'll dislike each other since Adrian's all neat suits and discipline, while Liz wears pajama pants to the grocery store and considers cutlery optional for most meals. But I shouldn't have worried because the two of them hit it off. Liz texts me later.

*He's a keeper. Don't F this up!*

One Thursday, Adrian invites me to a work event. The restaurant is on the top floor of an office tower, all floor-to-ceiling glass and over-designed pendant lights. I panic at the inevitable dress code, but Adrian assures me it will be okay and tells me to just be myself. That doesn't make me feel much better. I show up in black jeans, heels, and the only satin blouse I own that still fits, and hope it's enough.

At the bar, a man with a red balloon nose and a laugh that could shatter glass waves us over. "So this is the Miss Grey I've heard so much about," he shakes my hand with both of his. I learn his name is James, and he is Adrian's boss and the firm's unofficial social chair, with a manic energy that's both intimidating and contagious.

"I've never seen Adrian this happy," James booms. "He used to be so dull. All work and no play. Now look at him. Practically human!" He elbows Adrian and nearly tips my water glass in the process.

Adrian parries with a joke about James's taste in watches. They banter back and forth until I'm laughing along and the awkwardness dissolves.

Throughout the evening, I watch Adrian work the room. He introduces me to several prominent figures in the community. The police chief clasps Adrian's shoulder with affection. The commissioner nods eagerly at whatever he's saying. Even the district attorney, who earlier looked bored with everyone else, animatedly discusses downtown revitalization plans with Adrian, sketching something on a cocktail napkin. James hovers nearby, as if afraid his star architect might vanish if left unattended.

When a sleek woman in a red dress approaches, eyes lingering on Adrian, my stomach tightens. But Adrian politely withdraws from the conversation. His hand finds the small of my back, anchoring us together and melting away my insecurities.

Dinner is up in a blur of tiny, pretty plates and alcohol that costs more than most of my camera equipment. The city's elite talk about their favorite buildings and mid-century furniture. Adrian is animated and includes me in every story, even though I don't understand their jargon half the time. When our knees bump under the table, Adrian gives me a knowing smirk, and the rest of the room blurs out of focus.

Somewhere between the main course and dessert, James leans across the table, voice low. "How long have you two been together? You seem like old souls."

Adrian shrugs. "Not long enough," he squeezes my hand, and my heart folds in on itself like a paper crane.

Later, as we wait for the elevator, Adrian pulls me close and brushes a kiss behind my ear. "Thanks for coming," he murmurs. "I know how much you hate these things."

Before I can protest, the elevator dings and James shouts, "Get a room!" from down the hall. Adrian hides his grin in my hair as we step into the elevator.

We're wrapped around each other on elevator glass for a moment, the city streaming neon in the windows. But then the doors close, and Adrian's mouth is suddenly on mine. His hands are at my waist, sliding up my ribcage, urgent and a little rough, like he's finally let go after holding himself back for hours. I lean into him, greedy for the attention, for the way his mouth finds the hollow just below my jaw and lingers there, a shiver racing down my spine.

I tug at his collar. "How close is your apartment?"

"Not close enough." His voice is rough against my skin, his hips pinning me to the wall. When I gasp, I feel him tense against me.

"I bet we could get there fast."

The elevator hits the ground floor. Adrian's eyes darken, and the next thing I know, we're half-running through the night air, his hand gripping mine. Two blocks pass in a blur of streetlights. Then we're in his building's elevator, and my back hits the wall as his mouth finds mine again, picking up where we left off.

Adrian lifts me in one motion, so I'm pressed between him and the cold wall, and I tighten my thighs around him on instinct. I'm laughing, I think, but his mouth, which tastes like wine and the ghost of dessert, smothers the sound. I barely notice when the elevator starts climbing.

Adrian's much stronger than he looks. The edge of the rail digs into my hip as he grinds against me, one hand cupping the back of my head, the other tugging at the buttons of my blouse. I let him, even as I fumble for his belt with unsteady fingers. We're a mess of limbs and half-muffled gasps, crashing into each other like teenagers.

I feel reckless. I want Adrian to ruin me, right here, in this elevator with its mirrored walls and bright LED lights. I want to leave smudged fingerprints on the glass, to hear his name echo in this mirrored space as I cry out in pleasure. I fumble with the buttons of his shirt, desperate and graceless, and when I finally get it open far enough to reach bare skin, everything else falls away. The city could be burning down, and I would only care about Adrian's chest, warm and solid, the faint peppering of his hair, the way he shudders when I scrape my nails along his collarbone.

The elevator dings, and I growl in protest. Adrian chuckles, breathless, and scoops me up as the doors slide open. I bury my face in his neck, inhaling. He smells irresistible and impossibly mine.

Adrian walks us straight to his apartment, barely pausing to unlock the door. He pushes me up against the oak panel inside and kisses me anew, deeper, one hand raking through my hair, while the other tugs his tie loose so it spills over his shoulders.

The apartment is dim, city lights bleeding through the windows and making everything look surreal. Adrian moves down my throat, his teeth grazing the spot just below my jaw, the one that makes my legs threaten to give out. I gasp, and he shudders against me, fingers already working their way under the hem of my blouse. He unbuttons my shirt and kisses his way down my collarbone, finding every sensitive spot like he's memorized a map of me. When my bra falls and his mouth closes over my nipple, the shock of pleasure is so sharp it almost hurts.

Adrian's hands are everywhere at once. They are sliding down my back and around my ribs, then flattening me against the wall so there's no space between us. I can feel how badly he wants me, the hard line of him pressing through his pants, and I want to laugh, or cry, or maybe both.

Adrian tastes like salt and wine and the faintest trace of sugar. He kisses his way down to my navel, sinking to his knees as he tugs the waistband of my jeans loose, his eyes never leaving mine. The hunger in his expression could consume me whole.

I'm so turned on I'm almost embarrassed, but if Adrian notices he doesn't show it. He strips my jeans and underwear in one motion, his mouth following close behind, hot and insistent. He slides his tongue over me and groans. "Fuck, Tessa. You taste so good."

Oh God, if he doesn't start moving his tongue right this second, I will combust. As if reading my thoughts, Adrian parts my lips with his fingers, then sucks on my clit. My knees nearly buckle at the sensation, and when he starts to explore me, slow at first, then faster, in a rhythm that is uncannily perfect, I almost come on the spot. He knows exactly where to slide his tongue, as if he's listening to every gasp, every stutter of my breath, and tuning his body to mine in real time.

The way he looks at me while he eats me is obscene. I squeeze my eyes shut, but he just growls and kisses up the inside of my thigh until I open them again. I'm pinned to the wall, legs trembling, and Adrian doesn't stop until I'm right at the edge, until I'm begging him, "Please."

When I come, it's with a force that makes my vision white out, a tsunami of sensation that leaves me gasping and half-sobbing into his shoulder. Adrian holds me through the pleasure, like he knew how intense it would be, how completely he would dismantle me.

He doesn't give me time to recover.

Adrian scoops me up and carries me to the bedroom down the hall, his mouth never leaving my skin. He lays me on the bed, kissing every inch of my body while he strips off his clothes with a quick efficiency that should not be this sexy.

Adrian's whipcord strong, with just enough softness at his waist to make him look human. I want to bite him, I want to scratch my nails down his back, to mark him the way he's marked me. I reach for him, but he shakes his head.

"Later," he growls, voice rough. "I need to feel you around me when I lose control." My entire body flushes hot at his words.

Adrian starts to slides inside me so slowly it's torture, his forehead pressed to mine. "Tell me if it's too much," he murmurs, and I shake my head, dizzy from the pressure building between us.

"Not even close," I gasp, and his smile is slow and dangerous as he slides all the way in. He begins to move, each thrust measured, like he's savoring every microsecond of buildup. I wrap my arms around his neck and dig my fingers in, needing him closer, needing something to anchor me. Our bodies fuse, breath and sweat and heat, and we move in a perfect, synchronized way.

Adrian's voice drops to a rasp against my ear. "Tell me you're mine. Tell me no one else gets to have you like this." The words vibrate through me, igniting every nerve. "No one but me."

I arch against him, fingers digging into his shoulders. "I am yours. Only yours."

Our mouths crash together, teeth grazing lips, his tongue sliding against mine with a possessive urgency that makes me dizzy. I nearly sob with relief when Adrian finally lets go, hips slamming into mine with a force that rattles the headboard.

I lose track of time, of reality, of how many times I come or call his name. When I finally peel my face out of the tangle of sheets and pillows, there's a giddy laugh bubbling in my chest.

Adrian's hair is a mess and his skin is damp, but his smile is pure sunshine as he rolls onto his back and pulls me with him, so I'm sprawled across his chest.

"Wow," is all I manage.

Adrian's chuckle rumbles through his ribcage into mine. "That was... yeah... wow." He kisses my forehead, then the tip of my nose. "You're fucking incredible, Tessa."

I bury my face in his neck, high from the aftershocks. "I can't believe we did that in your elevator. Did you see the camera?"

Adrian grins, teeth flashing. "They're only active from eight to six during the week. I checked."

I half believe him, half hope he's lying. The thought of someone seeing us like that should be mortifying, but it's not. Just remembering the desperate need of the moment makes me shiver.

Adrian traces lazy circles on my back, fingertips dancing along my skin and making me want to purr in pleasure. His hand pauses just below my shoulder blade, where the edge of my tattoo peeks out. He presses his thumb against the spot where the nerve feels more sensitive.

"You covered up your scar."

I stiffen without meaning to. I know the instinct to flinch is dumb. The scar's mostly faded, but it's still the first thing I see in the mirror on bad days. I'm not even sure why it bothers me so much. I'd gotten the tattoo to cover it, which was an impulsive decision, but ultimately a choice I don't regret. Most people don't notice my scar, or if they do, they don't mention it. But of course, Adrian is not most people.

"It's nothing," I force my voice to sound breezy.

Adrian keeps his hand there, palm flat, fingers splayed across my shoulder blade. "It's okay. We all have scars we don't want to talk about."

We lay there for a while, the only sounds the city outside and our breathing, slow and matched. At some point, I drift off, face pressed to the hollow of Adrian's neck, and for the first time in years I don't want to be anywhere else.

***

I'm insatiable after the night of Adrian's work dinner. I want Adrian every possible moment, every possible way. By the time the sun is up, we've made love in his shower, and against his enormous picture window looking out over the city, which is oddly satisfying for both of us. I never thought I'd crave sex before coffee, but the change is welcome. It feels like getting reacquainted with my body, or with a version of myself I've almost forgotten.

We spend the weekend trying our best to leave the apartment and failing. We order Italian delivery in our underwear and fail at watching a movie marathon thanks to our giggly make outs on the couch.

My camera gathers dust for the next couple of weeks, and when I finally pick it up for a job, Adrian jokes that he's jealous of the way I hug my equipment. I tell him it's nothing compared to the way I look at him, and funnily enough, I don't feel like I'm overselling it.

I don't think I'll ever get tired of learning the valley of Adrian's spine or the way his shoulders tense when he's about to lose control. He memorizes me, too. Maps every inch of my skin, traces the scar beneath my tattoo until I forget to be self-conscious about it. I let myself exist in this haze of sweat and dopamine, happy to surrender the parts of my brain that usually run overtime with worry.

One morning, while I'm humming along to a song and sliding a fresh can of food into Toast's bowl, I spot a white envelope halfway under the front door. The melody dies in my throat as I slide open the envelope and scan its contents. I read it once, then again.


*IMPORTANT: BUILDING MAINTENANCE NOTICE*

*Dear Resident: Due to extensive mold remediation, all tenants must immediately vacate the premises for a minimum of seven days. See attached for alternate accommodation.*


"You've got to be kidding me!"

Toast stares at me, unimpressed, as if to say, *Get a grip, woman.* Adrian is half-asleep on the edge of my bed with his phone in one hand and his other hand absently massaging the back of his neck. I wave the letter in his direction. "There is a mold problem in my building. They are kicking me out. Can you believe this?!"

"Let me see." Adrian takes the notice from my hand, eyes scanning the page. "Is this the first time you've heard about the mold?"

"Yes," I say, indignant. "And I'm very attached to my stuff. Where am I supposed to go? A seedy motel off the highway? Because that's about all I can afford right now, thanks to all the work I've missed lately."

Adrian doesn't miss a beat. "You can stay with me. I'll even let the cat sleep on the bed with us."

The offer is so casual, I almost miss the enormity of it. "For a week?" I ask, feeling flustered.

Adrian cocks an eyebrow. "You say that like it's a bad thing."

"I just mean…" I trail off, not sure how to explain the anxiety that ripples through me at the idea of living in someone else's space. It's not that I don't want to move in with Adrian. I do. I want to live with Adrian so much it kind of scares me, but the thought of moving my chaos into his meticulously curated apartment is… daunting.

Adrian must see the moment my neurons start to combust, because he crosses the room in three strides and cradles my face in both hands. "Hey," he says, voice gentle. "One week. If you hate it, you get your apartment back and a year's supply of scones, no strings attached. Deal?"

I snort, pressing my forehead to his. "Fine. But you better not judge me for how many bottles of shampoo I travel with."

"Noted. But just so you know, I use three conditioners on rotation. It's good for my hair to mix them up."

I squint at him, and the tension unravels in my chest. Adrian kisses the corner of my mouth. "It's settled then. We're roommates."

"Great." I sigh, feigning defeat. I don't like the thought of giving up my own space, but deep down, the idea of having Adrian to myself 24/7 doesn't sound so terrible.

Adrian helps me pack. I start by tossing the contents of my underwear drawer into a garbage bag, but he brings out an actual suitcase with wheels that must have been hidden somewhere in my closet, and lays it open atop my bed. He then proceeds to sort my clothes by color and folding them into perfect squares.

Once finished, Adrian eyes my modest collection. "You know I could fit three of you in my closet, right? We'll need to get you some more outfits to wear."

I roll my eyes and toss in a pair of mismatched socks. "My clothes are fine, so stop with your rich guy flex."

"It's only a rich guy flex if I show you how many shoes I own. Spoiler, it's a lot."

"Wow. Okay then."

There's something about packing up my things and letting someone else untangle the wild ball of string that is my life that makes it weirdly easy to imagine a future where living with Adrian is not just a one-week arrangement. I blink away the thought and pass him Toast's gravity water bowl. "You have, like, three hours to cat-proof your place. Toast has a history of criminal behavior and you should be very afraid."

Adrian accepts the challenge, sweeping the cat bowl into his arms like he's been handed the best present ever. "Already done. Fostered a cat, remember?"

It doesn't take long for us to have my entire closet and pantry boxed up, including the pet food, snacks, and even a mug with Toast's face on it. Adrian wraps the fragile pieces in towels, which is a move so domestic that it makes my heart clench. As we make the last sweep, Liz texts.

> Liz: This is how horror movies start. Do NOT let the hot boyfriend talk you into a remote cabin, I repeat, do not enter the woods

> Me: Too late for that LOL.

I pocket the phone and take a last look at my apartment. There's a pit in my stomach as I shut the door behind me. It's part nerves, part excitement. Mostly I just want to know what happens next.

Adrian's apartment is still styled within an inch of its life, but it feels somehow less foreign now. When he opens the door to his closet, I expect to see an array of pressed shirts and color-coded suits, the way you'd find in a magazine spread for men who actually iron their clothes. The first section is exactly like that, with shirts, pants, and accessories lined up with military precision. But then, toward the back, a section sits empty except for a couple of my sweaters, and on the lower rack, I see hangers loaded with a half-dozen female shirts. Adrian gestures as if unveiling a masterpiece. "You can use this side."

I stare, blinking. "You... set this up in advance?"

He shrugs. "I guess I hoped you'd eventually want to stay. For longer than a day, I mean."

I'm not sure what startles me more; the gesture itself, or that it doesn't make me want to run for the hills. Adrian's thoughtfulness sparks a giddy excitement in my chest, the kind I get when I see the first proof of a photo shoot and realize I've captured something real. I reach out and run my fingers across the hangers, a smile creeping onto my face.

"I can't decide if I should be concerned or grateful."

Adrian's lips curve. "Maybe a little bit of both." His gaze travels over me, lingering like he's savoring the sight of me and my belongings in his immaculate closet. "You can show me how grateful you are after you settle in."

In the bedroom, Adrian gestures to the bed. "Which side do you want? Left or right?"

When I point to the left side, he clears the nightstand, transferring his belongings to the opposite table. I watch as he relocates a pair of reading glasses, a half-empty tube of hand cream, what looks like an ancient phone with a shattered screen, and one of those book lights that hangs around your neck when you read at night.

We unload the rest of my stuff, and I go to plug in my hard drive and laptop at the kitchen counter, only to discover Adrian has already cleared a nook at the end of his long, glossy desk. There's an empty power strip, a cup of Sharpies and pens, and a little ceramic dish for SD cards. My camera bag fits perfectly underneath. The space is so precisely set for me that I have to blink twice, half convinced Adrian's swapped my ordinary life for a better, custom version.

"Did you... plan this, too?" I ask, voice trailing up at the end. If this is some kind of subtle intimidation strategy, it's working.

Adrian's grin grows. "You said you needed a better editing setup."

"I did?"

"I pay attention. I like knowing what matters to you."

For a minute I just stand there, staring at the way he's folded my chaos into his life so seamlessly. So this is what it means when someone makes space for you, literally and metaphorically.

Even Toast adapts to the new place instantly. At some point Adrian must have raided every cat store in the city, because the first thing Toast does is hop onto the window ledge and discover not only a fresh cat grass planter but a carpeted tower that puts my old cardboard box to shame. There are tiny toys on every flat surface, and when Toast finds the scratching post, which is dusted with catnip, he goes full gremlin and starts purring like an old diesel engine.

Adrian kneels beside him and lets Toast butt his head against his hand. "I missed you, buddy," he murmurs, smoothing Toast behind the ears.

I don't know why the sight makes me want to cry a little. Maybe because it's so easy, so natural. Maybe because I always thought of myself as someone who couldn't do domesticity, who'd break any relationship before I let it get this settled.

But here we are. Cat, boyfriend, and a shelf in the bathroom with my name on it. Every time I round a corner and see my things mixed in with Adrian's, it sends a shock through me, like I've accidentally walked into a scene from someone else's life. Someone braver and less likely to sabotage herself at the first sign of contentment.

We spend our first night as "roommates" sprawled on the couch with a box of pizza, Toast head-butting our ankles in turn. Adrian ruins the mood by dominating at Mario Kart, but redeems himself by letting me pick the movie. He drapes a blanket over both of us, and when I snuggle into his side, it takes all of three minutes before I'm drooling on his shoulder.

At some point I wake up to find the apartment dark except for the TV illuminating the room, and Adrian is still there, wide awake. He's not watching the movie. He's watching me, like the sight of my tangled hair and mascara-streaked cheek pressed against his sweater are the most beautiful thing he's ever seen.

"Why are you looking at me like that?" My voice is all scratchy, thick with sleep.

He doesn't answer for a moment. "I just like knowing you're here, with me." He finally says, so quietly that I almost don't hear him. I want to say something profound, but my brain is stuck in buffer mode, so I just kiss him with as much intention as I can muster.

Adrian responds like it's the only answer he'll ever need. The kiss is slow, lazy, but underneath it I feel a current of wanting that makes me shiver. I melt into him, the city outside fading into a blur of blue and gold.

The next morning, Adrian hands me a key to his apartment. It's on a ring with a tiny silver camera charm. I turn it over in my palm and inspect the lens rendered in perfect miniature, down to the tiny fake shutter.

Adrian looks almost sheepish as he asks, "You don't think the keyring is too much, do you?"

"It's perfect," I say, and I mean it.

# Chapter Six

## Fractures

The weeks fly by in slow-motion, each day oddly domestic. Neither of us brings up the fact that I could technically move back into my apartment now. We fall into a rhythm that feels so natural, so complete, I almost forget that it used to be just me and Toast against the world.

Adrian claims to have no preference about décor, but our bed now carries soft throw pillows that seem suspiciously hand picked. At first, I side-eye the accumulation of stuff and assume they are relics from a girlfriend past. I ask Adrian about it once, and he just shrugs and tells me he likes how they look with me here. I don't tell him, but I start to like them too. The apartment feels less like a showroom and more like a place where two actual people live.

Most mornings, I wake to the sound of Toast knocking something off a counter, followed by Adrian's voice scolding the cat as if he understands English. I will never get used to waking up next to someone and not immediately wanting to flee into the street, but Adrian has a way of making my presence feel not just tolerated, but essential. Like I am a missing part of a puzzle, and he's been waiting for me to fall into place.

When I try to pay for groceries, Adrian looks so genuinely perplexed that I have to laugh. "The least you can do is feed my woman," he tells me, and that's that. I still find ways to contribute by replenishing things like toilet paper and laundry detergent, and by buying takeout on the days neither of us feels like cooking.

Liz visits often, allegedly to check that I haven't been murdered, but mostly to raid the wine rack and rate our relationship milestones. She and Adrian have developed an ongoing, mutual prank war involving the worst tasting wines and jelly beans. The energy is chaotic, and I wouldn't have it any other way.

Work is steady. Marissa officially books me as the gallery event photographer, which comes with an actual contract and a monthly retainer. Thanks to the high-paying gig, I now have the luxury of saying no to the people who want me to shoot engagement announcements for their chihuahuas. Not that we need the money. Adrian's career is so successful you'd think he was handcrafting the foundations of capitalism itself. I love the way his eyes crinkle when he tells me about a design going up, or a client seeing the architectural plans for the first time. I think he's just as obsessed with creating beautiful things as I am, only his medium is steel and glass instead of pixels and paper.

This life, this ridiculously domestic and perfect life, feels like a fairy tale. Our shared Netflix account, favorite sides of the bed, the matching slippers, Adrian's toothbrush leaning against mine as if that's where it's always belonged... It's all. So. Perfect.

And yet.

The familiar self doubt creeps in when Adrian isn't looking, making me wonder when he'll get bored of me. How much time do we have before he realizes I'm not pretty or interesting enough? He says that will never happen, but the doubt lingers. Each perfect day feels like another step toward an inevitable cliff edge, and I'm terrified of how far I'll fall when he finally decides to move on.

***

One gray afternoon, I'm sitting at the desk we now share, finishing a round of edits on last night's gallery photos. Toast is asleep on the windowsill, chin tucked under his paw, and Adrian is at the far end of the table, laptop open, sketching something on a legal pad that looks like a doodle of our building. I'm half-watching him, half-working, when a folder on my desktop catches my eye.

*MISC: 2023*

Hmmm. Curiosity prickles under my skin. I don't remember creating that folder. Maybe it's a backup from my old laptop? I double-click the folder, expecting to see client photos or maybe Toast in a series of shots, but I find thirty or forty pictures of Adrian instead. Some are perfectly in focus, others blurred by motion, all taken from odd angles and distances. He's seated at a bistro table downtown in one photo, sunlight slicing across his face while he reads something on his phone. In another, he's entering an office building, the camera peering through a window. There are nighttime shots of him walking alone under a neon sign, and of him stopped at a crosswalk, peering up at the sky like he's gazing at the stars.

I don't remember taking any of these pictures. The metadata all matches my camera, and they are clearly photos of Adrian working and existing. Two years before we met.

I frown, clicking through the images again, wondering if my mind is playing tricks on me. In every picture, Adrian appears to be unaware of me, caught in the everyday business of living. It's as if I'd been stalking him, collecting pieces of his life before it ever intersected with mine. Except there's no way. I had never met Adrian before that first gallery night, never even noticed him in passing. At least, I don't think I had.

I flip through the dates, then cross-check my social media posts. My head pounds as I try to find a logical explanation; anything that will help me make sense of what I'm seeing. Maybe I was doing a street photography project? Maybe I captured him by accident?

Adrian is still lost in his sketchbook, mouth moving silently as he counts windows with his pinky finger. He looks up, sees me staring, and smiles in that slow, sleepy way he has after hours of hyper-focus.

"You okay?" he asks, scooting over to my side of the table. "You look like you saw a ghost."

"Just caught off guard," I hear myself say. I shake my head and make some excuse about a weird spam email. Adrian accepts my explanation, kisses my cheek, and goes to refill our water glasses. He doesn't see the tremor in my hands, or the involuntary shudder that runs down my spine.

I close the folder when he returns, my heart pitter pattering in my chest. Adrian sets my cup down, his gaze gentle, and strokes my cheek with the back of his knuckle. "Take a break," he coaxes, and I let him pull me into his embrace, burying my confusion in his warmth.

That night, after Adrian falls asleep beside me, his breath slow and even, I tiptoe back to the computer and scan the photos again, searching for a sign to explain the holes in my memory. Had we crossed paths before? Some chance encounter I'd forgotten? But the more I stare at Adrian's face captured in pixels, the more my stomach twists and the growing sense of unease settles deeper in my bones.

I file the folder away into a hidden subdirectory, labeled *Sorting*, but the images blink at me from behind my eyelids every time I close my eyes.

The next day, I trip over myself stalking Adrian's entire digital footprint while he's at work. I need to find something that would give me a clue as to why I have all these photos of him from before we met. But no matter how hard I look, I find no explanation. His work account is all real estate developments and fundraising. His personal accounts show mostly pictures of buildings and the occasional artfully blurry shot of me and Toast. There are no hidden tags or pseudonyms; there's nothing odd.

I even call Liz and try to joke my way through my sudden unease. "Let's say I have a folder of photos from, like, months ago, and my boyfriend is in all of them... is that... weird?"

Liz snorts. "Umm you're dating in the digital age. It would be weird if you didn't have pictures of your boyfriend."

But when I push, saying, "No, really, I don't remember taking them and the timeline doesn't add up," she laughs me off. "You're a photographer, Tessa. You're always taking photos. It's kinda your thing, you know." Her voice softens. "Honestly, if you're getting cold feet, just say so. You don't have to create problems where there aren't any."

The thing is, I don't want to create problems. It's the opposite, actually. I want to freeze life right here, in this perfect little world where nothing hurts, except for my head occasionally. But even the migraines have mostly vanished since moving in with Adrian. The mold at my place must have been causing them, and I'm pathetically grateful to be free of the pain.

So, I swallow my doubts. Whatever explanation exists for those photos can't be worth risking what Adrian and I have built together. The life we share matters more than whatever strange coincidence came before. I need to focus on the rush of Adrian's hands on my hips and the way he reads my mind with a look. I need to appreciate the way he always, always knows how to make me feel safe.

But no matter how much I try to plaster over the hairline fractures in our perfect world, they only seem to widen over the next few weeks. I notice little things, mostly. Like the way I sometimes zone out for half an hour in the morning, only to realize I've started a chore or an email and have no recollection of doing it. Or the time I spot a mole on my arm in a photo, even though I could have sworn I had it removed two summers ago. I try to chalk these up to minor details that may just be evidence of my chronic sleep deprivation or the effects of too much screen time.

One Saturday, I catch Adrian watching me as I edit, his gaze too sharp to be casual. It's as if he knows something is wrong, but isn't sure how to bring it up. When I turn to look at him, he covers his expression with a tender smile, then crosses the room and wraps his arms around me.

"What are you working on?" he asks, nuzzling into me.

"Just cleaning up old photos. You're actually in a lot of them... Hope you don't mind."

He squeezes me and kisses the top of my head. "Of course I don't mind. You can photograph me anytime."

Liz drops by later that day. She's all sunglasses and energy and invites us out for a late afternoon walk. We end up at a bakery where she orders six different pastries and makes us try a bite of each.

Liz wipes a crumb from the corner of her mouth. "So when's the wedding?"

Adrian chuckles and finds my fingers under the table. "We're taking it day by day, but I like where we're headed."

Liz pivots toward me, eyebrows raised. "What about you? Ready for the picket fence?"

I trace the rim of my mug. "Sure, someday." The folder of photos flickers across my mind, but I push the image away. "So which pastry is your favorite? I think I like the raspberry filled one..."

We talk and laugh until dusk starts slanting against the window, and Liz takes off, promising to crash our place with cheap wine and scandalous TV at the soonest possible opportunity.

On the walk home, Adrian links his fingers through mine. "Liz's great. She cares about you a lot."

"Yeah. We only met a few months ago, but she's already like a sister... just a little more annoying," I chuckle. "You better watch out though. I'm pretty sure she'd bite your face off if you hurt me."

"As she should. But I hope you know I'd never hurt you..." Adrian glances at me sideways, and I don't miss the glint in his eyes as he adds, "Unless you asked me to. In that case, I could come up with some delicious ways to inflict pain. And trust me, you'd love every moment of it."

"I can't say I'm not intrigued," I grin, "but I'll have to work up to that. So let's save that experience for another day."

We climb the steps to our building, chatting about our week and making plans for next weekend. I fan my face when Adrian gives me a wolfish grin and describes all the ways he'd love to incorporate a little pain into our Saturday evening plans.

At the door, Adrian catches me by the wrist and turns me to face him. "I know you said you'd like the picket fence someday... but if you ever feel like it's too much…" his voice trails off, eyes searching mine, "if you ever need your own space back, just tell me. Promise?"

I study the new creases at the corners of his eyes and the furrow between his brows that wasn't there yesterday, my chest tightening. Here I am, making this incredible man doubt us because of some dumb photos I can't explain. "I promise," I whisper, rising on my tiptoes to kiss him.

Safe in the apartment, I set down my bag and let Toast wind around my ankles, purring like a demon. Adrian slips away to the bedroom, the door clicking softly behind him. I lean back against the couch, trying to clear my mind, but thoughts of the folder lurking on my desktop keep intruding despite my best efforts to barricade them behind mental walls.

My feet carry me to the desk where my laptop waits. Just delete the folder and be done with this nonsense, I tell myself, my hand hovering over the trackpad. The screen illuminates my face as the folder expands, revealing dozens of images, daring me to make sense of them. My cursor finds the delete button, hovers there for a second… but a photograph I hadn't properly noticed before stops me.

It's a shot of Adrian standing in the rain across from the Plum Pot, umbrella held high, mouth half-open as if he's about to speak. I zoom in and spot a blur behind his shoulder. It's a second figure, also holding an umbrella. And there's the ghostly impression of a third person's face reflected in the glass behind both of them. It's my face, I realize with a jolt, but not quite right. The hair is longer, the mouth a little off, as if my own features have been transposed onto a stranger's skull.

A spike of dread jolts up my spine. I snap the laptop shut, the clack echoing in the quiet living room.

Adrian calls my name from the next room. I force my voice to work, call back, "Yeah?" like nothing's wrong, like my heart isn't skittering in my chest. I tell myself the photo's just a fluke or a trick of the light. Nothing for me to worry about.

I lie in bed beside Adrian that night, his arm snaked under my back, his breath slow and even. I stare at the wall and try to piece together the last few months of my life. I think back to every skipped beat, every flash of familiarity that shouldn't exist.

There was one time here, at Adrian's, when we sat together on the couch and I felt like I'd lived through that moment before... but no, that was just déjà vu. Then the time at the hike when we were under the oak tree and a sense of unease hit me out of the blue, though I told myself it was nothing. Then two weeks ago in the park, my finger hesitated on the camera shutter as Adrian smiled... because I'd already captured that shot, hadn't I? My knees nearly gave out from the vertigo that hit me just then.

Am I remembering a future that hasn't happened, or forgetting a past that has? But these flashes can't be from the past. If Adrian had been a part of my life longer than I can remember, he'd tell me. Wouldn't he?

When I finally drift off, my dreams are a flicker-show of a strange montage. I see Liz's face, overexposed and grinning, then the gnarled oak with the scarred heart. The oak slowly transforms into shadows with glowing orange eyes, their light singing my skin and making me want to hide. But my legs won't work, and there's nowhere for me to run. I wake in a sweat, the taste of something bitter on my tongue, convinced someone has been standing at the foot of our bed.

But Adrian is still asleep, and the city outside is just beginning to light up.

# CHAPTER SEVEN

# Fixation

I've convinced myself the migraines were from black mold and insomnia, a problem I could solve with good ventilation and a week's worth of hibernation. But the mold from my place is gone, my migraines are back, and sleep has become as elusive as the answers behind the photos of Adrian on my laptop.

I pop vitamins as if they're sugar cubes. They no longer work. Or maybe they do, and I'd be dead without them. Who knows?

I go through the motions of editing, grocery shopping, spending time with Adrian, and texting Liz. I'm present in body, but my soul wants to curl into a ball of exhaustion and confusion.

Adrian is attentive, bordering on psychic, about my moods. He notices when I get the flicker of pain behind my eye, and will steer me to the couch, toss a blanket over me, and click the TV on to a mindless reality show that helps me not think for a while. He makes me fresh camomile tea and sometimes just holds my head in his lap and strokes my hair while I try not to cry from the pressure. "You okay?" he'll ask, and I'll say, "Just tired." Which is true, if not the full truth.

I try not to think about the folder, but it's like trying not to roll your tongue over a loose tooth. Every time I close my eyes, I see the distorted image of me behind the lens, staring at Adrian, before I was supposed to know him. Rationally, I know there's a logical explanation. Maybe I was on an assignment for work and just forgot? Maybe it's a B-roll from a project I never finished? But the dates on the files don't add up.

I want there to be an explanation, any explanation, but it feels like the world is tightening around me, squeezing until the only thing left is the throb behind my eye and the taste of copper on my tongue.

Would Adrian think I'm crazy if I told him about the pictures? I run through a dozen scenarios in my head. I picture him bracing himself at the kitchen island while I confess, "Hey, so, I have a folder on my hard drive full of stalker shots of you from a couple of years ago. Best case, I'm sleepwalking with my camera. Worst case, I'm a crazy person who'd followed you around before you ever knew me." The thought of having that discussion with him makes me want to crawl out of my skin.

I don't tell Adrian about the pictures. I keep the words zipped up, triple-encrypted. I tell myself the photos must be a coincidence, even as I check the folder every night, as if the evidence might have rearranged itself and I'll wake up one morning to find it was all just some weird hallucination.

Adrian's firm lands a big and fancy downtown revitalization project, and suddenly the apartment is a blur of meetings and phone calls. Adrian is burning the midnight oil at the dining table, with blueprints spread across every surface. He still makes time for me, but I can feel the shift in the air, a new current pushing us along. It pulls me further away from the version of myself who only had to worry about getting through the day without a migraine.

It's not all bad, though. In fact, some of it is so good it makes me question why I'm looking for ways to self-sabotage. We go out for drinks with Adrian's colleagues, who are earnest to talk about buildings and the latest office gossip. I'm the oddball at the table, but Adrian makes an effort to involve me in the discussion. He drapes his arm around my chair, tracing small grounding circles on the top of my shoulder like he's reminding me, you're here, you matter. I want to ask how he makes me feel so seen, but I'm afraid if I say the words out loud, I'll jinx them. If I acknowledge I want to keep Adrian, want to build a life with him, maybe the universe will snap my wish away like a rubber band.

On Wednesday night, we're at a work dinner and I'm doing my best impression of a functioning adult. My head is full of static, but I've curled my hair and put on mascara and am faking my way through a conversation about the merits of open-plan office design. Adrian is in his element, charming as ever, and every so often he glances over like he's checking to make sure I haven't bolted for the exit. I pick at a beet salad and nod along as one of Adrian's coworkers tells a story about a client who requested a fireplace in every room of their new house.

Adrian squeezes my thigh under the table, and for a second I let myself sink into the comfort of his touch. The migraine is hovering behind my eye, but Adrian's warmth pulls me back to the present.

After dinner, we walk the long way home, past shuttered cafes and half-lit windows. "You okay?" Adrian asks, fingers twined with mine.

"Yeah. It's just been a long day."

He doesn't push, just squeezes my hand in reassurance.

I collapse onto the bed fully clothed when we get home. Adrian kisses me once, quietly, then undresses me with reverent care. There's no rush. He is gentle as he pulls off my tights, then climbs into bed beside me, his hands warm and steady against my skin.

He kisses my shoulder, then moves to the spot just below my ear where the pulse jumps when I'm anxious. I feel the world quiet when his lips touch my skin. Adrian doesn't ask for anything, doesn't push. He just holds me until I melt, until the hurt in my skull and the ache in my chest shrink down to something small and manageable.

We make love slowly, as if we're both afraid we'll break this thing between us if we go too fast. Adrian's lips trace the curve of my neck, leaving a trail of goosebumps in their wake. I arch into him as his mouth finds my breast, my fingers tangling in his hair.

The pressure builds with each careful thrust, his breath hot against my collarbone, my legs wrapped around his waist. Our eyes lock in the half-light, pupils wide, and something unspoken passes between us. I tremble beneath his weight, the world narrowing to Adrian's heartbeat against mine. The familiar coil tightens as he moves deeper until the taste of salt on his skin and the sound of the soft groan he makes when I dig my nails into his shoulders finally push me over the edge.

When we're both sated and spent, I lie with my head on his shoulder, heart thumping unevenly. Adrian traces his thumb along my collarbone, slow and rhythmic, until my breathing syncs back up with his.

"You're shaking," he murmurs, brushing hair off my forehead.

"Just a headache," I lie, and he kisses the spot above my eyebrow like he could will the pain away with touch alone.

We stay like that, the lights of the city flickering against the ceiling. I wonder what it would take to stop time and live in this moment forever. With Adrian's skin against mine, and the faint aftershocks of orgasm still humming in my bones.

When I finally drift off, I dream of the tree on the mountain ridge again. This time the heart carved into the bark is bleeding sap, gold and slow, and Adrian is there, tracing the liquid with his fingers. I reach for him, but when I look down at my hands, they're covered in red. I wake up gasping, eyes wet, throat raw, head pounding with pain.

I crawl out of bed and pad into the living room, where the city glows through the windows and the only sound is Toast snoring in his cat tower, sprawled out on his side like he owns the place. The pain is severe enough to make my eyes water, and I take two more of the vitamins Adrian reordered for me, swallowing them dry.

My laptop waits on the kitchen island, its dark silhouette taunting me. I won't open it. Not now. Not tonight, when there's nothing I can do but let the images fester in my head like a fever. But the compulsion is there, hot under my skin.

I curl into the corner of the sofa, pulling one of our embroidered fleece throws around my shoulders. My eyes drift across the darkened apartment, trying to see it through an outsider's eyes. I take in Toast's new bed Adrian splurged on, the ridiculous dinosaur popcorn bucket from our third date perched on the bookshelf, then the embarrassing matching slippers we bought as a joke but actually wear every day. Not a single thing seems out of place; nothing that would explain those impossible photos waiting on my laptop, anyway.

I rub my temples and squeeze my eyes shut, fighting off the next pulse of pain. I need to stop this spiral and just let those pictures go.

I hear a soft ping from the couch. It's coming from Adrian's phone, forgotten there overnight, screen lighting up the darkness like a beacon. Who would send him a message in the middle of the night? I lean over and dig the phone out of the crease of the couch. My thumb hesitates on the unlock button. I know the passcode is 1021, which Adrian uses for everything.

I unlock the phone, and the text message fills the screen. It's from a jewelry store, something about a discount for loyal customers. Just spam. My shoulders drop as I exhale, the knot in my stomach unraveling.

What had I been bracing for? A mysterious woman texting Adrian heart emojis while I slept two feet away?

My eyes drift down Adrian's other messages. They are mostly texts from clients, a handful of banter with James, and a few affectionate check-ins from me. I scroll further, my guilt warring with curiosity. There's a note from another coworker, brief and stiff, and a shipment notification for a package. Then I come across a reminder for an appointment with the dentist. It's all so boringly normal.

I should set Adrian's phone down. There's obviously nothing to find here. My rational brain knows this, yet some dark gravity tugs at my fingertips, and before I can stop myself, I'm scrolling through his recent calls.

An unknown number appears over and over, calling every few days. Most of them went unanswered, but there's one connected call, lasting two minutes and thirty-two seconds. That must have been another telemarketer, a spam call Adrian finally answered to tell them to stop.

I switch to the photo gallery, feeling my heart rate double-tap against my ribs. The most recent images are what you'd expect. I see shots from our hikes, along with unflattering dinner selfies. I chuckle at the photo from the time Toast squeezed himself into Adrian's failed pottery project.

But going back further, almost at random, I find dozens of photos of my neighborhood. My eyes land on images of the Plum Pot's painted sign at different times of day, and on the tiny yoga studio where I met Liz. Then, I see a photo of the vet where I take Toast for his checkups. I scroll further and freeze when I find images of my apartment complex, one specifically focused on the third-floor corner unit where my bedroom window is, curtains half-drawn, how I always leave them.

They're not stalker shots, exactly. But they're not normal, either.

I check the timestamps, and sure enough, the photos are dated months before we met. A year or two before, in some cases.

What the hell?

Maybe Adrian was working on a project in my neighborhood? Maybe he just liked the architecture? The explanations arrive fully formed, but none of them fit the way my heart is galloping in my chest, or the way my hands have gone clammy.

The coincidence is too much. Adrian taking pictures of my building, my life, and me somehow having photos of him I don't remember taking. Like an invisible force had pulled us toward each other before we ever met.

I hear a soft sound behind me. The bedroom door hinges creak, then footsteps approach. I flip the phone facedown on the coffee table and curl up at the far end of the couch.

Adrian pads over in his boxers. His hair's a sleepy chaos, and he squints at me from bleary eyes. He crosses the room, sits beside me, and pulls the blanket over our knees. "Couldn't sleep?"

I say nothing for half a minute, and the silence goes from soft to screaming. I can feel the shape of every thought in my head, queuing up to tumble out. I should let the photos go. I really should. But the words are burning behind my tongue, and if I don't say something, I might actually combust.

"I was looking at your phone… I know I shouldn't have. But I did." My hands twist the blanket. "I saw the pictures you took from before we met. Of my neighborhood, even my apartment windows."

Adrian stiffens next to me, and I look up to see a twitch across his features. Then he shifts his shoulders, and the blanket falls, forming a wall between us.

There's a tightness to his tone when he asks, "Why were you going through my phone?"

"I don't know... I guess I just—," I almost say I needed to know why I have photos of you on my laptop from before we met, but that sounds deranged, so I finish lamely, "couldn't sleep."

We stare at each other. I'm expecting a fight, or maybe a denial, but Adrian just sighs and rubs his palm across his face.

"I can explain," he grumbles, "but you have to trust me when I say it's not what you think."

"What do I think?"

He looks at me, really looks, as if he's trying to decide how much of the truth I can handle. "You probably think I'm some kind of creep, taking photos of your home, following you around. But it's not like that."

"Then what is it like?" I ask, and I can hear the quaver in my voice. "Explain the photos to me."

Adrian lets the silence build as he stares at me, his mouth in a tight line. When he finally speaks, it's in a voice so careful it sounds like he's afraid of breaking me. "My firm was bidding on a redevelopment contract in your area. I was documenting the neighborhood. Taking pictures of the businesses and the people. It's part of the proposal process. Community engagement, or whatever buzzword they assigned to urban planning. Tessa, I took hundreds of pictures. Most of them never made it into anything."

His eyes find mine. "But these photos, the ones I kept... after I met you, they became something else entirely. Now when I look at them, I don't see potential development ideas. I see where you close your eyes in bliss over that first bite of pastry. Where you whisper to Toast through his carrier when you think no one's watching. Where you called out my name with your windows thrown open, and God, Tessa, I wanted everyone for blocks to hear you screaming you were mine."

It takes a minute for Adrian's words to sink in, and my cheeks fill with heat. I exhale, my shoulders dropping. Of course there's an explanation; there's always an explanation. I want to kick myself for doubting him, for letting my sleepless brain concoct a conspiracy out of a set of work photos. I stare at my hands, knuckles white, fingers knotted in the blanket.

Adrian's face is still drawn, but the tension in his jaw softens as he watches me process. I must look like I've been wrung out and hung to dry with my puffy eyes and thinly pressed lips, curled up in the oversized T-shirt I stole from him.

"I'm sorry. I shouldn't have..." My eyes fill, hot and humiliating, and I press my fists to them, willing the tears to reverse direction.

Adrian reaches for me. The blanket collapses between us as he pulls me into his lap, settling me against his chest. He smells like sleep and cedar, and his arms are steady around my shoulders.

"It's okay," he murmurs, his lips grazing my hairline. "I know you're just tired. You haven't been sleeping right for weeks. I see it every morning when I wake up and you're laying there wide awake."

He's not wrong. I spend my nights tossing and turning, and more than once in the past few days I've woken up in the kitchen with no memory of getting there. Sometimes I find my phone in the refrigerator, or wake up with bruises lining my skin that I don't remember getting. These episodes scare me, but the idea of telling Adrian about my sleepwalking and letting him think I'm crazy scares me even more.

"I just..." I start, then trail off. I just what? Couldn't stop myself from sabotaging something good? Couldn't let go of the fear that I'll turn out to be the villain in my story? My tongue is heavy, stuck to the roof of my mouth.

Adrian sighs into my hair. "You know, last night you were talking in your sleep. You kept saying my name over and over... You sounded scared."

I flush, embarrassed. Adrian strokes my back in slow, even arcs, grounding me. "Maybe you should talk to someone," he murmurs, the words so low I almost miss them. "A doctor, or Liz. Anybody. I'm worried about you."

I nod, because I don't know what else to do. He's right; I should have called a doctor months ago, when the headaches started tunneling through my skull. I keep meaning to, but every morning I wake up and think, today is the day I'll get better on my own.

Adrian nestles his face into my hair. "I would burn down the world before I let anything or anyone come between us," he whispers, voice rough at the edges. "You know that, right? There's no other woman out there for me, Tessa. Not a single soul. And if going through my phone every day helps you believe that, then you're welcome to look at it whenever you want to."

Adrian's words burrow beneath my ribs and leave me feeling raw.

"You can trust me," he continues. "I know you've had a rough go before. But I'm not them. I promise I'm not going anywhere."

I open my mouth, then close it, unsure of what to say. I never had broken hearts, just a few not-quite-anythings. Brief flings that didn't go anywhere beyond a first couple of dates. Adrian must have filled in the blanks himself, built a narrative for me where I am the tragic, wounded thing in need of saving.

But maybe he's right. Maybe that's all I've ever been.

Adrian wipes a stray tear off my cheek, then holds my face in his hands. "You keep looking for reasons to blow this up... But I love you, Tessa. And that is the honest to God truth."

*I love you, Tessa.*

His words sink into my chest, my brain, every inch of me buzzing from the impact. Adrian loves me. Imperfect, trying-so-damn-hard-to-ruin-this me. My lips can't form a response at first. But then realization dawns and I hear myself whisper, "I love you too." My voice is shaky and barely there, but I mean every word.

I love Adrian. With everything I have.

Adrian tips my chin up to kiss me.

"I'm sorry," I mumble when he pulls away, feeling ashamed for violating his privacy and for accusing him of... I'm not even sure what.

"No need to apologize. Just trust me when I say you mean the world to me and that will never change. No matter what." Adrian kisses me again, and I believe him; I do.

He picks up the blanket and wraps it around us like a cocoon. His body radiates heat against mine, and his heart beats with a steady rhythm under my palm. My muscles go slack, tension dissolving as his arms tighten around me. When he whispers against my hair, his breath warm on my scalp, I close my eyes and let myself believe he can want me this completely. That I can be enough.

We sit on the couch until the city begins to pulse with the hint of sunrise, limbs tangled, Adrian's chest a steady thrum beneath my cheek. I drift in and out, held tight in his arms, and the pain in my head recedes to a faint, ignorable ache.

# CHAPTER EIGHT

# That Simple

I am lounging on the living room rug with my camera battery charging on the side and Toast sprawled across my lap, dead to the world. My episode the other night, as Adrian likes to call it, seems like a long forgotten fever dream. The sting of my embarrassment still lingers, though.

After all, normal people don't dig through their boyfriend's phones, and they don't create conspiracy webs based on a few random photos. I still cringe thinking about how I must have looked when Adrian walked into the living room that night. I've been trying to do better since then, to take care of myself and my mental health, by walking more and eating better. Adrian was the one who threw out those suggestions, and they've definitely helped.

Speaking of meals; my stomach growls an angry sound, reminding me I haven't eaten breakfast. I drag myself upright to make a bowl of cereal when my phone buzzes. I think it's Adrian at first, but then I see Liz's name.

I type back with one hand, while using the other to pour the whole grain protein cereal Adrian picked out into my bowl. It tastes like cardboard and misery, but I force it down anyway.





I search for a flat look GIF and send Liz a cat looking utterly unimpressed. She ignores it, of course.



I want to say no, but Liz is relentless, and tempura crab with sticky rice does sound incredible. My stomach growls in agreement.

I exhale and let the phone drop onto the counter. It'll be good to see Liz. It'll make me feel normal, grounded.

I wolf down the cereal and start editing photos, falling into the old rhythm of highlighting, cropping, color balancing, repeat. By the time noon rolls around, my eyes are swimming, and there's a tidal wave of unprocessed caffeine in my system. When Liz arrives, she's carrying a white plastic bag stuffed full of containers, and their smell alone makes me feel instantly ravenous.

Toast stretches and regards Liz with the disdain of a creature who knows he is too cute to be trifled with. Liz croons to him, "Handsome boy, did you miss me?" before turning her attention to me. She flops onto the couch, kicks her shoes off, and pulls several boxes from the bag.

She squints at me over the rim of a plastic container. "You look exhausted. When was the last time you slept?"

"Last night?"

"Liar. You have corpse circles under your eyes." She rips open a packet of chopsticks and hands them to me. "Spill. What happened with Adrian? He must have done something to make you this stressed."

I poke my chopsticks into the rice. "Nothing happened. Things with Adrian are great. Amazing, actually. We had a little weirdness the other day, but we're fine now."

Liz's eyebrows shoot up. "What weirdness?"

I shake my head, trying to laugh it off. "Just me being crazy. I thought he was hiding something, but it turns out he's just a workaholic... Aaaand before I realized that, I might have gone through his phone..."

"Oh my gosh, you didn't!"

"Yeah." I cover my face with my hands. "You can revoke my cool status now."

"Babe, you never had cool status. That's why we're friends." Liz leans back, pressing a fist to her sternum. "Was it worth it? Did you find nudes?"

"No nudes. He's basically a monk. But he forgave me, and then he told me... he told me he loved me."

Liz gapes at me, chopsticks frozen midair. "He caught you going through his phone, and he told you he loved you?"

I nod, my attention firmly on a piece of tempura.

"That is not the reaction I expected. So what did you do? Did you say it back to him?"

I nod again, cheeks burning.

Liz thumps her hand on the coffee table, nearly upending her rice. "This is huge! You, falling for a guy who's practically a saint. Where is the drama? Where are the bad boys with mommy issues?"

I laugh. "Maybe I'm growing up?"

Liz makes a skeptical noise, then narrows her eyes. "So why do you look like you're about to crawl out of your skin? There's something you're not telling me."

I shrug and focus on the shrimp. But Liz will not let it drop, obviously. She licks a dab of sauce off her thumb and fixes me with a stern look. "You know what your problem is? You keep waiting for the other shoe to drop, but you won't even let yourself buy the pair. Just wear the damn shoes, Tessa. Try to be happy."

I want to protest, but she's not wrong. "I know I need to get out of my head. It's just... Adrian is so out of my league. He's successful, he's got money, and on top of all that he's actually sweet and caring? He's the total package, and that's exactly what scares me. No one is *that* perfect."

"Look. Everyone has flaws, and you'll find his eventually. I'm sure he does some weird things, like smelling his socks before putting them into the laundry, or dipping his fries into apple sauce."

"Eww."

"But what matters is that he obviously loves you. And you love him. Sometimes it really is that simple."

***

After lunch, Liz sticks around long enough to offer an unsolicited TED Talk on the five stages of healthy attachment. I half listen as I stack takeout containers and wipe sauce blobs off the table. When she leaves, she hugs me tight enough to crack my back, then threatens to stage an intervention if I try to ghost her again.

The door clicks shut behind Liz, taking her perfume cloud with her, and suddenly the apartment feels like it's vacuum-sealed around me.

"Alexa, play some music," I say to the little black box on the bookshelf, desperate to have something in the air besides my own thoughts.

As the tunes of a catchy pop song play, my mind drifts to the memory of Adrian's hands around my body, to the way his voice sounded when he said he loved me. The moment felt so real. A goofy smile spreads across my face. Liz is right. I love Adrian, and he loves me; it is that simple.

I'm humming to the music while I go to refill my coffee, and end up sloshing dark liquid over the mug Adrian got me as a gag gift. Usually, the *MUG SHOT* text on its side makes me grin, but today I can't muster up my appreciation as I take in the spreading puddle with a sigh.

"Well, at least I'll finally clean the countertops," I declare, but my forced brightness falls flat even to my own ears.

I reach to grab a paper towel to mop up the mess when a movement catches my eye in the room's corner. I swear I see the shadow of something tall and thin for a split second, just beyond the threshold to the hallway. The darkness seems to lean forward, as if peering at me.

I freeze, crumpling the paper tower in a white-knuckled grip. Alexa keeps playing that stupid upbeat song, but I won't tell it to stop. What if someone is in the apartment and they hear me? I know an intruder would know full well where I'm at already, but I can't think rationally in the moment.

Quiet. Just be quiet. Yeah, that seems like a good plan.

The drip of coffee hitting the floor sounds like a bass drum under the chorus singing something about summer love. Even my breathing seems too loud, rasping in and out while I strain to hear any footsteps or rustle of clothing, a sign that I'm not alone.

I ease a butcher knife out of the block on the counter and take a steadying breath. My legs want to carry me straight out the front door, but my mind won't let them. There's only one way to find out if there's an intruder in here, after all...

Metal handle cold against my palm, I creep toward where I saw the shadow, scanning each potential hiding place. My eyes wonder over every corner of the room, looking for a hint of movement, my senses on high alert.

Toast opens an amber eye from his spot on Adrian's pillow in the bedroom. He stretches and yawns, front paws extending forward, unconcerned with my racing heart. My knuckles whiten around the knife handle as I scan the corners. What am I even looking for? Some ski-masked intruder? A deranged stalker? But the only thing intruding on this quiet afternoon is the shadows cast by the afternoon light and the echo of my pulse hammering against my ribs.

I search the entire apartment twice over, knife at the ready, checking behind doors, inside closets and cabinets, and even under the bed. I find nothing but dust bunnies.

I eventually make my way back to the kitchen and double over, one hand braced against the counter while I exhale slowly, waiting for the surge of adrenaline to subside. Good Lord! The caffeine must be getting to me, or maybe I just need to go outside to clear my head and get some fresh air.

I stay hunched over for a couple of minutes until the shakiness leaves my limbs. Once my pulse settles back into a normal rhythm, I straighten and swivel back to clean up the spilled coffee. But as I move, my elbow catches the edge of the mug, and my coffee tips, plummeting to the floor. I watch in dismay as it shatters on the hardwood, the ceramic splintering into a fan of white and blue shards.

A strangled sound escapes my throat as I drop to my knees, fingers hovering over the broken ceramic. The letters "*MUG SH*" stare up at me from one large piece, the rest of the word obliterated. No amount of superglue could resurrect this gift. Adrian will say it doesn't matter, but that won't stop the pang of guilt clawing at my chest.

Could this day get any worse?! I cast a glance toward the bedroom, picturing Toast's delicate paw pads meeting these razor-sharp edges. Yes, actually, this day could get much worse. But Toast is thankfully still spread eagled across Adrian's pillow, utterly uninterested in the mess I made.

The bigger pieces come up easily, but there are still tiny specks of glaze and coffee peppering the floor. I'm on my knees, dabbing at the broken ceramic, when a fluff of cat hair wedged under the fridge catches my eye. I must have missed that spot when I was cleaning the other day. I reach for the hairball and freeze when my fingers brush against something crinkly. Pinching it between my fingernails, I pull out a small yellowish square, its edges curled and grimy from months beneath the refrigerator.

I examine the dirt and the film of god-knows-what that's caked on the sticky note. Suspicious stains mottle the yellow paper, and I fight the urge to drop it and wash my hands immediately. I straighten to toss the note in the trash when I notice the writing in black ink:

*Ask him about Kate*

I turn the note over in my hand, but the back is blank. There are just those four words on the front.

The handwriting is loopy, the letters slanted. I suppose this note could be mine, but I don't remember writing it. Did Adrian leave it for me? Or did I leave it for myself?

*Ask him about Kate.*

I wreck my brain, trying to place the message. There is no Kate among my family, and I don't have any clients named Kate either. I decide to text Liz, hoping she'll know who Kate is.

*Liz: LOL what? Like a mutual friend?*

*Me: Yes. I just found a note under the fridge that says "Ask him about Kate"*

*Liz: Ooooo. Could Kate be a secret love child??*

*Me: Haha no, I'm serious*

*Liz: Ok, gimme a sec, checking the old group chats, socials…*

*Liz: The only Kate I know is that girl from the yoga studio? I think she moved to Portland after she got dumped*

*Me: I would not put her name on a note*

*Liz: Unless she's Adrian's secret love child :)*

*Me: Thanks. That's extremely helpful*

*Liz: You're welcome. This is what I'm here for*

I close the text and look at the sticky note again. The stained paper sits on my palm, stubbornly refusing to offer an explanation. I will not ask Adrian about it, I decide. It's not worth the potential embarrassment. The reminder about Kate must just be a brain fart, a ghost of a memo past. It doesn't mean anything. Besides, I have work to do.

I spend the rest of the afternoon mourning my favorite mug, blasting through edits, attending a consultation, all the while glancing at my phone, waiting for Adrian to text. At five, my phone vibrates with his message.

> Wine Guy: Ready for dinner? Or are you still meeting with happy couples?

> Me: Just finished. Can you come and pick me up?

> Wine Guy: Sure, I'll be there in 15. I love you!

I read his last sentence twice, a swarm of butterflies rising in my belly before typing "I love you too" back.

***

The note migrates from the kitchen counter to my nightstand to my hoodie pocket, getting softer and more crumpled every day.

*Ask him about Kate.*

I mean, it's not like I'm going to ask Adrian if he's hiding a secret wife or child. He's forgiven me for the phone incident, and I'm not about to claw at the curtains again. But every time I see his name on my phone, every time he texts something sweet or sends a selfie of Toast perched on his laptop, the note pricks at the back of my mind. Who is Kate?

I try an experiment while Adrian is in the shower one morning. Maybe if I Google "Adrian Mercer" and "Kate" together, I'll get a social media connection or an embarrassing college photo. I'm just being thorough. Scientific.

Adrian's last name brings up four architects, one of whom is now retired, and a few links to his work portfolio. The man is practically unsearchable. I scroll further and find a comment thread from four years ago. There's a photo of Adrian and a pack of people at a rooftop party, dated and a little blurry. Below it, a single comment stands out: *Miss you, Kate.*

I click on the commenter's profile, and my eyes travel to the circular photo showing blurred city lights, which provide absolutely no clues. I dig deeper, scanning through a few old posts that must be set to public, but they are all just random photos of landscapes and a few memes. There's no sign of a Kate.

I close the app and exhale, my shoulders dropping with a mix of relief and disappointment. Kate is no one important. I should throw the note away. My fingers curl around it anyway, tucking it back into my pocket.

The sticky note stays buried there until the next day, when Adrian kisses me goodbye and leaves for work. During a lull in my schedule, I fish the crumpled paper from my pocket and smooth it against the desk, then reach for my phone, social media already loading beneath my thumb. I punch in the words "Kate," "Adrian," and "Mercer", along with the name of every nearby city I can think of. The algorithm churns, and I get a hit when an account named KateShoots1 pops up on the screen. The icon is a grainy black-and-white photo, offering zero helpful information about the account holder... again. What is it with all these mysterious photos?

I examine the rest of the profile and roll my eyes at the bio that says something pretentious about losing ourselves in the light. How profound. The rest of the account is practically an empty shell and offers no location or personal details. Not only that, but its owner hasn't posted anything since 2023.

I scroll back through the earlier feed, alternating between curiosity and self loathing for my obsessive need for answers. There are only a handful of posts showing urban landscapes and animals in random places. They are annoyingly vague and impersonal, but I must admit, each photo is stunning. Whoever owns this account either has an eye for beautiful shots or is fantastic with photo filters. Either way, it seems they can make a hairless mole look like modern art, which is just annoying. I hate how the light bends to this person's will. I hate that I'm jealous of someone I don't even know.

I keep scrolling, searching for something more about who Kate is, but the captions are vague: #sunset #urbanlandscape, or an occasional quote. There are no photos of a woman, not even a tagged friend.

Was Kate a fling? An acquaintance? And why does imagining this faceless woman make my stomach twist into such a tight, angry knot? I close my eyes and take a breath. This isn't normal. This isn't me.

I roll my shoulders back and scroll to KateShoots1's most recent posts. The early shots of meticulously framed photos give way to motion blur and shadows creeping in from unexpected angles. It's as if the account owner stopped having the luxury of time to set up her shots properly.

In a few, there's a human shape in the background. I squint at the man who appears to be standing at a distance, just at the edge of the frame in one photo. I zoom in. He looks tall, dark-haired, with broad shoulders under a heavy coat, face turned away. Maybe it's a trick of the lens, but he looks like he's stalking the poster, trailing down the block half a stride away. My skin prickles.

I browse the other photos, but the man stays out of reach, like a shadow that won't become a real person. There's no matching caption, just hashtags and a poetic line or two. I want to tell myself I'm imagining things, that it's just coincidence, but I can't shake the feeling there's something here I'm not seeing.

The way the silhouette stands, shoulders hunched against an invisible weight, tugs at my memory.... Where have I seen him before? Then it hits me. He reminds me of the man who kept creeping into the background of the work photos I was organizing the night Adrian and I met. The similarities are there, but there's no way it's the same person.

I continue browsing and come across a picture of a three-story apartment building with blue shutters, titled *Home sweet home*. Finally, something useful. I save the image and drag it into a reverse Google image lookup.

The search reveals an address: *1288 Redfern Lane*. According to the map, I could be there in fifteen minutes. My fingers hover over the screen before I save the address in my Notes app. "What am I even doing?" I mumble, but I still check twice to make sure the note saved properly.

I navigate back to social media and scroll until I reach Kate's last post from two years ago. It's just a photo of orange light melting into a dark sky over some mountains. The caption reads *New beginnings*, but there's no explanation, nothing else. After that, there's only silence. As if Kate had simply vanished, her account frozen in time. I tap my finger against my thigh, feeling unsettled.

Should I fess up and ask Adrian about Kate? I picture myself sliding the stained sticky note and my phone across the table, pointing to the feed, and asking Adrian, "So... who's Kate?" If I learned anything from our previous argument, it's that I need to, as Liz says, keep my damn shoes on, and not sabotage myself over something silly.

Kate is just a girl who came before. She's no one important.

I close the app and set my phone face-down on the counter. My mind needs something real to latch onto that isn't Kate and what she might have meant to Adrian, so I clean the kitchen and then the bathroom. I scrub the toilet until my knuckles ache, walk six blocks to clear my head, then do a month's worth of laundry, grocery shop, and meal prep for the next week like a responsible adult.

When Adrian comes home that evening, he brings chili and a cute little batch of cornbread muffins, and Kate becomes a ghost I can't quite remember why I was chasing.

Adrian's in his element tonight, sleeves rolled up, telling me all about his pitching session gone sideways at work. "You ever have this moment where you know exactly what to say, but your mouth just betrays you?" he asks.

Every day of my life, I think. "Yup."

"I had it all written out. But then my brain glitched mid-sentence, and I called the major's concept half-baked, instead of, you know, forward-thinking."

We laugh, and the sticky note doesn't seem so important anymore. Not when Adrian pulls me close and tells me he loves the way I smell, or when we argue playfully over whether Bullets and Mistlejoes counts as a Christmas movie. Kate's name is nothing but a distant memory as we settle in to watch Joe Maclean save the hostages at Imotakan Tower, with Toast stretching his furry body across our laps.

# CHAPTER NINE

# Spiral

My favorite way to end the day is with Adrian between my thighs. I can't get enough of his lips against mine or his hands tangled in my hair, while our bodies stick together, damp and perfect. The world narrows to the roughness of his stubble against my chin, to the shallow rise and fall of his chest against my breasts. If I die from pleasure, at least I'll go with my body and heart full of him.

I'm not sure how we made it to the bed. Last I remember, Adrian was stirring risotto in the apron I got him that says, *Kiss the Cook*. He got a smudge of flour on his nose and looked so endearingly proud of himself that I couldn't help but tackle him. Food burned, the smoke detector yowled, and we laughed so hard the other tenants in the building must have heard us. We made love on the kitchen floor, grains of risotto pressed into my shoulder blades, my thighs splayed on the cool floor as Adrian buried himself inside me. Now we're in bed with the sheets twisted around us, the last bit of blue dusk leaking through the window. I'm sweaty, sated, and happy. So damn happy.

"Are you okay?" Adrian asks, voice hoarse.

I can't answer right away because my brain is still rebooting. "Fine. Good. No, like, fantastic," I manage, and I see the corners of his eyes crinkle with something that might be pride. He rolls off me, stretching all six plus feet of himself across the mattress. I ogle his body, taking in all the muscles and the dark hairs on his chest that catch the fading light.

"That might be the fastest anyone's ever gone from stirring risotto to..." He gestures at our naked bodies, and the sound of his laugh makes my insides flip.

I let my hand drift over his ribs, feeling the tremor there. "I should be embarrassed that I have zero self-control with you in an apron, but I'm really, really not."

"Don't be. As a matter of fact, I'll wear that apron every time I cook from now on."

We lie like that, side by side, our bodies cooling in the open air. The silence is easy, punctuated only by the hum of the fan and the faint sound of the TV through the wall. It's only when my breathing slows and my thoughts start to drift that the question surfaces, unbidden.

"Hey," I say, tracing a lazy pattern on Adrian's chest with my finger. "Do you know anyone named Kate?"

Adrian's body goes still under my touch, like I flipped a switch and transformed him into a statue. For a second I think he didn't hear me, but then he turns his head, eyes finding mine.

"Kate?" He draws out the word, soft and slow, as if testing the taste of it. "No. I don't think so. Why?"

I almost laugh, because this behavior is such an abrupt change from the warm, relaxed man I love. "No reason. I just... someone mentioned a Kate at work, and I thought maybe you knew her. I guess it's a common enough name." I say the words as evenly as possible, like I'm not at all invested in the answer. But inside, my curiosity has sharpened to a point, and I watch Adrian's reaction closely.

He rubs the back of his neck, eyes flicking to the ceiling. "Can't say any Kates come to mind. Do you know her last name?"

"Didn't catch it. And her first name could've been Katie, maybe."

"Hmmm. Not sure who that might be, sorry."

I study Adrian's face. I watch as his lips flatten and the way a small muscle jumps in his jaw. Then, as suddenly as he tensed, he relaxes again, wrapping his arm around my waist. He kisses the curve of my ear.

"But I love you and that beautiful mind of yours, always working in mysterious ways."

I let myself melt into him, feeling his breath warm against my neck. But Adrian's reaction lingers in my mind. I replay the way his muscles tensed at hearing Kate's name, how his eyes darted away. Could she be an old girlfriend? I suppose everyone has exes they'd rather not talk about. If someone asked me about mine, I'd probably act weird too.

I push the thought away. Whoever Kate was, she isn't here now. Adrian's past relationships aren't my business unless he wants to share them with me. When he whispers against my skin that I'm his every-thing, when his eyes follow me across the room like I'm the only person who exists, I believe him. That has to be enough.

We stay like that, curled up so close I can feel Adrian's pulse through my skin. But when the darkness settles and Adrian's breathing evens out, I lie awake, staring at the ceiling, my mind replaying every second of that conversation.

Adrian didn't blink. He didn't even flinch, not really. His body language changed like a curtain dropping; one minute open, the next shut. But Adrian has no reason to lie to me. He is honest to a fault, actually. My brain must be manufacturing problems again where none exist.

I turn to study Adrian's sleeping face, which has softened into something boyish. His lips move with each breath, and he looks so peaceful, so unguarded. Part of me wants to wake him, to ask again about Kate and watch his eyes for any flicker of recognition. But what would that prove? That I don't trust the man who takes care of me and loves me unconditionally? Who's never once made me feel less than cherished?

"Keep your shoes on," I whisper to myself, curling my toes under the sheets. I blow out a breath and nestle against Adrian's warmth. His heartbeat thumps steadily against my ear as I count the shadows on the ceiling, sleep as elusive as usual.

***

The next morning, Adrian makes me eggs exactly the way I like them. He's set out the vitamins I keep forgetting to take, and when I mention I have a shoot across town, he volunteers to drive me.

When I get in the car, I find Adrian has adjusted the seat and turned on the warmer for me.

"Want a podcast or music?" He asks, then puts on my favorite podcast, Flaws In Laws.

I blink at him. "How did you know I like this one?"

"You mentioned it a while back. I listen to it sometimes, too. It's entertaining, isn't it?"

I nod along to the familiar intro music. "I love how Ashton digs into all the questions nobody else asks. Makes you see the victims and their cases in a whole new light."

"Especially the cold ones. You're left wondering what actually happened."

"Exactly. And Brie's commentary is so fun. I love the dynamic between her and Ashton. The only downside to these podcasts is the ads that play every few minutes."

Adrian reaches over and squeezes my hand, his thumb brushing over my knuckles. "Check your phone. I got you the top tier Flaws In Laws fan club subscription. No more interruptions."

My mouth falls open as I stare at the man next to me, the morning sun highlighting the sharp edge of his cheek. "Adrian, that's... I don't even know what to say."

"You don't have to say anything, Tessa." His smile is soft. "The way your face lights up when you're happy is worth every penny to me."

My heart swells against my ribs, and I wonder how much more I can love this man before I burst at the seams. "Thank you. You're amazing."

"I know I am. Now hush, so I can hear what Ashton's saying."

A chuckle escapes me as I turn up the volume. We stay in the car after we arrive so we can finish the podcast episode. Adrian eventually drops me off with a kiss, just long enough to make a couple of workers at the loading dock gawk at us. I'm embarrassed, but also not, and as I lug my equipment inside, I smile, the glow of my joy hot and bright behind my ribs.

The rest of the day is a blur. My subject is a CEO with the personality of unfinished drywall, and his public relations woman keeps making condescending comments to me like I'm a child with a toy camera instead of a grown woman with two degrees and an upscale gallery contract in the works. Ordinarily, I'd stew about it for hours after, replaying each rude comment. But by the time I'm done with the shoot, my phone is lighting up with a text from Adrian.

*Did you eat lunch? Should I bring you food?*

*I picked up one of those warm rice bowls you like. I'll be there shortly*

I reply with heart emojis and a yes, please, and fifteen minutes later, Adrian's picking me up with a bag of food and a grin that makes my heart swell.

This is what it's like for the next few weeks. Adrian appears every time I need something, like the universe's answer to a wish I didn't know I made. He anticipates, preempts, plans, and solves. I complain offhand about the heat in the apartment, and the next day there's a new oscillating fan on our doorstep, still in the box with a bow on top. I forget to buy cat litter, and a delivery driver shows up with a bag of expensive scented kitty litter. Then, I offhandedly mention an 80s action movie I haven't seen in a while, and that night, Adrian cues it up on streaming, popcorn and pop at the ready.

Adrian is so thoughtful that I feel almost worse about my insecurities. On the one hand, I'm flattered by his attention, but on the other, I feel even more obviously lacking in our relationship. Adrian never leaves wet towels on the floor, never forgets a date, or even a minor detail about me. He never even snores, unless he indulges in a few glasses of alcohol. Some days I wonder if he is real or just a figment of my imagination. I've been alone for so long that I'm half-convinced I dreamed this perfect man into existence.

*"I want to take care of you… you'd never have to work another day if you didn't want to."*

Adrian's words echo in my mind. I picture myself waiting for him each evening, dinner simmering on the stove, nothing to worry about except making him happy. Would that really be so bad?

I shake my head, glancing at my calendar app with its color-coded blocks. Meetings with Marissa, followed by back-to-back holiday minis, fill my schedule. Even if I was willing to give up my career to become a stay at home girlfriend, I wouldn't cancel on my clients out of the blue. Maybe someday I could scale back. But not today. Not yet.

By Friday night, I'm so keyed up from my marathon of deadlines and back-to-back shoots I can barely sit still. I spend an hour waffling over whether to start the show we've been watching early or wait for Adrian to get home, and in the end, I channel my nervous energy into cleaning. I scoop cat litter, wash the dishes, declutter the apartment, and even go after the streaky bathroom mirror with a rag and pink spray that smells like chemicals and fake lemons.

I take breaks to scroll through Liz's texts. She's just gotten back from her company's team-building retreat, and the story she's telling is pure Liz.

> *Liz: Almost made out with a guy in HR but  he looks like a boiled egg…. so NVM*

There's a burst of laughing emojis and then a picture of Liz on a barstool, hair slicked back, giving the camera an obscene finger while the other hand holds a canned margarita. I snort and text back.

What I really want is to make Adrian feel the way he makes me feel, like every small detail matters. I finish tidying the living room, carefully stacking the books on the coffee table and fluffing the pillows on the couch. As I vacuum the bedroom, I pause and look around, noticing all the subtle ways the place has changed since I'd moved in. The walls display framed photos of Adrian and me. There's a sweater of mine draped over the bed frame, a pair of my earrings glinting on the nightstand, and a stack of our shared books by the window. Half of the novels are unread, which has become a running joke between us.

It feels so natural to think of this space as ours. Not mine, not his, but something woven together, like a beautiful mixture of our lives. The thought makes my chest tighten in a good way.

I'm bending down to clean the spot under the hard-to-reach headboard that always collects dust bunnies and lost socks. I push the vacuum's nozzle all the way in, and something clinks into the canister with a metallic thud.

I sigh and sit back on my heels, prying open the vacuum's trapdoor. Emptying the canister is my least favorite part of cleaning. I hold my breath to stop myself from inhaling the gray cloud of skin cells, and whatever else the rug has been collecting, puffing into the air.

There, nestled in the dust, is a delicate gold chain. I reluctantly stick my hand into the canister and I tug the chain free, my eyes landing on the tiny letter K dangling from the end. It's tangled and worn, but appears to be mostly intact.

My first reaction is to set the necklace aside and scrub my hands until there's no skin left on them. The thought of all the dust and God-knows-what covering my fingers right now makes me want to heave. But then I stop, the breath catching in my throat as my brain catches up. My fingertips prickle as I study the K, the way it gleams against my palm even under layers of grime.

*Kate.*

Her name echoes in my skull, louder than it should be. I stare at the necklace, willing it to be a family heirloom or a previous tenant's belonging, anything but what it probably is. I set the necklace on the nightstand and try to forget about it. Except I can't. I text Liz, fingers flying with the story of my find, and she replies with a GIF of a cartoon cat with its eyes popping out.

> *Liz: OMG, Tess. That's so sus. You gonna ask him about her?*

"Yes," I type, then delete it.

I appreciate Liz's protectiveness, but my smile quickly transforms into a frown as the gravity of my situation starts to sink in. I grab the gold K, twirling it between my fingers. Maybe it's Adrian's sister's. Or his cousin's? But Adrian doesn't have a sister, and he hasn't mentioned any extended family beyond his estranged father, who, according to Adrian, hasn't spoken to him in years.

Adrian told me he didn't know any Kates. I want to believe him, but the tiny golden K mocks me. Tossing the necklace into my hoodie pocket, I mechanically finish vacuuming, hating myself for doubting Adrian, and hating him for making me doubt him.

I scrub the pendant until I can see my reflection in it, then wash my hands three times. The woman in the mirror looks haunted, with dark circles under her eyes. I'm drawing in deep breaths and wiping my hands when my phone vibrates against the counter.

I press my forehead against the bathroom mirror, which feels cool against my skin. I thump my head against the glass once, twice, a dull ache spreading behind my eyes. Get a grip, Tessa.

I open the medicine cabinet to look for my vitamins, but all I find are Adrian's prescriptions, a bottle of allergy medicine, ointment, and some cotton swabs. Of course, my vitamins aren't where I left them. I slam the door shut harder than necessary, and the cabinet swings askew, something behind it popping loose with a metallic ping.

Just perfect. I stare at the wreckage, tears welling in my eyes. All this chaos because of what? A necklace with a letter dangling from it? It feels like my sanity is slipping through my fingers, and I can't cup my hands fast enough to catch it.

The cabinet won't stay flush with the wall no matter how hard I try to push it back into place. A screw or a bracket must have broken loose behind it. I huff in annoyance, gripping both sides, and channel all my frustration into the movement until the whole thing comes off its mount. The cabinet's heavier than it looks, and I almost lose my balance before staggering backward and lowering it to the floor with shaky arms.

I survey the scuffs on the wall and the bracket that appears firmly attached. The cabinet must have slid off it, but it looks salvageable at least. My eyes travel to the drywall next, and I suck in a startled breath at the small recessed storage nook the damage exposed.

Why would Adrian cover up the built-in shelves? That's a strange choice for an architect who loves unique features and clever ways to save space. And what's even stranger is the box tucked into the bottom shelf, positioned where it would be completely inaccessible with the cabinet in place. Why would Adrian leave something there? My phone pings on the counter, making me jump.

*Wine Guy: Running late, stuck in traffic*

*Wine Guy: ETA 40 min. Sorry!*

I force myself to inhale, exhale, and count to ten. Then I reach for the box. My fingers tingle as I pull out the container, heart hammering. It appears to be a black shoebox, battered at the corners, nondescript enough to be easily overlooked. I stare at it for a full minute, hesitating. If this is something Adrian deliberately hid, maybe I shouldn't open it.

I flip the lid anyway.

At first, I just see a mess of tissue paper and old receipts, but then a glint of gold catches my eye. I close my fingers around delicate links with a single turquoise bead at the clasp. The bracelet looks soft and unmistakably feminine, and the tag is still attached. Okay, that's a little strange. Maybe Adrian bought the bracelet as a present for me and hid it so I wouldn't find it. I set the jewelry aside and dig deeper.

Next comes an aged strip of photo booth film. The first photo appears to be of Adrian holding a brunette's face between his hands, gazing at her with such intensity that I go a little hot behind the ears.

She's laughing at him in the second photo, with her head tipped back, hair wild and flowing down her back. Her eyes are closed, lips parted in delight.

They're kissing in the third one. Adrian has his hand splayed across her cheek, the other cradling the back of her head.

In the fourth photo, he's holding her against his chest and looking dead into the camera with an expression I can't decipher. Her face is buried in his shirt, with only the crown of her hair visible.

I flip the photo over and find, unsurprisingly, *Adrian & Kate* written in black ballpoint. There's a date, nearly two and a half years ago. I stare at it for so long that the numbers begin to blur.

I flip the strip back, my eyes drawn to the woman. Though she's angled away from the camera, I can make out glimpses of her profile. The tilt of her nose is similar to mine, and her hair appears to be a shade darker than my chestnut. Even the way she tilts her head looks similar. God, her resemblance is unsettling. Adrian obviously has a type. The way he holds her in the photos, the way their bodies fold together, it's all suddenly too much.

The urge to drop the box and run is overwhelming, but I force myself to keep digging. Underneath the photos there's a spiral-bound notebook, the wire along its spine warped from too much use. I pull it out and open it to the first page.

The handwriting is loopy and feminine, similar to the writing on the *Ask him about Kate* note. I flip through the pages, eyes skimming until the words make my stomach sour:

*I can't shake the feeling that someone is following me. I know that sounds paranoid. Marc says it sounds paranoid. But I keep finding things moved in my apartment. My phone was in a different spot. Did I forget where I put it? My journal was facing the wrong way. Am I losing my mind?*

The entry is dated a few years back. My heart pounds as I flip further. There are more entries about dinners and date nights with Marc, about fights. I read about an argument over a text, over a work trip, over a misplaced house key. Then, I come across an entry that makes me pause:

*I confronted him about my suspicions. He has an explanation for everything. He made me feel crazy for even asking. But I KNOW what I saw.*

The rest of the page is scratched out in thick, angry loops. My eyes wander to the next page:

*He knows where I am. Yesterday he showed up at the Polkadot Goose while I was eating lunch, then today I ran into him at the park. He says it's a coincidence. I'm not sure I believe h*

I close the notebook and stare at the recessed shelves for a minute, my brain refusing to line up the facts. The necklace and the notebook are real. Kate's real. And most importantly, Adrian's lie is real too.

My head pounds so hard that my vision goes pixelated at the edges. Nausea churns in my throat as I sit in the middle of our—no, his—bathroom, clutching the battered notebook and staring at the strip of photos like they might divulge their secrets.

I should put everything back and pretend I never saw the bracelet and the journal. That would be safer. Smarter. But I can't seem to let go of the notebook, and I can't stop seeing Kate's profile in those photos. I didn't ask for this, I remind myself, even as guilt and jealousy gnaw at me. It's not my fault the cabinet came loose or that Adrian's hoarding some other woman's journal in his bathroom nook.

I swallow twice and force myself to keep reading. The pages near the end are smeared, the ink running in blotches where Kate must have written with her hand pressed too hard, or maybe she cried as she wrote. The entries get shorter.

*I know he'll say I'm not thinking clearly. But I have to get out. I'm packing tonight while he's at work.*

*He showed up early. He knows. I can see it in his eyes. He's acting normal, asking about my day. But he KNOWS.*

The last entry is shaky and uneven across the ruled page:

*I have two hours. I'm packing now. If anyone finds this... if something happens to me*

The journal ends there. There's no sign off, no next page. The rest of the notebook is blank.

I can feel my brain short-circuiting as I try to make sense of what I just read. I squeeze my eyes shut so hard that I see stars. Despite the rational explanations, the thousand sweet gestures, the way Adrian is so perfect for me I sometimes think he's a hallucination, I can't shake the fear that overtakes me in that moment. I flip the notebook shut with a slap, then open it again, hunting for something that will help me understand why Adrian lied to me.

Didn't he say he had a brother named Marc? Kate talks about Marc in the journal. I flip to the beginning, looking for context, but nothing makes sense. If Kate was Marc's girlfriend, why was she kissing Adrian in the photos? And why does Adrian have her journal? Did Kate leave it here on purpose? Does this mean they are still seeing each other?

I feel sick, and I realize I'm sweating through my t-shirt. I want to scream, to throw the notebook out the window, to smash the photo strip and forget I ever found it. I grab a bag and shove everything into it, yanking the zipper so hard it almost pops off the track.

I check the time. Adrian's ETA is now twenty minutes. What am I supposed to do? Just pretend I never found any of Kate's belongings? Sit through dinner and let him feed me cake while I die inside? I decide to text Adrian.

> *Me: Liz crisis. Can't do dinner tonight. I'll make it up to you later. Love you.*

I add a heart, then delete it. I hit send before I can overthink it. My hands are shaking as I dial Liz. She answers on the second ring, voice thick with laughter and static from whatever she is doing. "Tess? Did you talk to Adrian about the secret baby?"

"Not yet," I say, trying to sound normal. "But, uh, I need a huge favor. Can I come over? It's... It's important."

Liz must pick up on the crack in my voice. The background noise cuts out as she moves somewhere quieter. "Sure, I can meet you at my place in 20 minutes... But are you okay?

"No, I'm so far from okay I'm not even in the same stratosphere as that. I found something about Adrian and Kate. But it's better if I show you in person."

Liz's all business now. "Ok. Want me to have a chocolate ready or just wine?"

"Maybe both," I tell her, and for a second I almost laugh, until the wave of nausea hits again.

I hang up and fumble with the medicine cabinet, trying to rehang it on the wall. My fingers won't stop trembling, and the frame nearly slips from my grasp. When I finally click it back into place, the cabinet sits slightly crooked, which is a small imperfection only noticeable if you look closely.

I rub my chest as I stare at my work, trying to loosen the tightness there. Toast wanders into the bathroom and bonks his head against my shin, oblivious to my existential crisis. I scoop him up and bury my nose in his fur, breathing in warm cat and whatever fresh hell I've gotten myself into.

When I get to Liz's townhouse, her hair is in a bun and she's wearing fuzzy socks. She's holding a bottle of wine and a look that could deflect bullets.

"All right, spill. What did you find that freaked you out so much?"

I shove the notebook and the photos at her. "I found these in Adrian's bathroom. Behind the medicine cabinet on a hidden shelf."

Liz' s eyes widen as she takes the journal and photo strip.

"That's not even… there's more. Just read the notebook."

Liz perches on the edge of her couch, flips through a few pages with furrowed brows, then goes still as her eyes lock onto the words, scanning line after line with growing intensity. Her face transforms from skeptical to horrified in a single pass.

"Um. Tessa. This is…" She doesn't finish. She just flips the photo booth strip over and studies the woman's face. "Are you sure this isn't you?"

I bristle. "That can't be me. Look at the date on the back. And Adrian told me he didn't even know a Kate. Why the hell would he lie to me about that?"

We sit on the couch, knees knocking together, the full horror of the situation hanging in the air. Liz flips through the notebook again, slower this time. "Do you even know if this Kate's alive?"

"I don't," I whisper, "but I need to find her. I need to know the truth of her relationship with Adrian, and whether Adrian is still seeing her."

My chest feels tight, a physical pressure like someone's fist is squeezing between my ribs. I glance at the door every few seconds, wishing this was all an elaborate prank. That Adrian would appear with a self-satisfied grin, exclaiming "Got ya!" I can almost hear his deep laugh as he'd gesture to hidden cameras. "Just a joke, Tess," he'd say, and everything would make sense again.

Liz nods, jaw set. "Okay. We find Kate. But we definitely do not confront Adrian until we know exactly what we're dealing with. Do you have Kate's last name?"

I press my lips together, blinking hard against the hot pressure behind my eyes. "No. But I have something better... I have her address."

# CHAPTER TEN

# Breaking Point

Liz parks her SUV three inches from a fire hydrant, throwing it into park with a violence that makes the car shudder. She's put on her gym leggings and an oversized hoodie, along with an aura of determination that radiates off her in waves.

We get out of the car and turn toward the midsize apartment complex at 1288 Redfern Lane. Kate's photo didn't capture the peeling paint or the rust stains bleeding down the fire escape, but the faded blue trim around the windows confirms we've found the right building.

Liz glances at me sideways. "Are you sure you don't want to go door to door until we find her?"

I nod. "The manager can point us to the right apartment."

"Hey," Liz steps in front of me, blocking the buzzer. "You want to talk first, or just... I dunno, punch something?"

I huff out a bitter laugh. "Maybe later. Let's just get this over with."

Liz nods, then hits the buzzer with her knuckle. When the door opens, the first thing I notice is the smell of body odor and boiled cabbage that clings to the walls of old apartment buildings and never quite leaves. I take in the tiny lobby. There are walls covered in peeling beige paint and a row of battered mailboxes. A crooked *MANAGER* sign marks the office door at the far end. We cross to it, our footsteps echoing on the linoleum floor.

The door creaks open when I knock, revealing a man with balding hair, a sweat-stained shirt, a thick gold chain around his neck, and the permanent squint of someone who's seen way too much human fuckery. A plastic name tag pinned to his shirt reads *Ross Ramponi* in faded black letters.

"Yeah?" he asks, sizing us up. "Rent's due on the first, not the fifteenth."

Liz's face breaks into her signature PR smile. "Hi Mr. Ramponi! Sorry to bother you. We're looking for our friend, Kate. Does she still live here?"

The manager frowns. "Kate..." He rolls the name around like he's tasting something sour. "No, I don't know no Kates."

Liz gestures at me with her thumb. "Are you sure? She looks a lot like my friend here. Same height, same age, same dark hair."

I shoot her a sideways glance, wondering where she got that information from, but Liz just winks back at me.

Ramponi's expression shifts, eyebrows lifting slightly. "Actually... there was a gal who lived upstairs. Her name might have been Kate, but I haven't seen her in... hell, two years now?"

Something cold settles in my stomach. The last page in Kate's journal is dated exactly two years ago, too.

"Right, she mentioned wanting to move a while back. Did she leave a forwarding address? Or, um, anything?"

The manager snorts. "If she did, that's long gone by now." He scratches his chin, looking directly at me. "You her sister?"

"No, Kate and I work together. Or we did." I force a smile.

"What can you tell us about the tenant who used to live upstairs?"

Ramponi studies me for a long and uncomfortable moment, then swivels towards Liz. "She paid on time, kept to herself mostly. Then one day she just disappeared. Her boyfriend moved her stuff out. Said she was in the hospital or somethin', then leaving town for a fresh start." He shrugs like that's all the explanation required.

A pressure grows behind my ribs. "Do you remember the boyfriend's name?"

The manager scratches his temple, cackling. "You serious? I can barely remember my own name." His laughter turns into a dry cough, and it takes him a minute to add, "He was a big guy. Drove some fancy black car."

I glance sideways at Liz, whose game face looks a little less solid than before. "Did you ever see your tenant again?"

The manager shakes his head and starts moving to the door, like he's put this entire matter to bed. "No. Now, if you'll excuse me."

He starts to close the door, but then pauses, as if remembering something. "Actually, funny thing. She left a few boxes in the storage area downstairs. Boyfriend said he'd pick them up, but never did. Been taking up space for years..."

He gives us a calculating look, and I can practically see the lightbulb flicker on above his head. It's clear he's thinking we're two suckers who might clear out his storage problem for free.

"Could we see her belongings?"

The manager grunts, confirming my suspicions. "Only if you take 'em with you. Follow me."

Liz gives my hand a squeeze as we trail him down the corridor. The building gets colder and darker as Ramponi opens a steel service door. He flicks on a yellow fluorescent light that buzzes so loudly it hurts my ears. "Down this way."

We descend the stairs, our shadows stretching ahead of us as the concrete floor tilts toward a wall of chain-link cages, each one padlocked and stuffed with forgotten possessions. Old electronics and boxes labeled *CHRISTMAS* are shoved into the cubbies.

Ramponi squints at a peeling tag. "She was in unit thirteen. Lucky, eh?"

He unlatches the door and swings it wide, revealing three cardboard boxes stacked waist-high, scrawled with a fading "KEEP" in black marker.

"That's it," he says, removing the padlock. "Be sure to shut the door behind ya when you leave."

As soon as he's gone, Liz lets out a low whistle. "Christ. This place is like a set for a slasher movie."

"You're not wrong." The basement air prickles my skin as my eyes adjust to the dim light. Cobwebs hang between the pipes, and dark patches, from water damage or something worse, bloom across the concrete floor. This place wasn't designed for comfort, but I guess that's the point. Tenants are supposed to get in, drop their stuff off, then get out.

I kneel and tug a sagging box toward me. The tape crackles under my fingernails as I pull the lid free.

I see books inside. So many books. Some are mass-market romances, water-stained and curling, but there are also composition notebooks, battered and well loved, just like the one I found in Adrian's closet. I pull one out and flip it to a random page.

"Wait. You want to do this here? Can't we take Kate's stuff and look at it literally anywhere else?"

I look up at Liz. "I need to see what's in these boxes. Just... give me a second."

She huffs and squats beside me, knees bumping mine.

The journal contains a few pages of mundane lists and doodles. I set it aside, moving carefully not to rip anything. I dig through the books and my fingers close around a manila folder underneath the novels. When I pull the folder out and open it, photos spill onto the ground in a mess of rectangles.

The first handful are ruined by water damage, their colors leaching into each other. But then I find one that's mostly intact. It shows a man and a woman, arms around each other, squinting into the sun. The man's face is unmistakable. It's Adrian, his hair a little longer, and he's wearing a crooked grin. The woman has a large sunhat on, and oversized sunglasses cover her eyes, but I can see the sharp line of her cheeks. It's Kate, with her hand on Adrian's chest.

I grind together my teeth. Liz leans over my shoulder, her mouth hanging open. "Holy crap. That's—"

"Adrian and Kate," I say, voice hollow.

Liz picks up another photo. This one includes two men standing shoulder to shoulder in front of a lake. Adrian is on the left, and next to him is a man I've never seen before. He could be Adrian's twin, except his hair is shorter and there's a scruff of beard along his jaw. His eyes are different, too. They are blue instead of hazel, and set deeper and harder under heavy brows.

"Who's that?"

I flip the photo over. On the back, there's a note in thick black marker: "Brothers, summer at the lake."

"Marc," I whisper, the name escaping before I can stop it. A shiver dances down my spine as I examine the photo.

Marc's shoulders strain the seams of his black polo, and he slouches against a picnic table with a confidence that feels animal. He looks like Adrian if you put him in a cloning machine with a cop and a bear, then poured the result into a pair of jeans. There's a smile, tight and wry, but it doesn't reach his eyes. I feel a weird, involuntary heat in my chest looking at the photo, and I'm instantly sick with guilt. This is Adrian's dead brother. What is wrong with me?

I flip through more pictures, hands working on autopilot. I see images of Marc and Adrian at a football game. Marc, with his mouth wide open, yelling something at the camera. Marc holding a dark-haired woman, her legs around his waist, facing away from the camera, while he grins. Not just any woman—Kate. I feel my stomach drop again, lower this time, like it's trying to evacuate my body.

Liz picks up the next photo. The corner looks warped, but you can still see what matters. Marc is holding the same woman in his lap, her face half-buried in his chest. Kate's hair falls like a curtain, and I can just make out her hand clinging to Marc's t-shirt, knuckles white. Adrian stands apart in the background, with his hands in his pockets, his head turned to the side. He isn't smiling. He isn't even looking at them.

I want to say something, but my tongue won't move. Liz's hand is suddenly on my arm, grounding me. "Tess, are you okay?"

I nod, but it's a lie. Everything inside me has gone strange and staticky. "Kate was close to them," I manage, my voice barely there, "and Adrian didn't want to tell me."

Liz is quiet for a beat. "Maybe he had his reasons?"

"He told me he didn't know her! He lied. He lied to my face, Liz."

We both look at the locked embrace between Marc and Kate. I stare at the shape of her profile and the tilt of her nose. If I wore my hair that way and put on a thicker layer of makeup, I could pass for Kate in a crowd. My skin crawls at the thought.

The next box is lighter, but I still have to drag it out by the fraying handle hole. The cardboard is pocked with water damage and ringed with a line of black mildew.

Inside, the top layer is clothes, folded in a rushed, haphazard way. There's a photo frame at the bottom, tangled in a knot of scarves and a ripped denim jacket. The glass has a crack, and the picture inside has faded, but I can make out the baby flanked by a man and woman, both smiling with joy. A thick gray mustache adorns the man's face, and the woman's hair is haloed in frizz. The image looks ancient, and it's impossible to make out all the couple's features, but If I didn't know better, I'd say they look almost familiar.

Kate was real, and she was loved. Somewhere, people who cared about her might be sitting in a kitchen right now, wondering where their daughter went, why she stopped calling.

Did she stop calling or am I making assumptions that aren't even true? For all I know, Kate could be out there, meeting with Adrian behind my back, as we speak.

I turn the frame over, thumb pressed against the sharp glass edge. On the back of the frame, my eyes land on the words written in black Sharpie: *Mom, Dad & Me.*

I swipe at my face, finding wet streaks on my cheeks. My chest feels like someone's reached in and squeezed everything tight, making it hard to breathe. I am truly losing my mind, unraveling here in this basement of doom, surrounded by a stranger's belongings.

I set the frame on the concrete and reach blindly into the box, half-expecting to find more photos, maybe a yearbook or a graduation cap. Instead, my fingers close around a thick stack of newspaper clippings. On the first folded page, the headline blares in black ink:

*LOCAL COUPLE DIES IN HOUSE FIRE, LEAVING BEHIND ONLY DAUGHTER*

The photo beneath is of a scorched colonial, windows blackened, a shell of char and smoke. Someone clipped and taped the article to a sheet of paper, as if they wanted to keep it from getting lost. There's a note scribbled in the margin: *Never forget. Never trust.* My head goes light, vision rimming with static.

I flip through the rest of the stack. There are three more stories about the fire. The investigators didn't find any sign of arson, only a pot on the stove that overheated, along with unfortunate timing. There's a quote from Kate. She says she was at a friend's when her world went up in flames.

My chest goes tight, my fingers feeling numb. I can't get enough air. When I manage to suck in a shallow breath, I think I'm going to puke right here on the concrete floor, so I clamp my hand over my mouth and squeeze my eyes shut.

"Tess?" Liz's voice sounds far away, like I'm underwater.

"Can't—need to get some air."

Liz hooks her arm under mine, lifting me as the journal and frame hit the floor with twin thumps. We stumble up the stairs, our footsteps echoing in the narrow hallway, until the door swings open and the chill air slaps against my face.

For a few breaths, all I can do is lean against the brick wall, palms braced. Liz stands next to time silently, with a hand pressed to my back.

After a minute, the pressure in my chest recedes enough that I can speak. "Why did Adrian lie to me?"

"Maybe he just didn't want to talk about—"

"He had Kate's journal. He had her stuff, Liz." The words tumble out, heavy and ugly. "And he won't tell me the truth. Why? What is he hiding?" I don't mention my eerie resemblance to Kate, but I know we're both thinking it. Add that to the pile of WTFs I need to process while I question everything I know about my boyfriend.

Liz wraps me in a hug. "I don't know, but we'll find out what happened to her and why Adrian is being so shady. We play it like a murder mystery, and you're Ashton  and I'm Brie. Okay?"

I nod into her shoulder. "Okay. Yeah."

Liz untangles herself from me and disappears back into the concrete tomb, returning with Kate's boxes one by one. I stay outside, watching her come and go, while gulping down winter air and trying to make my brain work again.

I let my head thunk against the brick, eyes closed, and inhale through my nose until the nausea retreats. When I open my eyes, Liz is lining the boxes up on the curb like she's prepping for an estate sale. She keeps glancing at me, concern clear in her eyes.

I gather myself and help her load everything into the back of her car, cramming the boxes around her yoga bag and a half-squashed case of hydration drinks. Liz waves me into the passenger seat and hands me a bottle. "You need sugar and salt. Blood sugar does weird things when you're in shock."

I chug the drink, too tired to argue.

Liz waits until we're on the road to break the silence. "Let's go to my place. You want to go through the rest of Kate's stuff, or should we take a break first?"

"Let's get it over with," I tell her.

"Okay."

We drive in silence, both of us lost in thought. My brain is buzzing with images of the ruined belongings and the newspaper clippings about the fire. Then, I think back to the photo of Adrian and Marc, side by side. One alive and one not.

Out of nowhere, a detail that's been gnawing at me surfaces. I jolt forward in the passenger seat. "Liz. The nightstand Adrian cleared out for me the day I moved in... there was a phone in there. An old phone with a cracked screen."

She glances over, one eyebrow raised. "Why would he keep that?"

"Exactly. He's perfect about his tech, right? He replaces everything the second a newer model comes out. So why keep that phone?"

Liz hums, considering. "Good question.... Maybe there's something sentimental on it that he didn't want to throw away. It's probably locked though."

"Probably. And dead. But if we can get it to turn on, maybe it'll have something that explains what happened with Kate."

"It's a long shot... I'll order a charger. We'll power up the phone and see what's on there." Liz grins, all teeth. "This is kinda fun. I mean, not for you, obviously, but—" She gestures at the boxes in the trunk. "This is the most exciting thing that's happened to me all month."

I shake my head, unable to match her enthusiasm. The life I'd built with Adrian, including our Sunday morning walks and our favorite shows we binge watch together, all feels like sand slipping through my fingers... But I've been waiting for this moment, haven't I? When I asked Adrian about Kate, something flickered behind his eyes before he lied. That calculated decision to hide the truth from me has haunted me more than any affair could.

Throughout the drive back, I press my forehead against the cool window and swallow hard against the rising tide in my throat. My reflection blurs, then sharpens, then blurs again as tears track down my cheeks despite my best efforts to hold them at bay.

# CHAPTER ELEVEN

# Surrender

It's been nineteen hours since I found the journal. Two hours since I decided I would never open another cardboard box in my life, and exactly two minutes since Liz set one on her kitchen island, folded her arms, and declared, "It's not going to unpack itself, Tessa."

I bite my nails down so far I taste blood while I watch Liz make a show of clearing her counters. She slides empty water bottles into the recycling bin and stacks her unopened mail into a neat pile. She even wipes down the counter with a rag, all in service of some mysterious girl's belongings, as if Kate might walk through the door at any moment.

"You want to do the honors?"

I shake my head. I want to run, actually, but I wedge myself between the kitchen wall and Liz's fridge and watch as she lifts out a heap of spiral-bound notebooks. "Jesus, how does anyone write this much?"

I squeeze my arms around myself. "Maybe it was her therapy. Maybe it made her feel in control."

Liz arches a brow, unconvinced. She hands me a journal, which I reluctantly accept, and open it to a random page. I catch phrases like, *Marc's such a great guy,* and *Everything I've ever wanted,* in looping handwriting.

I think back to the photo strip I found in Adrian's closet. The image of Kate's lips pressed against Adrian's and of his hands tangled in her dark waves swims behind my eyes. I turn the page, nausea churning in my stomach. Kate writes about flowers delivered to her door, weekend getaways, inside jokes, and the intoxicating feeling of being in love.

"This doesn't add up," I mutter. "If she was so crazy about Marc, why was she with Adrian in those photos?"

"Maybe she was playing them both? And they found out?"

"God, that's messed up." My eyes catch another entry:

*He remembered I had that early meeting today and texted me good luck.*

The thoughtful gestures and the texts make me feel like I'm reading about my own relationship. Kate might have been dating the other brother, but the parallel between her life and mine is jarring.

*He makes me feel like he really listens.*

*He showed up with the Christmas tree cakes I mentioned over the summer.*

*I told him to stay away while I was sick. Found him asleep on the couch after holding my hair all night.*

*I can't believe he's taking me on a surprise trip. I caught him measuring my ring finger while I was sleeping. Does this mean what I think it does?*

The words blur on the page as my mind flips between images of Marc's face, then Adrian's, superimposed over each other. Goosebumps prickle along my arms despite the seventy-two degrees in Liz's apartment.

"Why is the journal all about Marc? How does Adrian fit into all this?" There isn't a single mention of Adrian, which somehow makes me angrier than if Kate had written, *Had a wild affair with my boyfriend's brother.* I want her to explain herself. I want to know what happened.

"I don't know, babe." Liz flips another journal open, her acrylic nails clicking against the pages. She scans the text, clearing her throat dramatically. "Here, listen to this. August 12th," she reads, "Marc recited my lunch order today. Roast beef sandwich with extra mayo, no cheese. Even remembered I like the jalapeno chips on the side." Liz scrunches her nose. "Ewww."

She turns the page. "August 15th. Came out of the shower to find him scrolling through my phone. When I asked what he was doing, he just smiled and said, 'You looked beautiful at the Michaels' wedding.' That wedding was nine months ago."

Liz flips forward. "September 2nd. Mom visited today. I'd planned a shopping trip for the two of us. When we were getting ready to leave, he showed up with the car keys jingling in his hand. 'You ladies need a chauffeur,' he told us, already holding the door. Mom looked so pleased, so I smiled and thanked him, but I wish I could have spent time alone with her. Maybe next time."

She skims down further, her expression hardening. "Here's a good one," she says. "We had dinner at Bartelome's tonight. Before I could look at the menu, he told the server I'd have the Caesar salad. When I mentioned wanting pasta, he squeezed my hand under the table and said something about me staying healthy."

Like how Adrian wants me to walk and eat healthy? No. That's different. Adrian actually cares about me and wants me to be well both mentally and physically.

Liz looks up, one eyebrow arched so high it nearly disappears beneath her bangs. "This Marc guy gives me the eek. Like hot but psycho eek? Is that even a thing?"

I force out a chuckle, but it scrapes against my throat like sandpaper. Part of me wants to defend Marc—you're not supposed to speak ill of the dead, after all—but another part feels a chill at what these journal entries suggest.

"I don't know what to think. These entries make him sound perfect one minute and controlling the next. And Kate sounds… I don't know if she was in love, or being brainwashed, or both."

Liz taps her nails against the counter. "So what actually happened to her? And why does it feel like we're the only ones who care? Where are her friends? Her family? It's odd that she just disappeared off the face of the earth and no one seems to miss her."

"Those are good questions." I think of Kate's family photo, and my throat tightens as I swallow back tears. I press my fingernails into my palms until it hurts. This isn't me; I don't usually fall apart like this. Yet here I am, watching the life I've built with such care crumble at the edges because of some woman who might as well be a ghost. Is Kate still somewhere in Adrian's life? A secret he's determined to keep buried, even if it means lying straight to my face? I stare at the journals, torn between wanting to burn them and needing to read every word.

"Sometimes I wonder if I disappeared tomorrow, would Adrian tear the world apart looking for me, or would he just... move on like he did with Kate?"

"Look, regardless of what he's hiding about Kate, I've seen how that man looks at you. He is obsessed with you. He would never let you go without a fight."

Obsessed. A few weeks ago, I would have savored that word, tucked it away like a love note. Now my stomach clenches, and I can't decide if it's with pleasure or dread. The photo booth strip of Adrian and Kate, lips locked, flashes in my mind again. Ancient history, maybe. But the lie Adrian told me with such conviction, "I don't know any Kate", sits like hot coal beneath my ribs.

"In the photos Adrian is looking at Kate the way he looks at me, like she's something precious he couldn't bear to lose. Yet here we are, with Kate gone and Adrian pretending she never existed. Or better yet, maybe she is still here, and Adrian is secretly seeing her behind my back. Either way, this doesn't exactly bode well for me."

Liz blows out a breath. "I don't know, babe... Let's just keep reading. Somewhere in all this word vomit, there has to be something that explains what happened."

We plow through journal after journal, flipping pages until our eyes burn. We go through the notebooks in chronological order, working our way from the oldest to the newest. The early pages burst with Kate's infatuation with Marc, but over time, a subtle shift occurs. She talks about him saying her dress is asking for attention, or him calling her several times when she doesn't answer his text right away. The red flags appear between declarations of love, which disguises Marc's possessiveness as devotion. Then there's a six to seven months gap in the timeline, right around the time Kate's parents died.

When the entries resume, Marc's name appears in the first line: *"Marc says writing will help me process my feelings. I told him I'm fine, but he insists..."*

The pages that follow are more boring than the last. It's like Kate was going through the motions of living, rather than experiencing her life. Her once vibrant voice has flattened to a catalogue of mundane events.

The next notebook is full of disagreements with Marc about the thermostat setting and about how many times he pressed snooze on his alarm in the mornings. There's a detailed log of every upset stomach Kate's had and a list of restaurants she and Marc tried. There's still no mention of Adrian, though. Not a single clue to explain Kate's disappearance from social media.

But then, near the back of a journal, I find a page torn from a legal pad. It's a list titled, *Things I want to do before I'm 30:*

*1. Go skydiving with Marc*
*2. Eat real sushi in Tokyo*
*3. See the Northern Lights*
*4. Tell the truth*

*Tell the truth* is crossed out three times; the ink pressed so hard it indented the page. Kate tried to obliterate the word, but not even three layers of black ink can hide it. Tell the truth. What truth, Kate?

I feel sick, and my head is throbbing. The sound of a cork popping makes me jump. I look up to see Liz filling a glass with golden liquid, then pushing it toward me across the counter. "You look like you could use a drink."

I will my heart to stop racing, and grip the cool stem, staring at the journals scattered across the island. "All these words, all these secrets, and she just... left them behind?" The alcohol tastes too sweet, coating my tongue like syrup. "Does that sound right to you? Who runs away and abandons their diaries?"

Liz twirls her glass between her fingers. "Someone who thinks they're coming back." She takes a sip. "Or someone who wants to forget."

"Or someone who never made it out of an abusive relationship."

The words hang between us.

"You don't think..." Liz leans forward, voice dropping to a whisper. "Marc or Adrian killed her?"

Golden liquid splashes over my fingers as I jerk the glass. "God, no." I grab a napkin, wiping at the droplets. "Adrian cries during The Lion King. He wouldn't hurt a fly."

"The same Adrian who looked you in the eye and said he'd never heard of Kate?"

I meet Liz's gaze, heat rising behind my eyes as my vision blurs. "You don't think I replay that moment every night when I'm lying next to him? You know how much Adrian's deception is killing me!"

"I'm just saying—"

"I know what you're saying!" I close my eyes and inhale. "I'm sorry. It's just... Adrian is the guy who's always there for me. Who loves Toast like a son. He is the man I love. He is the man whom—," my voice cracks. "Whom I thought I could trust."

Liz tops off my glass, her rings clinking against the bottle. "Babe, I know you love Adrian. Believe me, I'm a big fan of his too. But you can't build a future on secrets. You need to talk to him and make him tell you the truth about this woman."

I press my lips together, staring at the spilt wine.

"Look, I know I've told you before to stop looking for problems where there aren't any. But Tess, this isn't one of your spirals. An actual woman might be missing, and your boyfriend, who swore he'd never heard of her, has her stuff hidden in his bathroom. That's not nothing." She punctuates this by draining half her glass in one go.

"I know you, Tess. If you don't talk to Adrian, this will eat you alive. You will obsess over Kate every waking moment. You'll find everything Adrian does suspicious. You'll wonder if he is secretly still seeing this Kate behind your back." She points her glass at me. "Trust me on this. I've spent months wondering if Jake, the guy I only dated for like a week, cheated with my yoga instructor. I still check his social media accounts daily."

"Do you really?"

"Yes. He rescued a stray puppy shortly after we broke up and named her Dill, which I'm pretty sure is short for Demon Liz. He posts pictures of the dog wearing sweaters and riding shotgun in his truck. He is a douche, but the dog is adorable. Makes me want to give him a second chance, actually."

I shake my head. "You're certifiable."

"I'm special," Liz corrects, raising her glass with a wink. "It's my most attractive quality."

Her smile is wicked, while mine barely holds. I exhale slowly, feeling the weight of everything pressing down on my chest. I want to believe Adrian'll hold me, reassure me that Kate's in the past, that I'm the only woman he loves. But then I see him again, with his jaw clenched and expression closed, when I mentioned Kate's name that night.

"I know you're right. Adrian is the only person who knows the truth. I know I need to talk to him... But what if the truth is worse than not knowing?"

***

The next morning, Adrian is waiting in his car outside Liz's townhouse. I see him before he sees me. His hair's perfectly styled, and he's drumming his hands on the wheel. He turns off the music as soon as I open the passenger door.

"Hey, beautiful." The smile that blooms on his face is so full of relief that I almost forget everything that's happened. He's wearing my favorite jacket, the one that fits his shoulders like a second skin.

"You can't do this to me," Adrian continues, "disappearing for an entire night. I barely got any sleep." He reaches for my hand, his thumb finding the space between my knuckles like it always does. "I missed you so much."

"Missed you too," I say, hating how true those words are.

I buckle in, and Adrian leans across the console to kiss me. "Let's get you home."

Home. Four letters that should feel like safety, but now sit in my chest like bricks.

We drive in silence for the first few blocks, the air thick with unspoken things. I steal glances at Adrian, searching for cracks in his composure, while my chest tightens with each breath, like my ribs are slowly folding in on themselves.

Adrian catches me looking, and I avert my gaze. "You're quiet," he observes, searching my profile. "You and Liz have a good night?"

"Yeah. Sorry if I worried you."

He reaches over and squeezes my knee. "It's okay." Then, reluctantly: "If I did something... I'm sorry."

For a second, I want so badly to believe that he means that. But Kate's necklace is still in my pocket, and the weight of it is a physical thing. At the next red light, I take out the chain and lay it on my open palm.

Adrian's eyes flick to the necklace, then up to my face. There's a split second where I see every gear in his head turning. "Where did you get that?"

"Found it in your bedroom."

"Our bedroom," Adrian corrects. He doesn't let go of my knee. He doesn't look away from the necklace either. "That's just a keepsake. Nothing important," he tells me, in a voice so even it almost makes me believe him.

I close my fist around the pendant. "I found more than this, Adrian. I found Kate's journal. I found her pictures with you. I know she's real."

Adrian's expression shutters, his face going blank. He withdraws from me and slumps against the seat. The car behind us honks, shrill and sudden. Adrian still doesn't move. He just closes his eyes, then blows out a breath. "It's not what you think."

My heart hammers so loudly that I can hear it over the engine. "What is it, then? Because it really seems like you lied to me about everything."

"You don't know what you're talking about, Tessa."

Adrian waves at the driver behind us and starts driving. He takes a right turn a little too hard, causing the water in his travel mug to splash over the rim. His knuckles are white on the steering wheel, but his voice is calm when he speaks. "I didn't lie to you, Tessa. I just didn't think it mattered anymore. Not after everything we've built together."

"So you didn't lie to me when you told me you didn't know any Kates?" I squeeze the necklace until the edges of the K dig into my palm. "I know Kate was your girlfriend. Or your brother's. So why did you deny knowing her?"

Adrian exhales through his nose, tight and controlled. "It's... complicated. I didn't want to dredge up the past. Didn't want to hurt you."

He glances at me, searching my face for something that might let him off the hook.

"Then explain why her things were hidden in your bathroom. Her journal, Adrian! That isn't something you keep for someone who doesn't matter to you."

Adrian pulls the car over and puts it in park beside a line of garbage cans. For a long moment, he says nothing. He just sits there, breathing evenly, like he's counting off seconds in his head.

"I kept it," he finally says, "because I didn't know what else to do with it. After Marc died, I had to sort out his place. Kate left all her things behind. It didn't feel right to throw it away. That's all."

"So what? You installed a medicine cabinet over a hole in your bathroom where you just happened to stash her stuff?"

Adrian's face tightens for a fraction of a second before smoothing out. "I renovated the bathroom, remember? Kate's box was on the old shelves along with a few other random stuff. Honestly, I just forgot about them."

Adrian's words make perfect sense on the surface, but something underneath them doesn't quite ring true. Then again, maybe I'm the one complicating things. The certainty I felt minutes ago begins to dissolve, replaced by a familiar doubt.

"Kate's in the past, Tessa. You're here, not her. And I love you."

"What happened to her? Please Adrian... I need you to tell me the truth."

Adrian's eyes lock with mine, his jaw working silently. "Kate and I were close friends at first, then... more. Our relationship was tumultuous. We were like water and oil, and Mark was the flame that lit us all on fire. Trust me when I tell you, it wasn't pretty."

"Then life hit Kate hard. Her parents passed away unexpectedly, and she needed a fresh start." He looks away, fingers clenching, then unclenching. "But you shouldn't be concerned about Kate. She's found her footing now, Tessa. Found someone who makes her smile, who makes her happy. Just like I've found you. So let the past go. If you love me as much as I love you, promise that you'll let Kate go."

Part of me wants to accept what Adrian's telling me, throw the necklace out the window, and curl into his chest. The other part wants to scream until my throat bleeds. The migraine pulses between my temples, and I close my eyes against the light.

I think of the journal hidden in Adrian's bathroom. I think of his lips against mine just minutes ago. I think of Kate's handwriting, looping across pages I was never meant to see. When I open my eyes, Adrian is still watching me, his face a perfect mask of concern. I hate that the sight of him makes my heart beat faster, even now.

"You promise Kate's alive and fine?" The question comes out smaller than I intend.

"Yes. I promise she got her happy ending. You have my word."

I study Adrian's face for any flicker of emotion, a twitch, a shadow, anything, but his expression remains smooth. "And you two don't talk anymore?"

"You're the only woman in my life, Tessa. You're everything to me. I wouldn't risk what we have for anything or anyone." He takes my hand, his fingers strong against mine. "You're my heart and soul. Other women might as well be invisible to me. You're the only one I see. The only one who matters to me."

I stare at Adrian's unblinking face, unsure what to think. The Kate-shaped hole in his story stretches between us, and I know, even as he squeezes my hand in reassurance, that I'm not getting any more information about his past relationship with her.

I offer a small nod, the motion feeling like surrender. Adrian leans in, his lips brushing mine with a gentleness that speaks louder than his declarations.

"You mean everything to me, Tessa. You know that, don't you?" The sincerity in his eyes matches every gentle touch, every thoughtful gesture he's ever shown me.

My throat tightens. "And you mean everything to me. That's why I need you to be honest with me. I couldn't survive if you lied to me… if you saw another woman behind my back."

"I won't," Adrian whispers, taking my hand and pressing it against his chest. "Feel that? My heart beats for you and only you, Tessa. You have to believe that."

He closes the distance between us, his mouth finding mine. There's such tenderness in the pressure of his lips, in the way he cups my face, that my body softens against his.

Is Adrian telling me the truth? He looks so sincere that it's hard not to believe him. When his fingers trace my cheek, when he whispers how much he loves me, my body believes him even as my mind hesitates.

I want to trust him. He is my Adrian after all, the one who pushed aside the coffee table in our living room and followed YouTube dance tutorials with me because I couldn't bear the thought of strangers watching me stumble. He is the one whose eyes soften when he notices I'm reaching my social limit at dinners before I've even said a word. Despite my efforts to stay aloof, I can feel my resistance crumbling.

I press my fingertips against my throbbing temples.

"Migraine flaring up? I figured you'd need these." Adrian extends his palm with two small white pills and a bottle of water, already uncapped. I swallow the vitamins without hesitation; the cool water offering momentary relief.

Of course, he brought my pills with him. Adrian always remembers the little things. He can tell when I need my vitamins, and he knows the exact pressure I like when he massages my shoulders. A man this attentive couldn't possibly be dividing his attention between two women, could he?

I watch the sunlight catch on Adrian's jawline as he eventually guides us back into traffic. The same jaw I've traced with my fingertips a thousand times, the same jaw I've seen pressed against Kate's cheek in the photos. I want to hate that jawline, but I still crave the rough edge of it against my neck, the brush of his mouth finding mine.

His thumb presses into my palm where the necklace has left tiny indentations, and I can't decide whether to pull away or lean into his touch. Part of me wants to scream at him to tell me more; another part whispers to let it go, to keep the life we've built. Adrian's eyes stay fixed on the road ahead, either unaware of the storm that continues to brew inside me or choosing not to acknowledge it.

Back at the apartment, Adrian makes me brunch exactly how I like it, with three eggs sunny side up and avocado toast on the side. He stands close while I eat, his chest against my back.

Later, his lips travel down my neck, then my stomach, and I close my eyes against the pleasure. When he whispers "I love you" against my hair, I whisper it back.

"You're so beautiful, Tessa," he breathes my name like a prayer. "You take my breath away."

Adrian kisses the line of my jaw as he tells me I'm everything he's ever wanted, that no one else could ever compare. He is so earnest, his eyes never leaving mine as he devours me, so loving in how he tucks my hair behind my ear with the gentleness reserved for handling something precious, that I almost, almost believe him.

# CHAPTER TWELVE

# Kate

Unbeknownst to Adrian, the journals come home with me, zipped inside my bag. When I get inside the apartment, I wedge the tote behind the couch where even Toast can't reach it. I ignore its presence, while the tension in my body coils tighter and tighter.

My cellphone buzzes with missed calls and text notifications from Liz. First, she sends me a couple of cat GIFs wearing detective hats, then a woman with one eyebrow arched high. Her message couldn't be clearer if she'd spelled it out; *keep digging and keep me posted*. But every time I consider looking further into Kate and Adrian's history, my insides clench like I've swallowed broken glass.

I know I'm being a coward, taking the easy way out. Adrain swore Kate was in the past, so I choose ignorance and try to forget about her by throwing myself back into normalcy.

It works for a while. Adrian and I fall into a routine involving work, dinner, sex, sleep. Things are great on paper. Adrian's hands find my body more often, lingering at my lower back in the mornings, and tangling in my hair at night. We walk together to the store for groceries, hands linked, and at one point he stops and kisses me so hard in front of the cash register that it makes the old lady behind the counter blush.

This is the life I've always wanted. So why does my skin feel too small for my body? Why do I wake up every night with my heart pounding and my mind running an endless loop of Adrian and Kate?

One morning, Adrian leaves to run errands. I hear the door click shut behind him, and immediately, the silence inside the apartment is deafening. I get up, grab a glass of orange juice, and stare out the window for what feels like a year. Then I find myself crouched behind the couch, hands digging for the journals before I can stop myself.

I lay the notebooks on the floor and read them again, one by one. I should put the journals away. I should trust Adrian. But I can't make myself close the notebooks and I can't un-know what I already know.

There are a couple of pages stuck together in one of the journals. Liz and I must have skipped over those in our haste to find answers. My heart is rattling against my ribcage as I carefully peel the pages apart. The first entry is dated September 13th. Kate's handwriting slants hard, the letters nearly vibrating off the page.

*I set up the camera in the living room. Hid it behind the plant so he won't see. If I'm wrong, I'll delete the footage and never speak of it again. If not... at least I'll know.*

The next entry:

*I watched the video. He came in at 11:46am while I was at work. He has a key from the time he watered my plants, so I guess it's not breaking in? He went straight to the bedroom and emptied my drawers, then lined up my medication bottles on the desk and counted them. He moved my notebook from the nightstand to the kitchen and read four pages. Then he ripped out one of them and stuffed it into his pocket.*

The last entry on the page is only a few lines, the pen digging so hard it almost cuts through the paper:

*I confronted him. He said he was worried about me. That he was just checking to make sure I wasn't hurting myself again. Said he'd never do anything to scare me, but I SAW IT. I know what I saw. He keeps saying I'm out of my mind, and maybe I am.*

I shove the journal closed, but the words have buried under the skin, festering like an infected wound. I don't even know Kate, and yet here I am, jealous of her and worried about her at the same time. I told myself I was done thinking about it, but I can't stop.

I try to pretend I'm fine, despite the itch under my skin every time I think of Kate and her notebooks. I focus on my editing and the next round of shoots for the gallery. I let Adrian touch me wherever, whenever he wants, and I try not to flinch when his breath gets heavy on my neck or when he squeezes me a little too tight.

He showers me with attention and makes me laugh until I temporarily forget my doubts. Still, I can't control the electric current that shoots up my spine every time he appears in doorways unannounced.

I dodge Liz's calls and ignore her requests for a lunch date. I know I'm being a crappy friend, but I don't want to see her face when she realizes I'm choosing the easy way out. I want to be someone who rips the truth out of the world with her bare hands... But I am tired. So damn tired. I am tired of being afraid, tired of the ache in my chest, and most importantly, I'm tired of doubting Adrian.

So, I go through the motions. I let Adrian plan a fancy dinner and light candles around the apartment. We make a show of slow dancing in the kitchen to our favorite song. I let him make me feel like the only girl in the city, and sometimes I even let myself believe it.

I keep up the act until November's first Friday arrives. Outside, sunshine glitters across fresh snow, deceivingly bright for how the cold bites. I'm shooting a set of engagement photos at the park when my cell buzzes. At first, I ignore the notifications, but my phone won't stop vibrating. I signal for a quick break and pull out the device to find increasingly urgent messages from Liz.

> *Liz: CALL ME*

> *Liz: WTF Tessa*

> *Liz: You need to see this*

> *Liz: STOP IGNORING ME*

> *Liz: It's about Kate!!!*

> *Liz: Seriously, Tess. Please. THIS IS AN EMER-GENCY*

The finality of the last message twists my stomach. I hit the call button, leaning my forehead into my palm as the screen lights up with Liz's face.

"Took you long enough," she grumbles, not bothering with pleasantries. "For the record, I've been this close to filing a missing person report for you. Started picturing Adrian wearing your skin as a suit."

"I'm sorry—"

"Save your apologies for later. I'm not letting you off the hook, but we need to talk about something much more urgent." Her voice drops. "Listen, I found something in one of Kate's boxes. It was wedged in the crease of the cardboard."

My pulse speeds. "What did you find?"

"Look at this," Liz holds up a crumpled piece of stationery. She angles the paper toward the camera, and I can make out Kate's looping handwriting in faded blue ink. "It says, *You have to remember, Tessa.*"

"What?" My voice comes out broken. "How would Kate know my name? And what does that message even mean? Remember what?"

"I was hoping you could tell me." Liz sighs. "Tess, are you sure you don't know Kate? Like, not even in passing?"

I shake my head. I want to tell Liz I would remember Kate if I knew her, but the words catch in my throat and all that comes out is a choked, "No."

"Yeah, I was afraid you'd say that."

Remember what, Kate? And why me? I'm spinning, vertigo rolling through my chest. I try to rewind every memory, every party, every day job, every odd run-in, hunting for a girl with a pointed nose and dark chestnut hair, but nothing lands.

"Are you okay? You don't look so good."

I swallow. "No. I don't know what to think."

"Me neither. I thought maybe she meant a different Tessa, but... what are the odds?"

"Nonexistent."

"Right. Which means..." Liz hesitates, letting the silence stretch between us, "you need to figure this out once and for all. I know you've been trying to sweep this under the rug, but there are too many loose ends here. Did you ever check that old cellphone in Adrian's nightstand?"

I shake my head no again.

Liz's voice hardens. "Well, I dropped off the charger the other day. You need to charge that phone and see what's on there. You owe it to yourself." She holds my gaze through the screen, unflinching. "Tessa, you can't keep running from this."

I know she's right. The truth is a weight I've been avoiding, but it's crushing me anyway.

"I'll look at the phone tonight," I promise Liz. "Thanks for not giving up on me. I'll let you know what I find."

After I end the call, I stand frozen, just watching the couple I'm supposed to be photographing. They're holding hands, swinging them between their bodies. Envy twists in my chest. How easy it must be to worry about nothing more than engagement pictures and dinner reservations. To fall asleep without ghosts crawling through your head. To wake up certain of who you are, who you love, and what's real.

The rest of the shoot is a blur of fake smiles and windburned cheeks. On my way home, I weave through the city crowds, catching glimpses of a stranger's face in store windows and car mirrors. The face might be Kate's or it might be mine; I can't tell the difference anymore.

The apartment is silent when I arrive, save for Toast wiggling around and pawing at his own tail. Adrian texted earlier that he's drowning in meetings until 6pm, which means I have the apartment to myself for hours. Plenty of time to gather my composure and dig through his nightstand drawer for that phone.

I wash down a vitamin with a gulp of water to steady my nerves, then march into the bedroom with my heart hammering against my ribs.

The cracked phone is waiting inside Adrian's nightstand where he left it, black and silent. I hesitate. Why would Adrian keep an old device if there was something damning on it? He's too careful for that kind of mistake. This is probably just a dead end, another breadcrumb leading nowhere.

I plug the mobile in, watching as the battery icon pulses red, then orange, then finally green. My fingers are slick with sweat as I punch in 1234 for the unlock code. Wrong. I try again, this time using Adrian's birthday. Wrong. I try 1021. The phone unlocks.

A striped orange tabby stares back at me on the screen. He is Toast's doppelganger down to the white patch on his chest. This must be the cat Adrian fostered before we met.

I open the Photos app and find hundreds of pictures. Some are mundane and show a woman whom I assume is Kate in bed, then Kate grinning at Marc over a plate of pancakes. Adrian's face starts to appear as I scroll. Sometimes he has a hand on Kate's shoulder, and sometimes he's just watching. I have to do a double-take because the angle and the light in the photos make Kate look exactly like me.

It gets worse. One close-up of Kate shows the side of her face, hair tucked behind her ear. There are three lobe piercings, the third just a tiny puckered scar where the earring should be. The phone slips out of my hand and lands on the hardwood with a crack. It feels like I am moving through quicksand as I reach up to touch the two earrings in my ear, then the faint scar of the third hole I've had for as long as I can remember.

The room shrinks to a pinpoint and bells clang inside my skull. Or maybe that's just my cell ringing, I can't be sure. The sound barely registers as I stoop to pick up Adrian's cracked phone, my hands shaking so badly I nearly drop the device again.

I search the photo album for any detail that might disprove what my eyes are telling me. A different mole placement. A scar I don't have. Anything. But with each new image, the truth becomes harder to deny. The woman in these photos has my lips. My eyes. The mole on the right side of my face, and the slight asymmetry to my smile that I've always been self-conscious about. It's not just that we look alike; Kate and I are identical.

The phone's contents blur as I scroll faster. The phone's owner is still logged into emails, but it takes several minutes for the messages to load. I have to wade through years' worth of junk mail before I come across a confirmation receipt for the exact Nikon lens I have, promotional messages from the sandwich shop down the road, and appointment reminders from Toast's vet. I feel numb from the chill spreading through my body, and I have to clench my fingers to keep from dropping the phone again.

Toast meows from the arm of the couch, but I can't look away from the screen, can't stop until I reach the beginning or the end. I go back to the pictures and scroll as far back as I can. The earlier photos are of Marc and Kate at a lake house. They are at a party, holding plastic cups in their hands. Then there are a couple of Marc and Adrian, arms slung around each other, faces blurred by motion.

In one image, Marc stands on the dock in swimming trunks. It's the same suit I've found balled up in Adrian's gym bag the week after our first trip together. The same brand. The same color. None of this makes any sense.

I tap over to the text messages. The phone's memory must be damaged because all I see are conversations with nameless contacts.

*Unknown: Did you change the locks?*

*Sender: Yes. I installed a chain too, like you suggested*

*Unknown: Good. Be careful. He's still watching you*

*Sender: I know*

Every nerve in my body feels electrified as I continue scrolling through the messages. The other thread is worse than the last.

*Unknown: You promised me dinner*

*Unknown: Don't ignore me. I know you're home*

*Unknown: Don't make me come up there*

These exchanges start three months before Kate's last journal entry, and they don't stop until the day she disappears. I feel the blood drain from my face as I read the last message:

*Unknown: DO NOT LET HIM IN*

The world tilts sideways, like I'm watching myself through warped glass. My body doesn't feel like mine anymore; it feels like borrowed skin wrapped around someone else's memories. I grip the edge of the kitchen chair, knuckles white, as vertigo washes over me in nauseating waves.

That's how Adrian finds me hours later. Hunched over the kitchen island, staring at the old phone in my palm with unseeing eyes. My breath is shallow, and my head feels full of static. I don't even notice him until I hear the clink of his keys on the counter.

"Tessa. Did you hear what I said?"

I glance up. Seeing Adrian's face, so familiar, yet so foreign, makes the floor tilt under me. He's holding a paper bag of groceries, balanced on his arm as if it weighs nothing. His hair is windblown and perfect, eyes bright and warm, and for a second I remember the world we built together. But then my gaze drops back to the phone in my hand, and my reality cracks open again.

"Are you okay? Tessa, what's wrong?"

I can't find my voice. I hold up the phone, the cracked screen alive with a photo of Marc and my face pressed so close together it's impossible to tell where one ends and the other begins.

Adrian sets down the paper bag, his movements slow as he reaches for the phone. "Where did you get that?"

I shake my head and back off the stool, my shoulders hitting the fridge. "What did your brother do to Kate?" My cry comes out too loud, echoing in the kitchen. "Why can't you just tell me the truth?"

"You don't know what you're talking about."

"STOP LYING TO ME!"

Adrian's demeanor shifts. For a second, I see something flat and unfamiliar float behind his eyes before he pulls himself back together. "Tessa." There's a warning in his voice. "Put the phone down."

I clutch it tighter. "Where is Kate? What happened to her? Don't give me any more bullshit, Adrian!"

Adrian's jaw tightens, a muscle flickering beneath the skin. For a long moment, he says nothing, his face drawn tight. Then his shoulders drop with his exhale. "Fine. You want to know where Kate is?" His eyes lock onto mine. "She never left, Tessa. She is right here."

I stare at him, blood roaring in my ears. "What do you mean here?"

He exhales, a slow, tortured sound. "Tessa... you are Kate."

The silence in the kitchen swells so big I feel my chest might collapse under it. I shake my head hard, hoping the world will snap back to normal. "No." Although I had already let myself consider it, the confirmation still hits like a fist to the gut.

I think back to what I know about Kate. Her talent for photos, her relationship with Marc and Adrian. Her eerie resemblance to me. The pieces are all there, but I can't seem to make them fit together. How could I be Kate? How could I have a past I don't remember?

Adrian steps forward, hands spread as if he's trying to steady a wild horse. "I know this is hard for you to understand. But you have to trust me."

"Why would I trust you? You've been lying to me this whole time." My voice comes out sharp enough to draw blood.

"A couple of years ago you were in a car accident," Adrian tells me, stepping closer. "It was a few days before Halloween, and the roads iced over. Marc was driving. You were in the passenger seat."

I recoil when Adrian reaches for me again, pressing into the fridge, my fingers aching where I grip the phone. "What are you talking about? I was never in a car accident."

"You were, you just don't remember it. You were with my brother that night. He was drunk and the two of you were fighting. You tried to get away from him, but he wouldn't let you. He lost control of the car and died upon impact. You, on the other hand, survived."

I shake my head, hard. "No. That's not... That's not possible."

Adrian steps forward, then hesitates, as if he's worried about spooking me. "You hit your head hard. The doctors didn't expect you to make it. And when you woke up, you couldn't remember anything before the crash."

"No," I say, voice breaking. My hands are shaking, the phone barely in my grip.

Adrian looks at me like I'm a frightened child. "Your first name is Theresa, but you've always gone by Katherine, your middle name. You once told me Theresa sounded like someone who collects ceramic angels and wears cardigans with embroidered flowers. But you're still you. You still order the same coffee, read the same books, listen to the same music, laugh at the same dumb puns."

He gestures to the phone in my hand. "That's why you can't stop obsessing over Kate's life. That's why you must have recognized her journals. They are yours, Tessa. You're Kate. You always have been."

My head pounds, the world spinning so fast I think I might throw up. I press my palm into the counter, willing it to anchor me. "You're lying," I manage. "Why would you lie to me again? Do you get some sick satisfaction out of torturing me?"

Adrian shakes his head in denial. "After the accident, you begged me to never bring up the past. You said you wanted to start over. So I did what you wanted. I gave you the life you asked for."

My breath comes in short, staccato bursts. "What about the photos? The memories I am supposedly missing—"

"Your mind is trying to heal. But some things won't stick, not when the trauma is that bad. You obsess over the past because you know something's missing, but you can't piece it together. I tried to convince you to let Kate go, but you always find new ways to tear at the scab."

"My mind is fine." I argue, thinking back to memories of my childhood. The time I got into trouble for wondering off without telling my mom. The butterflies I felt during my first kiss with a boy named Thomas. The cringeworthy neon pink dress I wore to my first school dance. The joy of getting accepted to college with a full ride. I remember all those memories vividly.

I stare at the phone, at the photo of Marc and Kate, my face, so close together. "If this is true..." my voice sounds warped, like I'm underwater, "if you're telling me the truth about my relationship with Marc and about the car accident, then why don't I remember any of it?"

Adrian inches around the island. He's so close now, I can see the pulse in his neck. There's nothing threatening about the way he holds himself, but the air in the kitchen has gone thinner, like my lungs can't draw enough oxygen from it. "Because trauma is a bitch. And because you don't want to remember. I know you don't believe me. But you're not safe when you start digging. You need to stop before you do something you'll regret."

"I wouldn't forget something as important as a boyfriend, or my parents—" Wait. Images of the newspaper clippings, obituaries I skimmed past flash through my mind. "My parents are alive, aren't they?"

The pitying look Adrian gives me makes my knees buckle.

"They are fine," I insist, but even as I say it, I'm frantically searching my brain. Mom called me... when? Last week? Last month? I remember her voice, but can't place when I last heard it. "She sent me a birthday card," I whisper. But did she? Or am I remembering a previous birthday from a few years ago?

"No," I say, because it is the only word I have left.

Adrian hovers, watching me try to refute the entire universe. I want to tell him the pictures could be faked, the journals forged. But the date stamps are there, and even if they were faked, why would Adrian put so much effort into a lie this elaborate?

"Take your vitamins," he says softly, as if I'm a child on the edge of a tantrum. "You're in pain. Let me make you something to eat. Then we'll talk."

But I don't want to hear any more of Adrian's truths. I want my mom, with her pale hair twisted into a bun, and her endless supply of patience. I want the version of my life where my parents send me postcards from the Florida Keys, where my dad is just a phone call away.

I dart to the living room, yank my phone from the coffee table, and dial my mother's number. The ring tone is different, which is the first thing that tips me off. I put the call on speaker so I can hear my whole world end at once.

The robotic voice answers: "We're sorry, this number is no longer in service. Please check the number and dial again."

I redial, slower this time, careful not to make the same mistake. I get the same message, the same flat voice. I try my dad's number next. It's disconnected.

I scroll to my messages. A dozen sent to my parents, all of them mine. There are no recent replies.

My whole body is shaking so badly I nearly drop the phone. The room is spinning. Adrian moves toward me, arms open, but I duck away, hyperventilating. "No, no no, this is all wrong. My parents are alive, they're in Florida, they're—"

Adrian tries to shush me. "Hey. Hey, you're okay. You're safe."

I round on him, sobbing. "Did you do this?" My words catch on a scream. "Did you do something to them?"

"Tessa, breathe." Adrian reaches for me. Toast's purr against my leg, the low hum of the refrigerator, Adrian's woodsy scent, my life, everything I thought I knew, close in around me at once.

I'm gone before Adrian can reach me, out the door, into the hall, socked feet pounding on the stairs. My vision tunnels, black spots dancing at the edges. I don't remember grabbing my jacket, but the next thing I know, I'm outside in the brittle sunlight, coat around my shoulders, hands clapped to my mouth to keep in my scream. I don't even know where I'm going; I just need out.

Adrian is close behind, calling my name, but I ignore him. "Tessa! You're going to hurt yourself! Come back!"

My lungs are burning as I sprint toward a yellow taxi idling at the curb. The driver, a middle-aged man with deep creases around his eyes, catches my reflection in the mirror as I hurl myself onto the back seat. His gaze flickers from my tear-streaked face to the doorway behind me, and he pulls away from the curb without a word.

I see Adrian standing on the sidewalk through the smudged rear window, his shoulders slumped, one hand half-raised as if to call me back. His expression isn't angry; it's a devastating blend of resignation and rejection that hollows me out more thoroughly than rage ever could. And somehow that makes me feel even worse.

# CHAPTER THIRTEEN

# Hollow

The adrenaline eventually fades, and my body remembers it's supposed to be a vessel for suffering. I welcome the pain and the bone-deep chill that floods my limbs while I curl into myself on the park bench, fingers locked around my knees.

I don't know how long I've been here. Long enough for the sun to slip behind the trees and for the wind to pick up and make my nose run. Long enough for every couple in the city to stroll by, their laughter echoing in the empty cavity of my chest.

I keep expecting the world to stop, but it just keeps going, the joggers and dog walkers oblivious to my world crumbling around me. Nobody cares about a barefoot girl in a puffy jacket, ugly-crying into her sleeves.

My phone buzzes, buried somewhere in my pocket. I don't look at it. It's probably Adrian messaging me again, saying something like, "Come home, I'm worried about you" or "We can get through this together." I press my forehead to my knees and try to breathe around the thought.

The breeze off the pond cuts through my clothes, stinging my cheeks until tears form at the corners of my eyes. But I know it's not really the wind making me cry. It's the empty space where my parents should be, the shattered mirror where my reflection no longer makes sense. Or maybe it's the cruel irony that the only person who could possibly understand what I'm feeling is the same person who just destroyed my entire existence.

How do you keep living after the love of your life detonates your world, and then tells you, actually, you're the bomb? How do you walk around in a body you're not sure belongs to you, with a history you don't remember?

I try to reconstruct myself from the inside out. My name is Tessa. My name is Kate. I had—no, I *have* a mother with a laugh like a wind chime and a father with an unbeatable sense of humor. My best friend is Liz. I have a feisty cat named Toast. I have a boyfriend, Adrian. Did I used to have two men in my life? Was I the one who loved them both and didn't know how to choose, so the universe did it for me?

The photos of Marc's expressive brows and eyes like chips of winter sky haunt me. When I think of what his voice must have sounded like, what his touch must have felt like, my body betrays me with a flush of heat despite the cold. I dig through the corners of my mind for him, searching for a single memory, a conversation, a kiss; but there's nothing but static and emptiness where Adrian's brother should be.

The harder I try to focus on the details, the more they slip away, and my head pounds with pain. I remember a spring formal where a boy named Steven showed up with a crooked grin that made my stomach flip. Except now I wonder if I made that up, or if it was Adrian who told me about it, or if maybe the truth was somewhere in the middle.

I remember holding hands with someone at the movies and laughing at the way the candy turned our fingers sticky, but the face beside me keeps swapping itself out. I see boys with braces and bad haircuts, then a guy I think I met in a philosophy seminar. I conjure images of Marc with his stubble-pebbled jaw and cerulean gaze, and Adrian with his golden eyes that seem to know me better than I know myself.

I think about the way Adrian orders my coffee before I ask, how he sticks the EpiPen in the zipper pouch of my bag just in case. I think of how my grumpy, traitorous cat accepted him instantly, which he'd never done for anyone, not even for Liz.

Then there were the snacks Adrian packed for our first road trip with all my favorites, even the specific brand of chocolate I like. I thought he was just hyper-observant with an exceptional memory, but what if his thoughtfulness was more? What if Adrian didn't just observe me? What if he'd already known me?

I stare at the glossy surface of the pond, the way the water ripples, and for a wild second I think about walking into it to see if anyone pulls me out.

A clattering noise somewhere behind me pulls my attention from the water. I turn to watch a little boy yell, "Watch this!" before launching himself off a stone ledge. His dad runs to catch him, both of them laughing.

I hate them for the audacity of their joy. Don't they realize how quickly it could all vanish? That they could wake up tomorrow and lose the people they love the most? Of course they don't. That's the most tragic part of it all. None of us imagines our lives could shatter until the moment the first crack appears.

The cold is deepening, and the park is becoming quieter the longer I sit here. My toes have gone numb inside my socks, and the last jogger vanished around the bend ten minutes ago. The street lamps flicker on one by one, casting pools of yellow that don't reach my bench. I should leave, but the mere idea of walking back to Adrian's place makes my stomach twist into knots. I can't bear the thought of any more of his explanations or his apologies right now.

I want to run to Florida and collapse into my mother's arms. I want to feel the rumble of my dad's voice as he hugs me and promises the world will right itself again. I've scrawled their new address on a piece of paper somewhere in my apartment... or is that just another lie my mind has crafted to torture me? My chest heaves as I try to swallow back tears, but they continue to spill down anyway, hot against my frozen cheeks.

I could steal Adrian's keys. I could drive all night, windows down, screaming until my voice gives out. I'd knock on every pastel door with an ocean-themed holiday wreath until I find the correct one. My mom would open the door, her eyes crinkling at the corners, and exclaim, "There you are, Honey. We've been waiting for you."

My phone vibrates with a fresh round of pings, shattering the mirage of my parents. I ignore the first three buzzes, but on the fourth I pull out the device with stiff fingers.

> *Liz: I'll put your face on a milk carton if you don't call me back*

I almost laugh, but the sound comes out as a sob. I text her back:

> *Me: Maybe you should do that*

Maybe if my face was plastered in grocery stores, someone would emerge from my past and tell me Adrian's revelations were nothing but an elaborate, twisted lie.

My phone vibrates with an incoming message again. Adrian's name blazes on the screen, a neon accusation in the gathering dark. I brace for another plea to come home, another string of platitudes, but when I open his message, I see an attachment of a video instead.

My thumb hovers over the screen. The thought of seeing Adrian's face or hearing his voice makes my stomach clench. Deep down, I know he didn't deliberately shatter everything I thought I'd known. He didn't drive me into Marc's arms, and he didn't drive the car that night. He didn't scramble my brain until my memories leaked out. But the deception afterward? The way he let me think I was losing my mind whenever Kate's name surfaced in my thoughts? I can't forgive that so easily.

Somewhere in the back of my mind, a voice whispers: Didn't you ask him to keep the truth from you? Weren't you the one who wanted to bury Kate forever?

I want to slap myself for that decision, but deep down I understand why past me had begged for ignorance. Taking the easy way out hurts much less than to face hard truths. Even now, the confusion and grief sit like boulders between my ribs, making each breath shallow and painful. If someone offered me amnesia tomorrow, a chance to forget how thoroughly my reality has shattered, I might take that bargain all over again.

I stare at the attachment. What if this video shows me another reality-shattering part of my life that breaks my heart all over again? I've endured enough of Adrian's revelations today, and a raw, gnawing need to fill in the gaps battles against my instinct to protect what little sanity I have left. I lock the screen, then immediately wake it up. I think about hurling the phone into the pond. Instead, I tap the screen before I can reconsider, hating myself even as I do it.

The video stutters to life. Kate's face—my face—fills the screen, and I feel the pulse falter beneath my skin.

The woman in the frame is sitting on Adrian's couch, bundled in a navy sweater, hair twisted up in the same messy bun I like to wear. She looks tired but determined, her hands twisting in her lap. I watch as she lifts her gaze, locks directly with the camera, and speaks.

"Hi, future me!" Her voice is my own, but warmer. "I'm Katherine Grey… and if you're watching this, it means you forgot about our past again. I'm sorry. I know it's scary." She makes a little grimace. "But Adrian is helping me. The photos, the reminders, are all to help me. I love him. We're going to figure this out together."

Video me glances away, nods at someone to the side, then looks back. "If you need proof that I'm you, check the birthmark on your left thigh. Or… look at the scar on your knee from when you insisted on riding a hoverboard and fell. Just… trust yourself, okay? You always knew something was off. So don't run now. Let Adrian help you."

She waves at the camera, awkward and earnest, and then the video ends.

I stare at my face, frozen on the screen. When did I record this clip? I search my memory but find no recollection of ever attempting to balance on one of those ridiculous two-wheeled contraptions. Yet I know if I pulled up my pant leg, I'd find a crescent-shaped scar on my knee.

I watch the video again, and this time notice the little details. There's the thinning enamel on my front teeth that makes their bottom look almost transparent. When I zoom in, I glimpse torn cuticles around my fingernails from nervous picking, then the tiny pockmark on my chin that I try to cover with concealer.

The woman in the video is really me.

I almost drop my phone when it buzzes to life with an incoming call. Liz's profile photo appears on the screen, her smile from happier days mocking my current mental state. I go to decline the call, but my blue-tipped fingers make the decision to press *Accept* before my mind can catch up.

"What do you mean, maybe I should put your face on a milk carton?" Liz asks, voice sharp. "What the heck kind of answer is that? Tessa, I'm seriously starting to worry about you."

I choke out a greeting, my throat thick with tears.

"Are you... crying? I swear to God, if Adrian—"

"It's not him," I tell her, which is partly true. "It just... I think I'm going insane."

The line goes quiet for a beat. "What happened? Talk to me. Is this about Kate?"

I squeeze my eyes shut and pinch the bridge of my nose, trying to squish the tears back into my skull. "Yes. I know who Kate is now, and the truth is worse than we could have ever imagined."

"Christ." Liz's voice drops, steadies. "Where are you right now?"

"The park."

"In this cold? With the sleet coming down?" Static crackles as she exhales sharply. "Never mind, I'm on my way. Do you need me to bring you a hot drink? An emergency blanket? Or a functioning prefrontal cortex?"

"No thanks. I want to just not exist right now."

"Well, too bad. I'm coming to get you, and you're going to eat hot ramen and tell me what the hell is going on."

"Okay."

I hang up, feeling empty. Liz is right. Despite the intrusive thoughts that urge me to walk into the freezing pond and never resurface again,

I'm not actually suicidal. I know I need to get out of the cold before it's too late. My fingers are losing sensation, and the cold is starting to be replaced by warmth that shouldn't be there, which isn't a good sign. The wind has numbed my lips and nose, and I can't feel the tips of my ears. And beneath all that, something inside my chest has gone calm and heavy, making my whole body feel foreign.

I thumb back to Adrian's video message again while I wait for Liz. I want to smash my phone against the bench until it shatters, but I can't stop watching this other me, who seems so warm, so composed. Her expressions are mine, but somehow different, like watching an impersonator who's studied me too well. "Trust yourself," she tell me, and I want to scream back, "Which self?"

How many times has Adrian watched me crumble like this? How many times have I recorded messages to myself, only to forget them again? I press my palm against the phone screen, wanting to erase her, wanting to erase myself. I long to sink into oblivion, to let the cold numb everything until this nightmare fades. I want to close my eyes and slip into darkness, yet I'm terrified of what else I'll forget again if I do.

But there's a deeper fear gnawing beneath the surface. What happens if the fog suddenly lifts? If I wake up tomorrow with every missing piece slotted back into place, will I recognize the person those memories belong to? Or will I discover someone I never wanted to become?

"I don't know what's real anymore," I whisper, hating the woman in the video almost as much as I hate myself.

***

Liz's headlights flicker through the park entrance, and I drag myself up, legs leaden. When I open the door, the hot air and the smell of Liz's hand lotion nearly bowl me over.

She pushes a to-go cup into my hands and cranks up the heat, eyeing my blue-tinged lips. "Jesus, you're practically hypothermic. We need to get you warmed up before you catch pneumonia."

I'm f-f- fine," I mutter, though my teeth won't stop chattering. "A-and besides, I d- don't think that's h- how pneumonia w- works."

"Maybe not. But do you really want to take the chance?" She taps the steering wheel. "My place is fifteen minutes away. Adrian's is closer. Where do you want to go?"

I curl my trembling fingers around the cup, seeking warmth. "A-a-anywhere but here. Just... d- drive."

We pull away from the curb. Liz gives me three blocks before she starts her interrogation. "Ready to tell me what happened?"

I dig my phone out of my pocket and queue up Adrian's video, thrusting it towards her. "It's—it's e- easier if you j- just w- watch this."

Liz glances at the screen, then parks in a fire zone and cradles the phone in her hands. Her face is a storm of skepticism and shock as she watches the clip. When the video ends, she looks at me with an expression I've never seen on her before. "So Kate isn't missing... You're her? And you recoded this and don't remember doing it?"

I nod, hugging the coffee cup to my chest. "Adrian t- told me I'm Kate. That I d- dated his brother, and we got in a car accident, and it..." My voice catches. "It k- killed Marc. I survived, but my m- memories didn't because of the head t- trauma."

Liz gapes at me, and I realize absently that this might be the first time I've ever seen her lost for words. She blinks a few times, as if she's trying to reboot her brain, then finally manages, "Holy shit. Are you serious right now? And you think Adrian's telling the truth?"

"I-I don't know. I d- don't remember the accident." I wrap my arms tighter around myself. "But I guess I w- wouldn't, right? If it messed up my brain."

Liz's gaze swivels back to the frozen thumbnail. "Do you think it's possible, though?"

I want to say n- no, of course it's not possible, but when I try to recall certain memories, it's like the edges blur. Dates slip away. I can p- picture moments, but they don't always feel... feel real."

I press my fingertips against my temples. "B-but what if this is all j- just some elaborate mind game? Adrian could be m- making the whole thing up, trying to gaslight me into believing I'm someone I'm not."

Liz hums in thought. "You've always been a bit scattered with details. Remember last month when you couldn't find your keys, even though they were in your coat pocket? Or that time we had plans to go see a movie, and you showed up a day early?" She hesitates. "Or around the time we first met? We spent days planning to check out that rooftop bar downtown, and when I texted you to confirm, you replied asking what bar I was talking about."

I do remember. Kind of. These brain farts didn't seem important, but now, in the context of everything else, my body flushes with embarrassment.

"I thought you were just forgetful. But this is..." Liz shakes her head. "This is a whole-ass identity we're talking about."

"I know."

"We should go to the hospital and get your head scanned. Confirm Adrian's story. There's a satellite ER not far from here."

"I d- don't want to go to a hospital. Please... I just want to forget everything for a little while."

Liz purses her lips and nods, putting the car back in gear and pulling away from the curb. "Fine. Let's go to my place then. I have ramen and ice cream calling our names." She glances over with a forced smile. "Okay, maybe not ice cream for you. But to make up for that, I can call a neurologist and schedule you an appointment in the morning."

I nod to pacify Liz, knowing full well no neurologist will see me tomorrow. Even if we find a doctor who takes my insurance, I'll be lucky to get an appointment before summer.

The ride to Liz's townhouse goes by in a blur of taillights and dark sky. My thoughts feel like they're underwater, slow and muffled, and I can't seem to make my fingers unclench from around the cup. I think the coffee has gone cold. I think I'm in shock.

Minutes or hours pass; it's hard to tell. The next thing I know, Liz is pulling into her driveway and cutting the engine. She doesn't move, just sits with her head leaned against the headrest, staring into the dark beyond her windshield.

"You know, if Adrian's lying, we could kill him. I know a guy who would make him disappear for, like, a hundred bucks and a case of beer."

It takes a few seconds for her words to slice through the fog in my head. When my brain finally catches up, I bark out a half-laugh, half-sob. My throat feels raw, like I've swallowed glass, but at least my teeth have stopped chattering and the world around me has come into focus again.

The heat inside Liz's townhouse is cranked so high that it makes my face sting. I slump on the pillowy couch while Liz fusses over an electric kettle and the ramen packets, letting out expletives when the seasoning spills. I flex my toes, relieved as the numbness retreats and the painful tingling that started in the car finally subsides.

Liz carries a thick blanket over, sits next to me, and covers us both. For a minute, neither of us says a word.

Her gaze weighs on me like a physical thing. I can only imagine what a fright I must look like, with my hair a wild tangle from the wind and my eyes vacant. I have my arms locked around my middle in an effort to hold the broken pieces together, the attempt futile. I wish I could fold inward until I disappeared completely, to become so small that even my thoughts can't find me.

Liz is the first one to break the silence. "So you're really Kate? The same Kate who dated Marc and wrote all those journals?"

I hesitate, unsure how to form my thoughts into a coherent sentence. "I don't know. It's like... there's this blank space where Marc should be. A person I supposedly dated, just gone. I don't understand how I could forget him like that... And do you wanna know what's even worse? I'm not sure if the memories I do have are real, or made up. My whole life could be a giant lie and I would never know it."

"God, what a mindfuck. But why wouldn't Adrian just tell you the truth when you first asked him about Kate?"

I wrap the blanket tighter around my shoulders. "According to him, it was my idea. I wanted to erase Kate completely, to start fresh. So he was just respecting my wishes."

Liz picks at a hangnail. She must be due for a manicure. "That's either sweet or totally manipulative. Adrian could be feeding you any story he wants. And you'd never know the difference."

"I'm aware of that."

"Well," Liz bites her lip. "At least now you know he wasn't cheating. Silver lining, right?"

I give her a flat look.

"Right. Too soon." She presses a steaming cup of ramen into my hands. "Here, eat this. Your lips are still the color of a corpse's."

My stomach revolts at the idea of food, but I accept the steaming cup anyway.

Liz blows on her noodles, steam curling around her face, as we both try to process the day's revelations. "So I'm curious..." she says after a while, "how do you feel about being Kate? I mean, if it's true... are you going to pick up where you left off? Try to reconcile your past with the person you are now?"

I close my eyes and imagine Kate—no, me—waking up in a hospital bed with nothing but a blank slate where memories should be. Starting over. Again and again, with each reset of my mind. I shudder at the thought of being trapped in an endless cycle of forgetting, of having to rebuild myself repeatedly, while the world around me never pauses, never waits... never even notices.

"A part of me wants to wake up tomorrow and forget about Kate again. To erase her completely. Never know about the fire that took my childhood home. Never have to think about my parents—" My words catch as my throat closes.

"Oh my gosh, Tess, I'm so sorry." Liz rescues the ramen cup from my trembling hands and wraps her arms around me. I crumble against her, my body convulsing with silent sobs that steal the air from my lungs. When I finally inhale, it comes out as a ragged gasp that burns all the way down.

"I'm so sorry." Liz repeats, brushing hair off my wet cheeks. "I wish I knew what to say to make you feel better."

"You being here is enough." My breath catches in hiccups as I try to regain control of myself. "You want to know what this feels like? Like I died in that car crash with Marc. And now I'm just... this echo. A ghost wearing someone else's skin, trying to live a life that isn't meant to be mine anymore."

"If you're dead," Liz says, nudging me with her elbow, "you're the best-smelling ghost I've ever met."

I snort into my jacket. "I doubt that."

Liz's face turns serious. "Jokes aside, though, you're here. You're real. And I'm not letting anything happen to you."

I manage a weak nod, and she continues, "Look. Your past is garbage, no arguments there. But the only thing that matters is what you do now. You can be Kate, Tessa, or someone entirely new."

"Ugh. I can't think straight right now."

"Of course not," Liz murmurs, her voice softening. "And you don't have to. But hey, just remember that you still get to decide who you are. Your life, your rules." She squeezes my arm. "If you want my advice, I'd start with validating Adrian's story though. He could be full of shit for all we know."

I huff into her shoulder.

"How about this? We get some rest, and tomorrow we can dig through your apartment. Look for old passports, birth certificates, whatever might prove you were Kate once."

"I'll save you the trouble," I mumble, my voice barely audible. "My name is Theresa Katherine Grey. Katherine, as in Kate."

Liz's mouth opens, then closes as she processes what I've just said. "Your middle name is Kate?"

I nod, feeling empty. "Kate. Tessa. Two sides of the same person."

"Um, why didn't I know that before? You know what? Never mind... Jesus. I can't believe the answer was right there the whole time." Liz tucks a strand of hair behind her ear, brow furrowed. "Makes you wonder what else we've been looking at without seeing the whole picture."

"Like my handwriting in the journals?"

"Yeah, like that. Though I never would've pegged those journals as yours. The handwriting in them is all..." She makes a flourishing gesture with her hand. "Your normal scribble is more like chicken scratch. Maybe trauma rewires your penmanship? I read this article once about how your emotional state shows up in your writing. Happy people's lines drift upward, while anxious people press harder on the page."

"I guess that makes sense."

"If we missed your middle name and handwriting, there must be other coincidences or inconsistencies we both just glossed over. Think about it. Are there things in your life that never quite added up? Little details that felt wrong but you just accepted?"

I search my memories for anything that feels off, any detail that doesn't quite fit. Nothing surfaces at first, just the usual blur of everyday life. Then suddenly, something clicks into place in my mind, like a key turning in a lock.

I pull my arm out of my jacket, then the sweater, and rub the puckered scar on my shoulder. It's been there as long as I can remember, except, apparently, that isn't very long at all.

Liz takes my arm in her hands and inspects the skin under my tattoo. "You never told me where you got this scar. You think this has something to do with your past as Kate?" She bites her lip in thought. "I figured it was a sports thing, or maybe you fell out of a treehouse when you were a kid. I didn't want to ask about the tattoo or the scar because you're obviously self conscious about it."

I frown at her. "I'm not self conscious about it."

"Please," Liz says, arching an eyebrow. "You wear shirts that cover up this part. And besides, nobody spends that much on custom ink just for decoration. You wanted to make sure nobody would ever see what's underneath."

"Perceptive, like usual." I pull my arm back, hugging it against my chest. "I guess I covered my injury with the tattoo because I couldn't stand looking at it. The weird part is that the scar was just there, like a birthmark. Something I was born with that didn't need explaining."

"You think it's from the car crash?"

My stomach tightens. "That's exactly what I'm wondering."

"You know what? Screw the ramen. This calls for something stronger." Liz pushes off the couch and strides toward the kitchen, returning moments later with two tumblers and a bottle of whiskey; the amber liquid reflecting the lamplight as she pours.

I stare into the drink she hands me, my mind racing. There are other gaps in my history, things I've never questioned. Adopting Toast without remembering how old he was supposed to be. The photo shoot consultation where my client said, "Welcome back!" like I'd been there before, even though it was my first time setting foot inside the building. The photos of Adrian on my computer.

These fragments could be pieces of a puzzle or just random coincidences. Either way, my temples pulse with each attempt to make sense of it all. I'm so tired. "I just want the pain to stop," I whisper, my voice small. "The not knowing, the doubting everything I ever thought was true."

Liz slumps next to me, elbows on her knees. "You could go home and ask Adrian to tell you everything from the beginning. Make him show you proof. If he really cares about you, he'll do it."

"He'll say whatever he thinks I need to hear. Just like he did when I questioned him about Kate." I chuckle bitterly. "God, what an idiot I've been."

"Then ask for the stuff he can't make up. Like, show you the accident records. Hospital bills." Liz offers me her hand. "If you want, I'll go with you. I'll make sure he doesn't brush you off this time."

I hesitate, then slide my palm into hers. "I'd appreciate that."

Liz squeezes my hand. "We're in this together. Remember, Ashton and Brie against the world. But first, you need sleep. You need a minute to process everything before you confront Adrian tomorrow."

I open my mouth to argue, but my body betrays me by swaying where I sit. I grudgingly agree to rest, and we finish the whiskey while a game show plays in the background.

Contestants jump and scream over blenders on TV, while Liz pretends to be absorbed in the show. I know she picked it to distract me, but the bright colors and canned excitement only make the emptiness inside me feel more vast. Every memory I thought was mine now feels like someone else's photograph, edges curling, details fading. Who was I yesterday? Who am I supposed to be tomorrow? The questions in my head spin like the big wheel on the screen, landing nowhere.

At some point, I drift into a sleep thick with half-memories and rapid-fire dreams of a hydroplaning car. I clench my jaw against a scream, and watch as the face in the rearview mirror shifts between my own and someone else's.

I come awake in the dark, my mouth bone dry. For one long moment, I have no idea where I am. Then I smell Liz's detergent, something sweet, always a little too strong, and reality crashes back. I remember the ramen, the whiskey, the couch, and the way I curled myself into a ball while Liz went to get ready for bed.

The blanket has fallen to the floor in the night, and goosebumps stand on my arms. I check my phone; it is 1:57am. The apartment is silent except for the pop and sigh of the pipes in the walls. Liz is dead to the world, sprawled face-down on her bed in the next room.

I lift the blanket and burrow deeper into the cushions. My phone battery's almost dead. I have fifteen missed calls and eight texts from Adrian, but I can't bring myself to look at them yet.

The brightness of the phone makes my head feel like it's about to split in half, all the way from my right temple to the back of my neck. I fumble in my coat pocket for my pill bottle, but then I remember it's back at Adrian's.

I thankfully find a bottle of extra-strength painkillers in Liz's medicine cabinet and return to the living room, collapsing onto the couch with a groan. I swallow the pill and pray that it helps lessen the pain so I can drift back into unconsciousness.

I toss and turn for a while, trying to quiet my mind. But every time I start to fall asleep, the throbbing in my temple, accompanied by night terrors, jolts me awake. In one I swear I can feel the hard edge of a desk digging into my forearm. My fingers are cramping around a blue pen as I write... write what? I'm hunched over a composition notebook, the tip of the pen moving so fast it squeaks. Then a shadow falls over me.

I look up, and there's Adrian—or is it Marc?—standing in the doorway. I can't see his face, but I know he's watching me.

"What are you writing, Kate?"

I snap back to consciousness with a gasp, though I'm not sure I ever truly drifted off. Each heartbeat feels like a hammer against my ribs, and the slightest turn of my head sends daggers of pain shooting through my skull, pinning me in place against the cushions.

For a long time I just lay there, waiting for the world to right itself. I replay the images in my mind again and again, searching for some detail that will prove it was a dream and not an actual memory. But the scratch of the pen, the sound of the question felt too real. Too sharp.

I eventually give up on sleep and squint at the brightness of my phone. I try to decide if I should text Adrian, or block his number, or set the whole thing on fire. I lay the phone on my chest and stare at the ceiling, lost in thought.

The next time I check my phone, the missed calls have multiplied to twenty-three. The texts keep coming, too:

*Wine Guy: PICK UP THE PHONE, TESSA*

*Wine Guy: Call me back*

*Wine Guy: I'm worried about you*

*Wine Guy: I can't sleep. Just tell me you're okay. PLEASE*

My head is a centrifuge. How do I explain to him that I'm lost? That I'm terrified? That part of me wants to hate him for making me question everything I thought I knew? I type out three different replies, delete them all, and then finally send:

*Me: I'm safe. I'm staying at Liz's tonight*

Liz's phone pings from the other room. I hear her groan and roll over. She's the worst about setting her phone on *Do Not Disturb*, even when she has back-to-back conference calls. My phone vibrates against my skin, and Adrian's reply appears on the screen

*Wine Guy: I'll be here. Whenever you're ready.*

I toss the phone aside and burrow deeper under the blanket. A chill must be seeping in from some unseen crack because the toasty warmth of the apartment is long gone. As I lie on my back staring at the ceiling, trying to ignore the goosebumps on my arms, something whistles in the darkness. The sound is different from the pipes. It's softer, like wind finding its way through a loose window pane.

My bladder aches with fullness, drawing a miserable sound from my throat. The thought of abandoning my blanket seems unbearable, but the pressure won't wait until morning.

I peel myself from the couch, wincing as my bare feet touch the cold floor. Each step toward the bathroom feels like wading through molasses. My body feels heavy with exhaustion, and I have to trail my fingers along the wall for balance as the throbbing in my skull continues.

The chill is stronger in the bathroom. I glance at the window and see that the latch is loose, the bottom edge rattling in the wind. The curtains flutter as a draft catches them. That's weird. Why would Liz leave her window open in the dead of winter?

I cross to the window and push it shut. The glass presses cold against my palm, and I blink at the empty backyard below. The alley is shrouded in darkness, and I can barely make out the moonlit dumpsters surrounded by a patch of brittle grass.

For a moment, I think I see movement where there should be none, a shape separating from the darkness at the corner of my eye. I snap the latch shut, jiggle it twice to be certain, then yank the curtain closed hard enough that the metal rings scrape against the rod.

It was just the wind, I tell myself. Just the breeze playing tricks on my exhausted mind.

I do my business with the bathroom door open, glancing up every few seconds at the window above the tub. I leave the lights off, hoping the darkness will hide me from whoever might be watching from outside... just in case. When I finish, I hurry back to the living room, pausing to listen for sounds of an intruder.

But there's nothing. Just the faint popping of the pipes in the walls again, and the distant city hum, muted by layers of glass.

I check the front door, then the bathroom window again, to make sure they are locked. I jiggle each handle three times.

Once I'm satisfied that the apartment is secure, I find a pair of scissors with red handles in Liz's junk drawer, beneath takeout menus and dried-out pens. I set the scissors on the side table so my fingers can find them in the dark. Again, just in case.

The throbbing behind my eyes intensifies as I imagine trying to explain my mental state to a doctor. Describing the worry that someone might be watching and the blank spaces where memories should be. Isn't this paranoia similar to what Kate, or I, described in those journals? The parallels between my past and my present aren't lost on me, but I'm too bone-weary to untangle them now.

I bundle myself in the blanket and sink into the cushions, facing the bathroom at the end of the hall. The glow of my phone is the only light in the room as I clutch it to my chest. I sit like that, staring into the darkness, until morning light seeps through the edges of the curtains and start to chase the shadows away.

# Chapter Fourteen

# *Rewritten*

Scalding water pounds against my skin, bringing warmth back into my stiff limbs. Liz knocks on the bathroom door, then tosses in a pair of black leggings and a hoodie.

"You're not wearing those jeans again," she hisses through the crack. "And you're most definitely not going barefoot. My clogs are by the door. Put them on when you're done."

I mumble thanks, but keep quiet about checking the window two more times before I stepped under the spray. She'd found me wide-eyed at 6am, clutching my phone and the scissors from the kitchen. No need to confirm what she must already suspect about my mental state.

We load up on coffee and drive in silence to Adrian's apartment. The sleet-soaked streets, along with the gloomy sky heavy with an invisible weight, match my insides perfectly. My brain feels like it's wrapped in cotton, my thoughts moving through sand after yesterday's bombshells and a night spent staring at shadows. I'm not ready to face Adrian, but I know delaying this conversation won't make it any easier.

The ride to Adrian's building feels impossibly short, and we make it there before I'm ready. In the elevator, Liz squeezes my shoulder and whispers something about how I deserve answers and Adrian deserves nothing, but her words barely register through the thundering pulse in my ears as we rise floor by floor.

Adrian opens the door before my knuckles graze it, hair rumpled, shirt untucked. I brace for an awkward hello, or perhaps a disapproving frown. But he just folds me in, arms wrapped around my back and his face pressed into the curve of my neck. I sag against him, breathing in the familiar soap and woodsy smell that is uniquely his. My ribcage, which has been locked tight all morning, expands at last.

"You're here," Adrian whispers. I nod into his chest, willing myself not to cry.

Liz shoulders past us, her purse clanging against the door frame. "We need to talk," she says, not bothering with a greeting.

Adrian's touch lingers, as if he doesn't want to let me go. His eyes flick from me to Liz and back. He looks wrecked, like he hasn't slept, and has been living off anxiety like I have since our confrontation yesterday.

Liz drops her purse onto the entry table. "Let's hear it, Adrian. The complete story about Kate and Tessa. Start to finish. No more bullshit."

Adrian's shoulders tense as he steps back from me. "With all due respect, this conversation should be between me and Tessa."

"Like hell! You think I'm leaving her alone with you after everything you put her through? After the way you lied to her? I'm staying right here with her."

I move between them, my hand finding the sleeve of Adrian's shirt. "I need her here. Please."

Adrian studies me, then nods after a beat. I watch the tension slowly drain from his face, replaced by something resigned as he murmurs, "Fine. Whatever you want."

"Thank you." I swallow, voicing the question that's been haunting me, "Liz is right. If you want any hope of salvaging our relationship, you need to tell me everything. Who was I before, Adrian? Tell me about my past, about Kate. And don't you dare leave anything out this time."

"Come sit. I'll tell you what I can." He leads us to the living room, where papers are spread across the coffee table.

Liz and I take the couch. As soon as we sit, Toast announces his presence with a meow. He saunters into the living room, tail swishing from side to side. My throat constricts at the sight of him, and the pressure I've been fighting all morning bursts behind my eyes.

Toast weaves between my ankles, oblivious to the world crumbling around me. I reach down to find the spot behind his ear, and his purr vibrates through my fingertips.

When Liz reaches toward Toast, the cat stiffens, back curving into a perfect arch to avoid her touch. A low hiss escapes from between his bared teeth.

Liz withdraws her fingers with a tight smile. "Okay, then."

Adrian clicks his tongue, and Toast trots over to him, the orange gremlin all affection again. He purrs as Adrian pets him head to tail, and I catch Liz's glare at the two of them. "We're waiting," she mutters, jaw clenched.

Adrian's eyes find mine. "Alright." He straightens and exhales. "You remember some of the past, like growing up a couple of hours from here, or graduating with double business degrees. What you may not recall is that you lucked into a job at a Fortune 500 company after graduating. You hated it, though. You were in marketing at this soulless firm downtown. Made a lot of money, got a lot of praise, but you said it felt like you lost a piece of your soul every day there."

His voice is steady and factual, like he's told this story a thousand times before. "You started taking pictures because they felt like something real, something no one could make you do or take away. Photography was right in line with your creative mindset, and it was something you really enjoyed doing. You'd only photograph objects at first, never people. Never yourself. It took forever to get you to take my picture." Adrian smiles, then catches himself.

"I met you at a bar right around that time. Marc brought me to a friend's birthday. You two had been on a couple of dates, but nothing serious yet."

I stare at him. I don't remember any of this.

"Marc fell for you first. He could be intense, even back then, but you thought it was just passion. Little things at first, like him texting twenty times a night or showing up unannounced. And then bigger things, like following you when you went out, picking fights with random men if they so much as looked at you. He said it was because he cared, but I could see what it was really about."

Adrian's eyes bore into mine as he continues, "He wanted to possess you. Like you were something he could own."

Liz sucks in a breath, and I can feel her eyes search my face with a mixture of confusion and concern. I don't know what to tell her. I don't even remember the man, much less why I'd be in a relationship with someone like that.

Adrian reads the bewilderment written across our features and pushes a document in our direction. "Here, these might help jog your memory."

My eyes catch my name printed in bold letters. *Theresa Katherine Grey.* God, will I ever stop feeling like an idiot for not realizing Kate was just a shortened version of my middle name?

"You kept to yourself. You were quiet, withdrawn. No close friends back then. Marc saw that and thought, here's someone I can make entirely mine..."

I stare at the dog-eared high school transcript, which shows straight As across every subject. Then I find a passport, which is mine apparently, with a photo of a woman who looks like me. The pages bear colorful stamps from Mexico and Costa Rica, countries I don't remember ever visiting.

Liz leans in, her finger tapping at the passport's address line. "1288 Redfern Lane. Isn't this the address for Kate's old apartment?"

I nod.

Adrian's voice is quieter as he asks, "You went back there?"

I nod again, heat climbing up my neck. All those nights spent obsessing over Kate, and I've been chasing my own ghost. The irony would be funny if it weren't so pathetic.

Liz's eyes narrow at Adrian. "What choice did she have? If you'd been honest with Tessa from day one, she wouldn't have had to play detective."

"Sure, because the last time I tried honesty, it worked out great. I knew how she'd react... she'd run again."

"You robbed her of the chance to process this on her own terms," Liz fires back, her teeth bared. "You only came clean when your back was against the wall..."

Their voices blur into white noise as my focus narrows on the passport in my hands. The birth date glares at me from the page, black numbers that don't compute.

"Thirty-two?" My cry is loud enough to cut off Liz's and Adrian's argument mid-sentence, and they both turn to stare at me.

I fumble in my coat pocket, fingers clumsy. My license slips free from my wallet, and I hold both documents side by side, comparing the identical dates with mounting disbelief.

"But I'm twenty-eight," I mutter, the math refusing to reconcile in my head. "I'm supposed to be twenty-eight." Either I've forgotten how to count, or I lost three years of my life.

No. No. NO! I let the passport drop and press my palms into the leather couch, feeling its buttery softness beneath my skin. I draw in Liz's flowery scent from the borrowed hoodie; something real to tether myself to while the room tilts around me.

Adrian steps forward, his hand half-extended toward me, before he catches Liz's glare. "The doctors warned us about memory gaps," he tells me. "They said you might lose chunks of time."

Liz squeezes my knee. "So you've got a few more years under your belt than you thought. Look at it this way. You're older and you're wiser. That's not a bad thing. And we owe you one hell of a makeup party for your thirtieth birthday."

"Sure. Because partying is what's on my mind right now. Let's invite the friends I can't remember, and my parents, who may... who may be..." I can't finish that sentence.

Liz's smile crumples at the edges, and my insides knot with shame. Here she is trying to lighten an impossible moment, and I'm throwing it back in her face. "I'm sorry. I know I'm being a jerk and you don't deserve that."

I set my wallet aside and avert my gaze back to the documents. There are medical bills and a transcript of a police report with my name blacked out in places. I skim the top sheet.

*"Incident: Domestic disturbance. Suspect: Mercer. Victim: Grey."*

My vision narrows, the edges of the page closing in.

Liz reads faster than I do, and her face puckers. "Did you report this?" She looks to Adrian, who nods.

His gaze shifts to me, jaw clenched. "Someone had to. You wouldn't do it yourself."

I wouldn't? I try to picture myself with this Marc. Who stays silent when someone threatens her? Probably someone who is so brainwashed that she makes excuses because she can't see the truth in front of her. Someone who says, "He didn't mean it," and, "It won't happen again." My cheeks burn hot as I realize I've become that woman. Or used to be her, before.

Liz's fingers curl around the edge of the police report, knuckles whitening. "This report doesn't tell us much. What did your brother really do to her?"

Adrian's jaw works before he answers. "Kate—I mean Tessa didn't have any visible bruises." He looks at me, eyes hardening. "But there were nights you called me at 3am because Marc'd thrown your clothes onto the lawn. Or smashed your laptop because you changed your password. Or stood over you while you slept, just watching." He takes a deep breath and looks away. "He was careful not to leave marks where anyone could see them, but I knew they were there."

Liz's gaze burns into the side of my head, but I keep my eyes fixed on the documents, refusing to look up. I want to argue, to challenge the narrative, but I can't dispute a history I don't recall.

I close my eyes and try to remember anything about my relationship with Marc. But there's only white noise and emptiness where memories should be. The urge to sweep everything off the table, to scream until my throat goes raw, rises in me like a wave.

Adrian keeps going. "I tried to talk to you. You found excuses and said Marc was just passionate. You were convinced he'd never hurt you, that he was just scared to lose you. Then one day you called me, sobbing. Marc had lost it over a text from a coworker. He'd locked you in the bedroom for hours and wouldn't let you out. You said you were done, but by the next morning you were apologizing to him."

"That doesn't sound like me," I say, my voice small.

"I know." Adrian's expression shifts, the hard lines around his mouth easing into something gentler. "But trauma changes people. It makes them do things they'd never imagine. You were trapped, Tessa. And you were so good at convincing everyone that you had it under control."

"Everyone but you?"

Adrian nods. "Of course, the police report didn't help. The only thing it accomplished was to make Marc more hostile. His drinking got worse, and he started throwing little digs my way, then outright challenges. I tried to keep the peace by staying away, but whenever things got bad, you'd call."

"I'm sorry." I murmur, "for destroying your relationship with your brother. If I could go back..."

"Don't be. I chose to stay by your side and I chose to get involved. That was my decision. You didn't force my hand."

I nod, unconvinced. "What about the accident? What really happened that day?"

Adrian lets out a deep sigh. "That night you left me four voicemails in a row. That's how I knew something was really wrong. I called you back, but you didn't answer. I tried Marc, but he never picked up. So I drove over."

Adrian looks away, as if he can't bear to see my face as he shares what happened next. "I found you outside your apartment, bleeding from your head. Marc was drunk, shouting about how you'd made him do it. And then he saw me and started screaming that I'd ruined everything."

A tear carves a path down Adrian's cheek as he stares off into the distance, lost in memories. "Marc grabbed you and started dragging you to the car. He accused me of being in love with you, that you cheated on him with me. I tried to stop him from taking you, but he was drunk and determined. He punched me without warning, knocking me out."

Adrian's tortured gaze finds mine, and I see so many emotions in them. Wanting, anger, guilt tangled with devotion.

"He was right. You were in love with me even then, weren't you?" The question hangs between us, though I already know its answer in my bones.

Adrian wipes his eyes with the back of his hand. "Does it matter now? You and I both know we were inevitable."

Inevitable. The word lands like an anchor, pressing the air from my lungs. "Was there ever anything between us while I was with Marc? Did I really cheat on him?"

Adrian's shoulder lifts, then falls. "Marc was never going to be your forever... I think part of you always understood that."

The truth of what that means hits me like a slap: I was unfaithful to Marc. With his own brother. What does that say about Kate, about me? A woman who stayed with her abuser while secretly betrayed him? The thought makes my stomach turn. If this broken, selfish person is who I was before, perhaps the memory loss was a mercy after all.

"I must have been out for a few seconds. I was laying in the snow when I woke up, my face half numb. Marc's car was already turning the corner. I ran after it... I ran until my chest burned, as if I just pushed hard enough, I could catch up." Adrian's laugh sounds forced.

"I heard the crash before I saw it. My mind refused to connect that sound with you, with Marc, with anything real. But when I rounded that bend in the road, the scene before me froze the blood in my veins. The headlights were still on, illuminating the wreckage where the car had slammed into a pole."

I float somewhere above my body, watching myself nod mechanically while Adrian's voice cuts through me like a serrated knife, one missing memory at a time. His words blur together as he describes the accident. The crushed metal. The way the red and blue ambulance lights lit up the scene. The blood pooling on asphalt and ice that made Adrian fear the worst. The helplessness he felt standing there, watching his loved ones slip away.

"They said you'd suffered a head injury, but it could have been so much worse. Marc was out cold, and he never woke up." Adrian's voice cracks. "He died at the hospital. I had to identify his body."

"Oh God, that must have been so difficult for you."

"It was, but the thought of you needing me kept me going. It gave me purpose. I wanted to hold you and promise we'd get through it together. I wanted to take care of you and help you through the grief. But then, I looked into your eyes and saw a stranger staring back." The pain in his gaze now nearly undoes me.

"You asked me every day for a week where Marc was, why he hasn't visited. And every time I told you, it was like you were hearing about the accident and his death for the first time."

Adrian pushes a manila folder across the table toward me, then slides a paper from it. "Here is the discharge summary from the hospital. You can see the details for yourself."

The page is dense with jargon, but some lines leap out:

*Primary Diagnosis: Closed-head injury with subdural hematoma, anterograde amnesia*
*Consults: Neurology, Psychiatry*
*Recommended: Follow-up with Dr. Chen, Neurobehavioral Clinic*
*Emergency contact: Adrian Mercer (relationship: significant other)*

The document is shockingly real. My name and my history, spelled out in medical jargon, are all there. Liz leans over and types something on her phone, thumbs flying, while I continue reading.

*The patient exhibits persistent deficits in short-term memory, especially for events prior to the index trauma... Patient reports amnesia for most of the prior twenty-eight years... Patient's affect is blunted, with flat mood... Consider therapy as an adjunct to pharmacology...*

My throat burns. I want to believe this is a cruel prank, but the details are there, impossible to refute.

Liz huffs, drawing my attention.

"Dr. Chen's online reviews are awful. One star for beside manner. Good grief. Is this really the doctor who's been treating Tessa? Are you sure you didn't want her to succumb to her injuries?" She ignores Adrian's glare and keeps scrolling. "And it doesn't look like he's even practicing anymore. Apparently, he moved to Taiwan last year."

"Dr. Chen retired a while back. We got transferred to a new provider, but Tessa didn't want to go."

My chest tightens with guilt for a decision I don't even remember making.

"You didn't want to relive the past, Tessa. You said the pain was worse than the not-knowing."

I want to deny Adrian's claims, but not wanting to relive the past sounds like me. Didn't I voice those same thoughts to Liz a while back? *What if the truth is worse than not knowing?*

I avert my gaze and realize I've been scraping my thumbnail into my palm hard enough to raise a welt. I unclench my fist, shaking out the pain.

"These reports are dated two years ago. What happened after the accident? There's still plenty of time unaccounted for. "

"You stayed with me," Adrian tells me. "You couldn't bring yourself to go back to your apartment. You had panic attacks every time Marc's name came up, so I stopped mentioning him. At first, I thought you'd get better, but the gaps just grew."

"That's when you started calling me Tessa?"

Adrian nods. "One night, you looked at me with these lost eyes and said, 'It's too painful to be me. I don't want to be Kate anymore.' You started introducing yourself as Tessa because you'd always complained Theresa sounded like an old lady's name. I thought... I hoped it was a sign you were moving on. But the doctors said it was classic dissociative amnesia. Like your brain just hit the reset button."

Next to me, Liz's lips compress into a fine line.

Adrian sits on the side chair, shoulders slumping. "I tried to do what was best for you. I thought if we started over, if I never mentioned Marc or your old life, you could build something new. And it worked for a while. You were happy."

"So over the last couple of years, you just what? Appointed yourself the guardian of my memories? Decided which parts of my life I could know? You didn't think I deserved to know the whole truth?"

Adrian shakes his head. "You asked about Marc once or twice after that. But every time I told you the truth, you got upset, then forgot about the past again. The doctors said it was possible you'd never remember for longer than a few months. And then they said it would be better not to force it, that you needed a safe space to heal."

His eyes glisten, and I feel the sharp edges of my frustration soften. "So I tried to give you that. I tried to be enough."

A heavy silence settles onto the room. I want to argue that it wasn't his job to decide what I could or couldn't handle. But part of me understands. That part wants to feel safe, to be held, to be protected from the hurt, even now.

Liz taps the table with a red nail. "Explain something to me. The landlord at Redfern told us that the boyfriend cleared out Kate's apartment. If your brother died that night, who was he referring to?"

"He was talking about me," Adrian admits. "Once Tessa was released from the hospital, I packed everything up myself. That apartment was full of memories of Marc. I couldn't bear the thought of Tessa seeing his things still there alongside hers. So I sorted through her belongings and brought them back to my place."

He hesitates, choosing his words with care. "It was the only thing I could do for her at the time. I wanted to fix what I could, even if it was just packing up boxes."

"So you just, what, erased her life in the meantime?"

"I tried to build something better for her." Adrian's eyes flick back to me. "For you."

I stare at him, thinking of the journals, the photos, the clothes, the trinkets I never remembered. "Where did you move all my stuff?" I ask, wondering how much of my belongings he threw away under the guise of protecting me. "Wait... when you told me you fostered a cat, you were talking about Toast, weren't you?"

Adrian smiles, but it doesn't reach his eyes. "You moved in with me for a while. We tried to make it work, but some days you'd wake up and not know where you were, who I was, or even who you were.

Sometimes you stayed confused for hours, sometimes for days. You'd get angry or scared. I hated seeing you like that. A few weeks after the accident, you said you wanted space. So I helped you find an apartment to give you a fresh start. I even signed the lease with you, so you'd feel safe."

All this time, every independence I'd claimed was just another inch on the leash Adrian'd placed around my neck. The thought makes me want to laugh and cry at once.

"And the memories?" I ask. "The ones I have of my family, of my life. Are any of them real?"

"Some are real. The rest... your brain filled in the blanks."

Liz looks at me, frowning. "So when you told me stories about your family, those were—"

"Not made up," Adrian interrupts, "just scrambled. Tessa remembers some things, just not always from the right time, or in the right order." His hazel eyes find mine as he adds, "It doesn't matter, though. You will always be the person I love, no matter what."

The adoration in Adrian's expression is so raw, I feel a physical ache to collapse against him and let his shirt absorb my tears until all the pain drains from my body.

"So that's why nothing about me ever surprises you. You'd known about my pork allergy and my hatred of cilantro since before our first meeting at the gallery." The air thins around me as realization dawns. "And that meeting at the gallery... you orchestrated it, didn't you? The spilled wine wasn't an accident, was it?"

"No, that wasn't an accident... Every time you forget me, I have to find ways back to you. You can't imagine what it's like watching recognition fade from your eyes. It shatters me every time..."

I have to steel myself against the anguish etched into Adrian's features. "But I'll keep finding my way back to you, as many times as it takes for you to love me again."

"I don't know what to say." Anger, betrayal, gratitude, tenderness collide in my chest.

Liz sits motionless in her chair, her usual sharp commentary silenced as she watches us. I study the tension in Adrian's posture, the hope he can't hide. How many times has he sat across from me like this, rebuilding what we've lost? How many times has he chosen to love me, knowing I might vanish again tomorrow?

When my gaze lifts to the deep circles under Adrian's eyes, at the tension in his jaw, I see a reflection of my own pain. But despite the bone deep weariness etched into his features, he stayed. Through heartbreak after heartbreak, he never left. He still fought for us.

I don't know where to go from here. Every truth I thought I'd known has been rewritten. I want to hate Adrian for his deception, for playing God with my memories. But he's also carried this burden alone, explaining my past to me over and over, only to watch me forget him again. Is it devotion or something else that keeps him tethered to me? And what does it say about me that part of me wants to run while another part can't imagine leaving him?

When I extend my hand toward Adrian, he rises in one fluid motion as if he's been waiting for my signal, drawing me in until our bodies meet.

"Just tell me you still feel it," he whispers, voice rough. "Tell me you still love me. That's all I need, Tessa. We can figure out the rest together."

I tilt my face up to Adrian's. The stubble on his usually smooth jaw scratches against my palm as I cup his cheeks. His eyes catch the light, amber flecks dancing in green depths that pull me in with an inevitability I can't fight. His betrayal still stings, but the realization that I could never *not* love Adrian settles deep into my heart and soul. Despite all the hurt and deceit, I can't imagine giving up this man, whose gaze holds me like I'm the most precious thing in his universe. This man, who stood by me and took care of me, even during my darkest hours.

"Of course I love you. I'm disappointed that you hid so much from me, and I need time to process all of this. But my heart knows you even when my mind forgets, and I don't think that'll ever change."

Adrian holds my gaze for a heartbeat, then his face transforms with a smile that threatens to steal my breath away. Before I can tell him he isn't out of the woods yet, he closes the distance between us, and the next thing I know, his lips are on mine. Our kiss is raw and desperate, but I can't seem to care. I relish the feeling of Adrian's desire, biting on his lip, then nearly moan at the growl he lets out. He tastes of mint and coffee and something uniquely him. He tastes like home.

Adrian's hands find the small of my back, pressing me closer until his heartbeat thunders against my chest. I surrender to the haunting familiarity of his embrace, even as a small voice inside cautions me to take things slow.

The truth is, in his arms, I feel tethered to something real. For the first time since learning the truth, the chaos in my mind quiets, and I realize this is exactly what I need. I need Adrian to make the pain better, to chase away my doubts. I need him to put my broken pieces back together. I need him to reach into the dark and find me there, to remind me that I am still someone worth finding.

I force myself to pull back, although every cell in my body protests the separation. My lips feel swollen, tingling with the ghost of Adrian's kiss. "From now on, I need you to be honest with me. No more secrets. Swear to me."

Adrian's eyes don't waver as he stares at me, pupils dilated against irises the color of forest moss after rain. His hands rest at my waist, his grip firm and warm against the fabric of my borrowed hoodie. "No more secrets," he whispers, his lips brushing mine to seal the promise.

# CHAPTER FIFTEEN

# Tethered

If you asked me to think of a moment that made me feel immensely uncomfortable, I would describe sitting in a too-bright exam room, perched on crunchy tissue paper, while Adrian and the psychiatrist discuss my sanity as if I'm not even there.

Dr. Whitemore's glasses perch on the tip of his nose. He's at least seventy, with a gentle handshake and a habit of humming whenever he's thinking hard.

"So," the doctor says, glancing at the clipboard. "You're having persistent headaches, anxiety, intermittent insomnia, and trouble with, ah, memory consistency."

Adrian is sitting beside the exam table, one leg crossed over the other, his hands folded in his lap. "And sometimes she has trouble keeping her days straight. This morning she got dressed for a photoshoot that's scheduled for next week."

My cheeks go hot. "It was an honest mistake that could have happened to anyone."

The doctor's gaze lands on me. "It's alright. Mixing up days is not uncommon, given the nature of your injury. Now tell me more about these headaches."

I shrug. "They're getting better. It's just... when I can't remember something, there's this tightness here." I press my fingertips against my temples. "Then, when Adrian tells me what I need to know, the pain goes away. Like a puzzle piece that finally falls into place."

Dr. Whitemore nods. "That's a typical coping mechanism after trauma. The brain prefers a coherent story and looks for ways to fill in the gaps." His eyes flick back to Adrian. "Have you noticed any compulsive behaviors? Repetitive actions or new phobias?"

"Not really. Although, she's been leaving herself reminders. Voice memos, emails, even sets alarms for small things." Adrian gives me a sideways smile, like he's proud of me.

Dr. Whitemore nods. "Good. Keep at it. Even if it feels too much sometimes, these habits will train your brain to accept your new normal." He clicks his pen once, then again. "And you, Adrian? Are you still coping?"

Adrian averts his gaze. "It's easier now," he says, but his words have an edge. "She's becoming herself again. That's all I want."

The doctor nods, then gives me a long look. "You're lucky to have someone so devoted. This boy right here really cares about you."

I force a smile, feeling uncomfortable under Dr. Whitemore's stare.

"If you want to get better, keep to your routine, stay in familiar places, and let the people you trust help you fill in the blanks. The more stable your environment, the faster your memories will return."

I want that. God, I want it so badly. But what if my memories never return? What if tomorrow I wake up and remember nothing, including Adrian?

Adrian's chair scrapes against the linoleum as he moves to my side. He wraps an arm around my shoulders, the wool of his sweater scratching my cheek. "Hey, talk to me. What's wrong?"

My voice catches as the words tumble out. "What if the opposite happens and the rest of my memories disappear again? What if I wake up tomorrow not remembering you?"

His lips press against my hair. "Then we start over. Together. As many times as it takes."

The doctor hums in thought. "Retrograde amnesia rarely progresses backward once recovery begins. And with Adrian by your side, you're ahead of most patients."

Dr. Whitemore's smile crinkles at the corners as he looks at us. "Come see me if anything gets worse, but otherwise, just give it time. Brains are stubborn, but they're also resilient. Your mind isn't broken, it just takes time for it to heal."

But my mind has already reset itself countless times, wiping away weeks or months without warning. I nod and smile anyway, pretending to believe Dr. Whitemore when he says the memories will stick this time.

That weekend, Adrian takes me to the cemetery. The grass around my parents' graves looks thick and green, with no trace of a raw dirt mound. My fingers trace the weathered edges of the marble, collecting a faint patina in the grooves of their names. I recognize the birth days etched into the stone, but the death dates seem impossible as they blur before my eyes.

Adrian's fingers tighten around mine while I stare at a bronze vase he tells me I chose myself. Someone has left fresh flowers on my mother's grave, their scent mingling with wet earth. I run my fingers over the dates again, hoping the touch might trigger a memory, a feeling, anything.

I keep expecting to hear my mother's laugh, to feel her arms encircling me in one of those crushing hugs that made everything better. But nothing comes.

Did I cry at their funeral, or did I stand here like an empty, broken daughter who can't even properly mourn her parents? How can I not remember losing them? The weight of their absence threatens to pull me under. It feels like I'm balancing on the edge of an abyss that I don't know how to come back from.

How do I process their loss? Where do I go from here? My mind grasps for a way to understand what I've lost, a path forward, but finds nothing solid.

So I do what feels like the only option. I gather the guilt and the unbearable sadness, and lock them away in a vault deep inside my mind. Someday, when I'm stronger, I'll open the box and work through these feelings. But today is not that day.

The next few weeks pass in a blur. I think I understand now why the journals changed the way they did, how the writing got monotone and distant. Something has gone quiet in me. The highs and lows have flattened out, and I don't feel truly happy or mad anymore. I suppose it could be worse; at least I'm not feeling too much.

My headaches mercifully lessen, shrinking from sharp, blinding spikes to a dull pressure at the back of my skull. When I forget something, Adrian supplies the memory, and the ache fades almost instantly. It doesn't take long for me to become reliant on his support, like a child looking for a parent's guidance.

Adrian's patient, but it hurts to see him scan my face every morning for recognition, as if he's bracing for the next time I might forget him again. On bad days, he'll come up behind me in the kitchen, arms around my waist, and just holds on. In those moments, I wish he'd never let me go.

Sometimes I catch myself doing things, like rinsing dishes that are fresh out of the dishwasher, or folding my towels into tight thirds, and I wonder if these are habits left over from my old life, or if I learned them from watching Adrian.

I can tell Adrian wants to help me remember who I was, but he lets me set the pace. He tells me about the first time we went to the market and got matching hot cocoa burns on our tongues, or the time I fell asleep in the movie theater and snored so loudly Adrian had to nudge me awake.

He regularly surprises me at the gallery with lunch. "I missed you," he says, kissing my cheek. "Remember how you used to light up when I'd show up unexpectedly?" I smile and nod, letting him believe I can see that moment he's describing, that version of me that may not exist anymore.

Adrian is protective, sometimes annoyingly so. He drives me to every appointment, even in the middle of the day when he has to step away from work. He makes it a point to accompany me to new consultations over the weekends and even sets up location sharing on our phones so we can track each other in case of an emergency.

One day, when Marissa introduces me to a startup founder who needs portraits, Adrian's hand tightens around mine. "I don't trust him," he whispers after the man walks away. "I don't like the way he looked at you." I glance back at the man. His smile seemed genuine enough, but Adrian's concern follows me like a shadow throughout the day.

That evening, Adrian shakes two pills into my palm. "But I took these this morning," I insist. His brow furrows as he checks his phone calendar. "No, sweetheart. That was yesterday. See?" He shows me the screen with its rows of checkmarks. "Should I track this for you where you can see the dates?"

And sure enough, he does. There is a calendar taped to the fridge the next morning. And every day following that, I wake to a trail of neon sticky notes guiding me through the apartment. Adrian's handwriting curves into little hearts over the i's. "Vitamins!" by the kitchen sink. "Phone charger!" on the nightstand. "Rain coming!" with a tiny umbrella drawing taped to the coat rack. "Don't forget to eat breakfast!" stuck to the refrigerator.

For the first few days, I just stare at the notes, wanting to crumple them in my fist and yell at Adrian to stop treating me like a child. But over time they become a regular part of my day, and when my missing memories become too much, Adrian's thoughtfulness feels like the only solid ground beneath my feet.

The nightmares still come on the rare occasions I fall asleep at night. I see headlights spinning, feel melted ice running down my arm, or glass embedded in my skin. A man's hand, which sometimes belongs to Adrian, sometimes to a stranger, reaches for my wrist as the car spins and spins. Most nights I wake up gasping in the dark, sweat soaking my tank top. The dream's gone, but the dread's still pulsing in my veins.

Adrian never scolds me for waking him. He just gathers me in, strokes my hair, and whispers, "You're safe. You're here, with me."

On days when the frustration of my fractured past overwhelms me and I sob into Adrian's chest, telling him he deserves better, he cradles my face between his hands. "That's not you talking," he tells me firmly. "That's just the stress. You need me here, and I'm not going anywhere."

***

Despite Adrian's reassurances that my recovery is progressing well, it becomes evident to me that I need more than just his version of my past. I want to connect with someone who remembers me, not just as I exist now, but as I was before. Someone who remembers me as Kate. The problem is, the couple of times I float the idea by Adrian, his face transforms into careful concern, and he tells me none of the people from my past are around.

So I do my research. At Toast's annual checkup, Dr. Patel's eyes soften with pity when I ask what I was like before.

"Your boyfriend mentioned your accident," he says, adjusting his glasses. "But honestly, you seem the same to me. Always fussing over this little guy." I watch the vet scratch Toast behind the ear, and if he hears my sigh of disappointment, he doesn't comment on it.

I spend hours rifling through past invoices, searching for familiar names. I consider reaching out to a couple of clients. But what would I say to them? "Um, sorry to bother you. I'm doing a survey and was wondering if you could describe your impression of me when I took your photos. Was I kind? Were you happy with my work?" God, that sounds weird. They'd probably wonder why a photographer suddenly cares about their impression of her from years ago.

It seems like I'm hitting wall after wall, every path leading to a dead end, and I can feel my patience wearing dangerously thin.

I ask Liz to bring over the rest of the boxes from the basement of doom, so I can meticulously dig through them. I'm hoping to find a high school yearbook with signatures from old friends, a college journal with names of roommates, anything that might lead me back to people who knew me before. When Adrian comes home and finds me surrounded by cardboard and packing tape, his smile falters.

"Oh, Tessa. Right after the accident, you made me promise to get rid of all that stuff. All the photos and the mementos. You said you couldn't bear looking at reminders of the past."

I swallow hard against the lump in my throat, but the disappointment refuses to go away. Throughout the rest of the day restlessness rises in me, and after dinner I walk over to Adrian, who's standing at the sink with his back to me, hands deep in soapy water. I slide my arms around his middle and lay my cheek against his back, feeling his warmth through his cotton shirt.

"Hey, which marketing firm did I work at again? I was thinking maybe I could reach out to some former colleagues, see what they remember about me."

"It's not that simple." Adrian says as he dries a plate and sets it aside. "Most of those people have moved on. Or didn't really know you that well to begin with." He says this while rinsing a wine glass, his eyes fixed on the swirling suds. "You told everyone you wanted a clean break when you left marketing. And besides, we both know where coffee breaks with coworkers land on the scale of meaningful relationships."

"Maybe," I concede, letting go of his waist, "or maybe you just don't want me to talk to anyone who might contradict your version of events." The words come out before I can stop them, bitter and ugly.

Adrian puts the glass down carefully and turns around. "That's not fair."

"I know," I say, regretting my words. "I just want to know if there's anyone out there who knew me as Kate. Someone who can tell me if I made sarcastic comments... or if I was someone who never returned borrowed books." I throw my hands in the air. "I know this sounds dumb. But I need more, Adrian." *More than you can provide*, an inner voice whispers, but I keep that thought to myself.

"I already told you—"

"I know," I repeat, softening my voice. "And I love hearing how you viewed me. But you loved me then, and you love me now. You're obviously looking at me through rose-colored glasses. Which I appreciate," I quickly add, "but that makes it difficult for you to stay objective."

A silence lingers between us, stretching wide enough to swallow the kitchen whole. Finally, Adrian wipes his hands on a tea towel and says, "There is someone. If you're sure you want to do this."

I look up, pulse quickening. "Who?"

Adrian's face tightens. "My father," he grinds out, like he's tasting something sour. "He's still around. But he's not... well, he's not himself these days." He leans on the counter, shoulders hunched. "It's been a while since the two of you met, and I didn't think seeing him again would be good for you."

"Why not?"

"Because he has dementia, Tessa. He lives in a care facility outside the city. He was never the best father, and now the disease has amplified his less desirable qualities. When I went to see him in the past, he'd hurl accusations and say awful things he wouldn't even remember five minutes later." His voice drops. "I stopped visiting after what happened with Marc. Father made it clear I wasn't welcome anymore. But," he looks back at me, resignation softening his features, "if you really think seeing him will help, I will take you."

Adrian's expression tells me it cost him something precious to even mention the man. "Are you sure?" I whisper, not because I need confirmation, but because I want him to have an out if he needs it.

Adrian steps closer and cups my cheeks, his thumb brushing my skin. "There's nothing I wouldn't do for you, Tessa. Literally nothing. If you think this will help you feel whole again, then consider it done."

I press my lips to his, trying to convey my gratitude. "Thank you for offering this. I know seeing your father won't be easy for you, and I want you to know how much this means to me."

Adrian's breath warms my skin as he pulls back enough to speak. "For you, anything. I'll call the facility tomorrow to give them a heads up. We can visit this weekend."

"Only if you're sure."

"I am." His voice doesn't waver, but his fingers tighten around me.

We don't mention his father again that night. After the kitchen is clean, we curl into the couch and watch a movie neither of us really follows. When the credits roll, I study Adrian's face in the television's glow. His shoulders form a rigid, tense line. Have I pushed too far? I'm forcing him to confront the man who tormented his childhood, all because I can't live with my own blank spaces. Adrian's spent years building walls around those memories, and here I am, hammer in hand.

But when I open my mouth to tell him I'll find another way, the words dissolve on my tongue. By Saturday, I'll be sitting across from the man who broke Adrian before he became the man I love. I should be ashamed of using his trauma as my bridge to the past, but the emptiness inside me howls louder than my conscience. Maybe that's the answer I've been looking for all along... about who I really am.

***

We drive an hour to reach the facility, a brown brick building tucked between a pristine golf course and a small church. The rolling hills of the countryside welcome us, but the tension is so thick in the air that I find it hard to appreciate the pretty landscape.

The care home is limestone, built to look like an old mansion. The grounds roll out in careful tiers of boxwood and late-season blooms, and I notice them despite everything. Near the hedgerow, a man in a green uniform crouches over something that doesn't need tending. Three black town cars and a rust- colored Bentley sit in the parking lot.

Inside, the halls echo with the squeak of rubber soles and the faint, ever-present scent of disinfectant. Adrian walks too quickly, his hand clenched tight in mine, as a scrubbed nurse leads us through a narrow hallway.

"Mr. Mercer's in there," she says, lowering her voice. "If he gets agitated, just press the button by the door. Enjoy your visit." She flashes a smile and disappears down the corridor.

I step inside first. The room is small, with walls painted a calming green, and a plush rug covering the floor. A small space heater's buzzing in the corner, making it feel like eighty degrees in here. The man in the bed looks nothing like the intimidating figure I'd conjured from Adrian's stories. He's shrunken, hollow-cheeked, his gnarled hands clasped in his lap. His hair is white, but the shape of his jaw is unmistakable. There's no question this is Adrian's father.

Mr. Mercer blinks at us, confusion flickering across his face. His eyes skim over me, then fix on Adrian. "It's about time you showed up. When are you bringing me your lunch?"

Adrian's lips pinch at the corners. "Father, it's me. Adrian. I brought Kate to see you. Do you remember her? We wanted to see how you're doing."

Mr. Mercer studies me with watery blue eyes, then frowns. "I want my mashed potatoes seasoned well. None of that tasteless shit."

"I'm sure your lunch will arrive soon. Why don't you talk to Kate while we wait? She's come a long way to see you."

A long silence follows. The older man's gaze sharpens, and for n second, his resemblance to Adrian becomes uncanny. "If you're the girl, then where's the other one? The pretty one with the dark hair." He stares at the blanket on his lap as if the answer might be tucked inside. "Marc's girl. The one that always smiles." He looks up, eyes unseeing. "Have you seen my boy?"

Adrian stiffens, and I step forward, hands folded. "Marc isn't here right now, Mr. Mercer. But he always said wonderful things about you."

The words seem to hit some switch, and Mr. Mercer's face softens. "Of course. Marc told me he was going to marry you, you know." His voice drops, and he pats the chair beside him. "Be careful with my sons. They're both idiots, but only one of them knows it."

I almost laugh, but his next words come out sharp as he adds, "The older one thinks he's smarter than everyone. He's cunning, that one."

Adrian doesn't move. He fixes his eyes on the sun-bleached curtains, his jaw set. "Marc's a good boy," Mr. Mercer goes on. "He's always been the best of the two. Handsome, smart. A real charmer." His gaze skips right over Adrian, as if he's just a piece of furniture, and I swallow the retort bubbling up in my throat. "He tells me about you. Says you're special. Says you make him want to be a better man. It's not easy, you know, living up to expectations." He lowers his voice and leans in. "The first time he brought you around, I knew. I just knew you were the one for him. I always know."

I glance at Adrian, but his expression is unreadable.

Mr. Mercer shifts forward in his bed. "I told him, hang onto the good ones. Don't let them get away. That was my mistake, you know," he confides in a rasp. "Did he propose yet? Did he buy you something nice? If he hasn't, you tell me. I'll make sure he does it right."

I feel my throat close, a bloody knot forming under my tongue. "He... I don't..." I clasp my hands in my lap, trying to think of something more eloquent to say.

Mr. Mercer brightens suddenly, saving me the trouble. "Did Marc tell you he's coming for my birthday? He's bringing me chocolate cake. Not the disgusting slop they serve here." His nose wrinkles as he glances at Adrian. "You! Go get me some lunch. What's an old man got to do to eat around here?"

Adrian's face is like granite, the way he stares at his father, a muscle in his jaw ticking. Mr. Mercer continues to ramble about Marc and how he will get him out of this hellhole soon, oblivious to the tension in the room.

I don't have the heart to tell him that Marc is gone. It's for the best that Mr. Mercer doesn't remember his son's passing. The irony of that doesn't escape me. Perhaps I should appreciate the empty spaces in my mind too, rather than desperately seeking to fill them.

"...before that one poisons me like he did his mother." Mr. Mercer's voice drops as he sinks back against his pillows.

"I'm sorry, what—"

"Lovely sunshine today." His attention darts to the window. "Warm for November. Do you enjoy walking outdoors?"

"I... yes."

"Good, good."

"Mr. Mercer, who poisoned your wife?"

Adrian's eyes flash a warning, but I can't let such an accusation hang in the air.

"Poison?" Mr. Mercer blinks. "No, no. My wife's at the market. Making Marc's favorite tonight." His gaze hardens. "The other one will be there too. Always underfoot."

I want to tell him he's wrong, that he is being cruel. I want to shout that Adrian is the best man I've ever known, that if there's someone leaking poison in this room, it's not the one standing quietly to the side.

But something in Mr. Mercer's slumped shoulders, the way his hands tremble, makes me hold my tongue. He's lost, I realize. Marooned somewhere between the past and the present, his bitterness calcified into made up truths in his mind.

Adrian clears his throat. "We should go," he murmurs. There's no anger in his tone, only a weary resignation that makes my heart ache.

"Go where? Who are you?" Mr. Mercer's questions draw my attention back, and I lean in, reassurance on the tip of my tongue. He flinches away from me so violently that for a second, I worry he might slip right out of his bed.

"Get out, get out of my room," he croaks. He pushes himself up with a force I wouldn't have guessed possible in a man so frail, and I have to backpedal to avoid his flailing.

Adrian is at his side, guiding him back into bed. "Father, it's okay. No one is going to hurt you." But the old man's face has gone waxy and slack, and Adrian's words only seem to make him more panicked. "Nurse!" he barks, voice rough. "Nurse, there's a stranger—he's—" His words dissolve into a wet cough. He sags back into the bed, his gaze fixed on the far wall. "Where's my wife? She's been gone a while," he mumbles, eyes wide.

I step back, heart pounding in my throat. A nurse rushes in, deftly inserting herself between Mr. Mercer and Adrian.

"It's okay, it's okay, Mr. M. You're just a bit tired, that's all." She glances over her shoulder at us and mouths, *Sorry.* "Let's get you some water, and maybe a cookie until lunch arrives?" She tucks the blanket around his chest and pats his shoulder reassuringly.

The door clicks shut behind us. For a moment, the world levels out, and I can breathe again. I look at Adrian, who is slumped against the cinderblock wall, his head hanging low. I want to reach for him, to say something wise or comforting, but all I can manage is, "That was... a lot."

Adrian's voice is hollow. "Sometimes he's lucid, but mostly he's trapped within his own mind. I wouldn't wish that on anyone." He looks up, and my heart pinches with guilt as I see just how worn down he is. "I'm sorry I brought you. That was a mistake."

I shake my head. "No. I wanted to come. And you did the best you could. We both did."

He gives a humorless laugh, then straightens and offers me his hand. "Come on. Let's get out of here."

We walk through the hallway, past posters about hand hygiene and heart health, before finally breaking into the sharp, freezing air outside. Neither of us speaks for a long time.

I watch the suburbs scroll by on the way home, lost in thought. I think about Adrian's father back at the facility, about how he remembered a version of me I'm not sure ever really existed.

"I'm sorry you had to go through that." I murmur, regretting my decision to push this visit upon Adrian.

Adrian's jaw works, the muscle twitching back to life along his cheek. He tightens his hand around the steering wheel, eyes locked forward. "I hated every minute," he confesses. "But I'd do it again if it meant you got some closure..."

My eyes burn with unshed tears. The image of Adrian standing there, hardening under his father's dismissal, plays on repeat in my mind. Whatever answers I'd hoped to find weren't worth watching him endure that. "I'm sorry," I breathe. "For making you stand in that room while he talked about Marc like you weren't even there."

"It's okay. I knew what I was signing up for," Adrian says. "Father loving Marc, his golden child, is nothing new. Marc was the one who could do no wrong. I was just the backup plan, someone who didn't matter." He shrugs, like the hurt can't get to him. "It was always Marc this, Marc that. Even when I was top of my class or won awards, I was just background noise. I think the only time Father ever really saw me was when I was punishing myself more thoroughly than he could."

I reach across the center console and take Adrian's hand in mine. "You're not background noise. Your father sees only what he wants to see, but I see you, Adrian. All of you." I squeeze his hand. "Even today, you put yourself through that for me."

He glances over, the corner of his mouth lifting slightly. "After a lifetime of disappearing behind my brother's shadow, you have no idea how refreshing it is to have someone actually look at me the way you do." His voice catches. "That's why you're different from anyone I've ever known. That's why I love you so much, Tessa."

"I love you too," I murmur and kiss him on the cheek, meaning every word. Adrian's father was cruel to him growing up, and he didn't deserve that. My quest for answers seems just as selfish now, trivial compared to what it cost Adrian to revisit his past and face his father's dismissal yet again. I squeeze his hand, feeling the warmth of his skin against mine. His fingers tighten around mine, and the small but genuine smile that crosses his face sends warmth spreading through me.

In that moment, the truth hits me like a wave. All those hours spent digging through memories suddenly seem like wasted time. My throat tightens, and I blink rapidly against the sting in my eyes.

Digging through the past is like picking at a scab that only makes the bleeding start again. The scars we carry are already part of us, whether or not we examine them. So maybe it's time to let them fade.

I look at Adrian's profile and feel the realization settle in my chest. What matters now is the life we create together, step by step, and I know with absolute certainty that I want to build that future with Adrian by my side.

# CHAPTER SIXTEEN

# All Yours

Weeks have passed since Adrian's revelation had torn my life apart. He has been there through every sleepless night and tearful morning, holding me close when the grief becomes too heavy to carry alone. The ache still spreads through my chest whenever I see a mother with her daughter, or I catch myself reaching for my phone to call home, but I've started to have moments when I can breathe without feeling like I'm drowning. The numbness is cracking and emotions are seeping back in through the fissures. Those feelings are unwelcome on the harder days, but on others, something close to contentment is starting to take root.

When I try to picture my first camera, or my parents' wedding photos, something behind my eyes tightens like a railroad spike being driven into my frontal lobe. Wanting more pieces of the past while simultaneously wanting to forget it all is its own kind of torture.

I can tell Adrian feels bad about tossing the photo albums and the trinkets. He makes up for it by telling me stories of my past.

He describes how I shrieked when he won me an enormous purple teddy bear at the summer street fair, then he laughs about how we demolished two large stuffed crust pizzas during a movie marathon. Marc doesn't appear in these narratives. Adrian's brother exists only in the negative space, in the careful way Adrian steps around certain dates, certain places.

Adrian's stories pull laughter from me one moment and tears the next. But what strikes me most is how Adrian never casts me as the villain in our history. In his retelling, I'm someone worthy of love, even when I was with Marc. Not once does he suggest I was foolish for falling for his brother, or for not seeing the red flags that should have been obvious.

We get up early most days. Adrian brews the coffee and lines up my supplements on the counter like a little row of white and pink soldiers. He kisses me on the cheek as I pass, and I pretend to roll my eyes, even though his presence makes me feel steady.

He encourages me to see Dr. Whitemore as often as possible. During the appointments, I can feel the doctor measuring how much of me is Tessa and how much is leftover Kate. The line between who I was and who I am blurs more each day.

I don't quit my job, but I scale back to focus on my recovery. I stop working wedding gigs and side hustles and prioritize the scheduled sessions for the gallery. Marissa says she's proud of my self-care, though I suspect she is just glad I'm not crying in the back room anymore.

Adrian comes to every gallery event, even the ones he probably hates. He arrives in tailored suits that transform him into something dangerous and delicious. He stands by the wine table while other guests mingle, his attention fixed on me as I walk around the room. Heat blooms beneath my skin when our eyes meet across the space, and I have to remind myself that gallery bathrooms are for patrons, not for indulging in the fantasies his gaze inspires.

I eventually admit that I have no intention of moving out of Adrian's apartment and cancel my lease. My shoulders drop an inch the day I hand over my apartment keys. Adrian's fingers find mine in the parking lot, and I lean against him, breathing in his familiar scent of cedar wood and citrus.

"Let's go home," he tells me, and for the first time in a long time, my heart doesn't feel like it's splintering into a million shreds at the sound of that word.

The holidays arrive with their particular ache. We keep Christmas small, just the two of us and Toast curled by the artificial tree, its colorful lights reflecting in the windows. Toast watches with his head tilted as we place ornaments on the highest branches, out of his reach. Hours later, we find him batting a glittery snowflake across the kitchen floor, looking entirely too pleased with himself.

We drink mulled wine from matching mugs and exchange gifts. Adrian's are wrapped with military corners and invisible tape, while mine are secured with paper bunched at odd angles and too much ribbon hiding the worst creases.

The setting feels intimate, but the apartment echoes with an absence that's impossible to ignore. I catch myself glancing at my phone, wishing it would light up with my parents' faces. When Adrian steps into the shower, I press my palms against my eyes until the pressure drives back tears, then busy myself folding discarded wrapping paper into trash bags.

Every day gets a little easier. I wake up remembering who I am and who Adrian is. Memories of what happened last week are firmly in place, which are small victories I don't take for granted. When the anxiety about the what ifs starts to creep in, I bury myself in work or in Adrian's arms, constructing something that feels like a future, brick by careful brick.

***

On the first day of spring, Liz texts to say she's kidnapping me for brunch and shows up at 10am sharp with a smile that promises retribution if I say no.

She thrusts a yellow dress at me. "You're wearing this."

When I protest that the dress is too much for a casual brunch, she says, "It's cheerful. You need cheerful."

I shimmy into the dress, its daffodil brightness blasphemous against the pallor of my skin. Liz zips me up, then spins me toward the mirror.

"Perfect," she declares, fluffing my hair so it sticks out in bed-head-chic.

I wince at my reflection, but Liz is already lining up powders and tubes. She then proceeds to sweep bronzer onto my cheeks while lecturing me on the importance of highlighter and bright colored lipstick. Her hands are gentle but relentless, and by the time she's finished, I look three shades more alive than I did before.

Liz's stereo vibrates with a popular 90s pop song as we cruise across town toward a new brunch spot. We belt out the lyrics, my voice breaking spectacularly on the high notes. When I do the dance from the music video, Liz nearly swerves into the next lane, her face flushing crimson as she gasps for breath between fits of laughter.

The restaurant is bright and loud, with every table crammed with women in florals and men cloaked in cologne. We get seated and Liz orders us mimosas.

"It's basically orange juice, but for grown-ups with good taste." She slides her sunglasses into her hair and leans forward, elbows on the table. "Besides, I need you nice and pliant by the time I return you to that hunky architect of yours. Just wait till he sees you in that dress." She wiggles her eyebrows suggestively.

Heat creeps up my neck as I snort into my mimosa.

"Listen, I had my doubts about him there for a while. But it's obvious to anyone with working eyeballs that man worships the ground you walk on," Liz continues, studying me over the rim of her glass. "You know that, right?"

"God only knows why. I keep thinking that he'll realize I'm a lost cause, but that hasn't happened yet."

"Don't be silly. Adrian's crazy about you. That's never going to change." Liz raises her glass and clinks it against mine. "To sexy and obsessive men!"

Whipped cream and rainbow sprinkles top our waffles, and they taste like heaven. I take a bite and close my eyes, letting the sweetness dissolve on my tongue, momentarily forgetting everything but this simple pleasure.

For the next hour we eat and gossip. Liz confesses she's been scheduling unnecessary follow-ups with her new client, who happens to be a devastatingly handsome and single CIO. I nearly snort mimosa through my nose when she demonstrates her strategy of picking up a dropped notebook near his desk.

It feels good to relax and talk about mindless topics. Today I'm just a woman in a dress, laughing too loudly, dribbling syrup down my chin, and not giving a damn about what happens tomorrow.

I barely notice the time passing until Liz checks her phone and declares she's running late for "a thing."

We leave Liz's SUV at the restaurant and share a taxi back. When we pull up to Adrian's building, Liz hugs me goodbye, and I catch a hint of mischief in her smile, but I'm feeling too relaxed to question it.

I float through the lobby doors, my veins fizzing with champagne. I find Adrian leaning against the wall by the elevators, his hands in his pockets, looking like he stepped out of a magazine. The white shirt clings just enough to hint at the muscles underneath, sleeves pushed up his arms.

A woman in heels by the entrance of our building does a double-take and almost stumbles, and I can't even blame her. Heat pools low in my belly as I imagine running my hands through Adrian's hair and making a mess of those perfect strands. I want to undo each button of his crisp shirt until I can trace every contour of what lies beneath.

"Did you have a good brunch?"

I look up at him through my lashes. "Brunch was delicious," I let my tongue linger on the word, "but I think I'm ready for something sweeter now."

Adrian's eyes darken as he pulls me against him, his hand sliding possessively down my back.

"Do you now?" he whispers against my ear, his voice rough. "Good. Because I've been thinking about bending you over since I saw you step out of that car. This dress makes me want to do filthy things to you." His words send a current of desire straight to my core. "But as much as I'd love to continue this, I have something else planned first."

Before I can act on my intrusive thoughts and start stripping Adrian down here and now, he tugs me toward the elevator.

"Where's the fire?" I laugh, tripping over my feet to keep up with him.

He's vibrating with energy as he leads me through the twists of our building, up a flight of stairs, then out a side door to the rooftop garden. The view up here is ridiculous. There are endless skies and skyscrapers crowding the horizon, all the way to the river glittering in the distance. But what makes me stop in my tracks is the sight of the garden itself. Everywhere I look, peonies burst from planters in shades of blush, cream, and coral. Their sweet perfume hits me, and I reach out without thinking, brushing my fingertips against the nearest bloom. Its impossibly soft, sunset-colored petals feel like velvet beneath my touch.

"This is incredible. Did you—" the words die on my lips as I turn to find Adrian on one knee before me.

The world shifts into slow motion. I know what's happening, but my brain can't quite catch up. Maybe it's the sun in my eyes, or that every one of my nerve endings is lighting up at once. Adrian is holding a ring. He's actually holding a ring.

"You remember when I first brought you up here?" he asks, a tremor in his voice. "You said it was the only place in the city you felt truly alive. I wanted to make sure you always had that. I wanted to make sure you always had me."

The ring looks like a shiny peony carved out of diamonds. He must have designed it himself.

"I love you, Theresa Katherine Grey. I love every version of you, and every version I don't even know yet. Will you marry me?"

I just stand there for a second, blinking back tears. I'm a mess, and I know I must look like a mess with my windblown hair and puffy eyes. I should say something funny, something clever, but all I can do is kneel beside him, bury my face in his neck, and let the tears fall.

"Yes," I manage, the word muffled by his collar. "God yes, of course I will marry you."

Adrian cups my face in his warm hands and kisses me. It's a sloppy kiss, ruined by my tears, but he doesn't care. His lips are hungry, the kiss all consuming, as if the world might vanish around us if he stopped. When he pulls away to look at me, his pupils are so dilated his eyes appear black, and there's a slight tremble in his exhale that tells me he's feeling as overwhelmed as I am.

A soft rustle breaks through my daze, and I turn to find Liz crouched behind a potted palm, phone aimed at us. Her mascara's tracking down her cheeks as she tries to hold the camera steady.

"Don't mind me," she calls, voice thick. "I'll just, uh, invoice you for the therapy after this."

We laugh, and Adrian slips the ring onto my finger. It fits perfectly, like it was always meant to be there.

Adrian's eyes crinkle at the corners, his lips curved into that crooked smile that makes my stomach flip, even now. Especially now.

"You're my everything," he whispers, his thumb brushing over my knuckles where the ring now sits, "in every universe that exists."

His words settle somewhere beneath my ribs, warm and permanent as a tattoo. In this moment, I know I'm the luckiest girl in the world.

***

Liz dabs at her mascara-streaked cheeks with a tissue, then holds up her phone to take more photos. She moves around so much that I know the pictures will be a blurry mess, but with Adrian's ring catching the sunlight on my finger, nothing can dim my smile.

Reality feels suspended, dreamlike. Adrian whispers my name against my hair, and I feel the warmth of his breath against my scalp. When I tilt my face up to meet his, his kiss tastes like promises and forever. His expression shifts between boyish triumph and something darker, more primal. When Liz turns to fiddle with her phone, his fingers trail up my thigh beneath the dress, leaving a path of goosebumps in their wake.

Liz clears her throat, gives us a knowing look, and makes a show of checking her watch. "Well, I should probably let you two celebrate properly," she says, hugging us both before slipping away.

We barely make it through the door before Adrian's hands are in my hair, at my waist, under my dress, everywhere at once. He kisses a trail from my collarbone to my ear, whispering promises that make me shiver. In the bedroom, I gasp at the sight of crimson rose petals scattered across our white duvet. Adrian has thought of everything.

His touch is reverent as he lays me down, his fingertips grazing my skin like I'm something precious. Then his touch turns urgent and consuming, his breathing ragged against my neck as we move together. He takes me hard and fast against the sheets, his fingers digging into my hips, leaving marks I'll admire tomorrow. I arch into every thrust, drinking in his whispered demands that flutter hot against my ear. Each kiss burns like a brand across my my throat, my lips, claiming his territory.

I don't hold back either. *Mine, mine, mine.* The words echo in my head like a drumbeat, the urge to mark Adrian's golden skin with crescents and shadows that will bloom purple by morning unstoppable. I trace the ridge of his collarbone with my teeth, suck bruises into the hollow of his throat, and drag my nails down the taut muscles of his back. Adrian's eyes flash dark when I bite the sensitive spot where his neck meets his shoulder, and he growls low in his throat, the sound vibrating against my lips.

God, I can't get enough of this man. The smell of his skin is intoxicating. The weight of him pressing me into the mattress, and the rough calluses on his fingertips that catch against my oversensitive skin drive me wild. He reads my body like a book, knowing when to curl his fingers just so. He uses his tongue in slow, deliberate circles until I'm trembling and crying out his name as the first wave crashes through me.

He's coaxing me toward a second peak before I can catch my breath, the climax more intense than the first, leaving me boneless and dazed. Only then does he relent, his body tensing above me, muscles rigid beneath my fingers as he shudders and spills inside me with a raw, broken groan that vibrates into my chest. Spent and sweaty, Adrian collapses beside me and pulls me close, tucking my head under his chin where I can feel the wild drumming of his pulse against my cheek.

He traces circles on my hip, his breath warm against my ear. "If I'd known getting engaged would make you this frisky, I might have proposed on our first date." He pokes my ribs playfully until I squirm away, laughing. Then he pulls me back against his chest, his voice dropping to a whisper. "I still can't believe you're going to be my wife."

I twist to face him, smiling. "Did you doubt I'd say yes?"

Something flickers across his face, so brief I almost miss it. "Never," he presses his lips to my forehead. "Hey, I should clean up. Then I'll make us something to eat. I've got another surprise waiting for you."

"Another surprise? You're spoiling me." I stretch languidly. "Though I wouldn't mind if this surprise involved you wearing nothing but an apron."

Adrian chuckles. "That can definitely be arranged." He slides out of bed with a wink, treating me to a view of his sculpted back as he disappears into the bathroom. The shower hisses to life moments later.

I burrow deeper into the warm sheets, floating in contentment. Sunlight catches the diamond on my finger, sending prisms dancing across the ceiling.

"Tessa Kate Mercer." I let each syllable roll off my tongue like honey, savoring how the name settles into my bones as naturally as if I'd been born with it.

The buzz of Adrian's phone slices through my post-engagement euphoria, its vibration rattling somewhere in the living room. I call out for him, but the water is still running in the shower and there's no response.

I sigh, annoyed that Adrian's work is intruding on the warm afterglow that still hums through my body. I've spent the last few months living by reminders and alarms, and today, I want nothing more than to float in this moment. But the phone keeps ringing, incessant and irritating.

I pull on Adrian's discarded shirt that still smells like him and stumble into the living room. There's his phone, vibrating across the glass coffee table, the caller ID flashing UNKNOWN on the screen. I swipe to answer, pinning the phone between my shoulder and cheek as I look for a pair of sweats to pull on.

The line crackles with silence before an automated voice cuts through. "You have a collect call from county penitentiary. To accept charges, press one."

My movements slow. Why is Adrian getting a call from prison? A ripple of unease travel down my spine as I stare at the device. I press down on the number one button.

I hear static, then a click. "Hello?"

At first, there's only silence. Then a rough voice cuts in. "Where's Adrian?"

"Uh... he's not available right now. Can I take a message?"

Goosebumps rise on my bare legs as I tug Adrian's shirt lower, suddenly aware of how exposed I am. After a moment, a single word slices through the static: "Kate?"

"I'm sorry, who is this?"

"Kate, it's me. I'd recognize your voice anywhere."

My mind seizes, and for a heartbeat all I can hear is the shower's hiss. "Who is this?"

The man on the other side of the line inhales. When he speaks, his tone is low. "It's Marc."

Marc? That's impossible. Unless Adrian has another relative or friend named Marc. After a beat of silence, the man's voice drops to a growl as he adds, "Marc Mercer." Well, that clears that up.

I blink a couple of times, unsure what this prankster is playing at. "Look, I have no idea what sick joke this is," I stammer. "Marc died years ago—"

"Died? Are you kidding me?" A bitter laugh rattles down the line, and an unwelcome heat floods my body at the sound. "And you believed that?"

Before I can articulate a response, the man continues. "Wait. He's there, isn't he? Say the word 'solicitor' if he's listening right now."

"I'm hanging up."

"That wasn't the word."

A brief moment of silence follows, then, "I don't know what lies my brother fed you, but trust me, I'm very much alive. And you need to get as far away from that lying son of a bitch as you can."

I open my mouth to tell this lunatic never to call Adrian's number again, but he presses on. "He's not who you think he is. Never was. You need to get out, Kate—"

"My name is Tessa."

"I thought you hated your first name?" The man on the other end of the line lets out a sigh, and the line cuts out for a few seconds. "...he would do. He made you call yourself Tessa to help you disassociate from your past, didn't he?"

I want to hang up, but I can't move. "Adrian had nothing to do with me choosing to go by Tessa. That was my decision," I manage. "Why am I even explaining—"

"Adrian," the voice spits. There's a rush of static again, like the line is about to die. "I tried everything to save you from him. How could you believe his lies after he stalked you for months, after he nearly killed you?"

"I don't know who you are, but you know nothing about me." I fire back, my rage surging. "Adrian is the best thing that's ever happened to me—"

"Listen to me, Kate, or Tessa. I don't know what you remember, or what Adrian told you, but he is not the best thing that's ever happened to you. As a matter of fact, the accident that supposedly killed me wasn't an accident at all. You may not remember this, but your precious Adrian pushed you down the stairs in a fit of rage before I could get to you. He is dangerous, and you need to get away from him now. I will come find you as soon as I can. But in the meantime, I need you to go somewhere safe, somewhere he—"

Footsteps approach from the hallway, and I end the call, tossing the phone onto the couch cushions like it's burned me. Then I immediately want to snatch it back, to hear more or to hang up properly; I'm not even sure. My pulse hammers in my throat as I stare at the device, its screen dark now. What in God's name has just happened?

The call has to be some sick prank. Adrian told me Marc died in that crash, and I have no reason to doubt him. The thought of Adrian fabricating his own brother's death is so ludicrous I almost laugh out loud. But something about that voice on the phone burrows under my skin, and a tiny seed of doubt takes root.

I've visited the cemetery, stood before the granite headstone with Marc's name etched into it. I've laid flowers beside the matching stone that marks his mother's resting place. But if Mark is dead, then who was that on the phone, with a voice that felt familiar in ways I can't explain?

My mind races through a hundred possibilities, each more implausible than the last. If Marc had survived, wouldn't there have been a hospital record? Something Adrian would have known about? And if Marc's been in prison all this time, why call now? Why call Adrian at all?

As if summoned by my thoughts, Adrian appears in the doorway, a towel slung dangerously low around his waist. The sight of him half naked usually makes my stomach flutter, but now something cold slithers beneath my skin, and I have to swallow hard against the acid climbing up my throat. His smile falters when our eyes meet. "Everything okay?"

"Just fine," I manage, stretching my lips into what I hope looks like a smile. I can still hear that voice, rough as gravel: *He's not who you think he is. He never was.* My fingers find the diamond on my ring finger, twisting it in circles. I know Adrian. I do. So why would someone call from prison claiming to be his dead brother? None of this makes any sense.

Adrian steps closer, water droplets sliding down his chest, and encircles me in a hug. His body feels solid and warm around mine. He guides me to the floor-length mirror he installed last week. In the reflection, his muscular forearms cross my chest, fingers splayed possessively against the borrowed shirt hanging open on my frame.

The woman in the mirror stares back with wild hair and kiss-bruised lips. Adrian's frame engulfs mine completely; shoulders twice as wide, head towering above. He makes me feel so cherished and protected. The way my journals described Marc at first... until things changed.

But something nags at me. In those pages, did I ever explicitly name who became possessive? The tender moments have Marc's name written clearly, but the darker passages only mention "he" and "him." I assumed they were about the same person, but now I'm not so sure... No. There's no way. Adrian couldn't possibly be the "he" from those later entries.

Adrian kisses the top of my head, reinforcing my belief that he is the knight in shining armor and not the villain that impostor on the phone tried to paint him as. Adrian holds me when I cry. He supports me in my darkest hours. He isn't some monster lurking behind a mask.

I trace my thumb over the calluses on his hands, evidence of a hard working man who fixes things around the house after ten-hour workdays, who still makes time to chop vegetables for dinner most nights. How many women complain their significant others don't even notice them? Meanwhile, Adrian catalogs everything about me with precision. He remembers every client I've casually mentioned, buys me perfume he knows I'll like, and selects clothes for me that fit perfectly without asking for my size. Sometimes I wonder if there's anything about me he hasn't memorized.

My stomach twists with guilt for entertaining doubts about him. Adrian is a good man, and he loves me. But then why does his smile tighten when I mention meeting a client for coffee? Why do I feel the need to explain myself when I bring up wanting to keep my job at the gallery? No, stop it. This is ridiculous. Adrian's protective actions stem from a place of thoughtfulness, not control.

*He is dangerous.*

The engagement ring catches the light as I slide my fingers to Adrian's forearm, feeling the muscles tense beneath my touch. His mouth grazes my hairline, his gaze fixed on our reflection.

"Just look at you," he whispers, a smile spreading across his face. "Absolutely perfect. And all mine."

I hope he doesn't hear the crack in my voice as I murmur, "All yours."


TO BE CONTINUED...

# A Word From The Author

If you've made it here, you've read every twist and heartache, and for that, I am so deeply grateful. You gave your time and trust to this story, and that means more to me than I can say.

I'm not quite ready to let Tessa go, and I have a feeling you might not be either. The story isn't over. The second and final book in the duet is coming soon, and I can promise you, the ending she deserves is worth the wait.

If this book moved you, please consider leaving a review. Reviews are the single most powerful thing a reader can do for a debut author. They help other readers find stories they might love, and they mean the world to me personally. Even a few honest words make an enormous difference.

Thank you for reading. Thank you for being here at the very beginning.

With love and gratitude,

Emma